The Eridanos Library 16

Virgilio Piñera

René's Flesh

Translated by Mark Schafer
Foreword by Antón Arrufat

Eridanos Press

Contents

Foreword

by Antón Arrufat

René's Flesh, along with two other important Cuban novels, José Lezama Lima's *Paradise* and Alejo Carpentier's *Explosion at the Cathedral*, belongs to the illustrious line of the so-called novel of education or instruction, novels that tell the story of a young adolescent and his or her growing understanding of the value of life and the world: family, school, friends, sex, intellectual relationships... Each of these three novels, written, strangely enough, within just a few years of each other—*Paradise* and *René's Flesh* were started in 1949, *Explosion at the Cathedral* in 1956—are fairly good examples of the *Bildungsroman*: in Lezama's novel, the protagonist learns to participate in the kingdom of the image or poetry; in Carpentier, the kingdom of history, and in Piñera, the kingdom of the flesh. Setting aside their tremendous thematic and stylistic differences, these novels nevertheless seem engaged in conversation, in a three-way dialogue within Cuban culture. Any of the three could be related to either one of the others. How, one might ask, does Lezama conceive of the human body in *Paradise?* What value does Piñera concede to history in *René's Flesh* or Carpentier to poetry in *Explosion at the Cathedral?* Furthermore, the three novels are examples of the complexity of Cuban narrative today: they proposed transcendent themes and knew how to present them intensely and adroitly.

Here it is appropriate to point out one of the differences that exist between Lezama's novel or Carpentier's and *René's Flesh*. In the first two, the protagonists are three young people whose personal histories are decisive, and who at the same time, seeming to converge, form an unseen archetypical protagonist. José Cemi, Fronesis, and Foción, at once fictional heroes and intellectual allegories, comprise a triad in *Paradise*. As they relate to each other, they seem to blend together, rectifying and completing each other until they converge in one single, ultimate interpretation of reality. Something similar occurs in *Explosion at the Cathedral,* where Esteban, Carlos, and Sofia —and it seems unusual that one of these young people should be a girl—also constitute a dialectically related trio. In both novels, the interplay of the central characters is that of three mirrors arranged so as to allow each one to see him or herself in the other, and all three at the same time. And they not only see themselves, but, redounding to something more profound and insidious, reflect each other. René, on the other hand, is alone. He has no friends his age and is an only child. No one accompanies, rectifies, or influences him. He lacks a teacher: neither Oppiano Licario nor Victor-Hugues imparts their knowledge to him. Every experience he has is particular, isolated, and self–involved. When he meets with his father, it is to listen to warnings and pieces of advice which he barely hears and doesn't want to understand. And then when his father, one of the major characters in this strange novel, decides to send him to school against his will, René doesn't interact with any of his classmates. Moreover, he cuts himself off, shuns them, guarding his lonely solitude at all costs. The three protagonists of *Paradise* and *Century of Lights* at least attempt in certain fashion to draw closer to the world in order to participate in the mystery of the image or to understand history. René, on the other hand, systematically and at times painfully attempts to separate himself from the flesh to which, according to Piñera's novel, he is nevertheless condemned. His every action, from the first chapter to the last, consists entirely of flight. A pathetic flight like a metaphysical bet as step by step he comprehends in horror that he is waging an impossible battle: he can never escape his own body.

The impossibility of René's desire makes him an essentially tragic figure. Like Oedipus, he must in the end accept the *fatum* of the flesh. The reader perceives that behind this impossible desire—the most outstanding aspect of René's personality—fear acts as his driving force. Fear of his own human body. Fear of accepting that he is made of flesh destined for pleasure and pain. The source of this fear is neither described nor explained in the novel. And it is one of the many enigmas of this work: Why is René afraid? What is the cause of his fear? I will venture an explanation, one of many possible. From his childhood, René has witnessed the constant peregrinations of his family, composed of the indistinct figure of his mother and the great tyrannical presence of his father for whom the flesh constitutes a priesthood and a crusade— suffering flesh that must be torn apart by the world while at the same time, defend itself—a peculiar family that flees from one town to another, from one city to another, pursued by enemies of the cause of the flesh. In anguish, René has witnessed such precipitous flights. Hardly have they acquainted themselves with one city when they must escape to another. I believe that his family's flights, actual and concrete, prefigure (and influence) René's own flight. In the same way his family flees around the globe, René flees from his flesh. He flees from the flesh in whose name his family has been forced to flee. René is the one who says no, the one who refuses. Employing the subtle strategies of apparent submission and tears, or an unexpected and short-lived fit of rebellion, he refuses to participate in the cult which his family, along with the other characters, try to impose on him through overbearing, escalating violence. His isolation undoubtedly increases the violence of the society that surrounds him. He is subjected to a savage process: that of other people.

They are the ones who by diverse means—though always coercive—try to initiate him. With each refusal other people take more forceful action. With each no, he seems to reveal the carnal cult of the people around him. And finding this intolerable, they tighten the noose to force him to surrender. They find René disturbing, disrupting. One of a kind. His negations imperil all the world's assumptions. Everyone seeks to initiate him and even the reader often wishes to lend a helping hand and push him along in his carnal process, place obstacles in the path of his peculiar escape.

If the novels of Lezama and Carpentier, along with *René's Flesh*, are fairly good examples of the *Bildungsroman*, as I wrote at the beginning of these pages, I now propose to establish a slight qualification. I would locate *René's Flesh* in the category of the novel of initiation. That is what the protagonist flees from in Piñera's work—flees from and approaches, paradoxical though this may be. While the other two novels are grand family or historical chronicles that refer to the real world, attempting to reproduce it in the consciousness of the reader, Virgilio Piñera's book is a dismasted narration that seems to take place in an empty and apparently unreal space. Nevertheless, and again paradoxically, he proposes to involve his charactrer in the only acknowledged reality: that of the human flesh. That is, to initiate him.

If the principal motivation for René's behavior lies in his efforts to escape his own body and any contact whatsoever with other bodies, the motivation of the other characters, including his parents, is to get close to and collide with his body. The single meaning of their lives is this: to initiate René into the cult of the flesh. They are all attracted by the flesh. Very near the beginning of his novel, Piñera offers a description—very brief, as his descriptions always are—of the flesh of his hero. René doesn't possess the muscles of an athlete. His beauty and attractiveness lie in the fine quality of his skin. His flesh is intact, which disturbs his father, while Mrs. Pérez, silently in love with René's flesh, finds his apparent appeal for protection against the furies of the world, his seeming to be a sacrificial victim, irresistible. She imagines his splendid flesh wounded with a knife or riddled with bullets. When she sees him for the first time, she has the sensation that René's flesh is about to be run over, that mere minutes remain before some demolishing object will fall on him, annihilating his flesh. This kind of ambivalent message emitted by René's flesh produces diverse reactions in each of the characters, but never indifference. In his presence, Mrs. Pérez sinks into "divine ecstasy." She sees such "vulnerable" flesh as promising unsuspected pleasures. A short while earlier, at the beginning of the passage, Piñera offers the key word to all these reactions. The word is *seduction*.

René does not set out to conquer. His behavior is in no way strategic. He lacks skill. He is ignorant of the art of gallantry. He is the anti-Don Juan. And yet, everyone is attentive to him. Lacking both poise and Don Juanesque manners, he *seduces*. With his ambiguity, his flesh that seems to cry out for protection, his gestures of a young man in flight, he is a seducer, and like so many other elements of this novel, he too operates by inversion.

In *René's Flesh*, the father recommends to his son nothing less than the service of pain. He calls René to his "office," so like a dentist's office filled with tourniquets, pulleys, and other instruments of torture, to speak to him of how he has dedicated his life to the cause of the flesh. With pride, he shows René his chest wounds, his scars, a hole in his ear the size of a coin. René, like any young person his age, must go to school.

But this school, rather than offering subjects to instruct the mind and intelligence, offers instruction of the body through "pain suffered in silence" to aid him in his understanding of the flesh as perishable, and the only certain property of man. There a dwarf preacher, instead of speaking of the immortal soul, speaks of the mortal body. That is, every one of René's experiences turns strange, and in strange locations. Similarly, this anti-Don Juan conquers without proposing to do so. He is a seducer precisely because he does not wish to seduce. Rather than approaching, he runs away. He hides his flesh from the voracity of others.

Virgilio Piñera, reader of the works of Kierkegaard, found in this philosopher, as did so many other writers of his time, a kindred intelligence, with similar problems and preoccupations. *Entweder-Oder* contains one of Kierkegaard's key texts: "Diary of a Seducer." Piñera read it very carefully, but having as he did the mind of a reactive artist, he transforms René into the antithesis, the inverse of the Kierkegaardian seducer: his method of seduction is not calculated as it is in "Diary"—a refined reflexiveness—but rather, involuntary in spite of himself. He seduces by subtraction, by withdrawal. And this distance has an irresistible effect on everyone. In *Jesus*, one of his plays, Piñera had earlier shown evidence of his reactive mind: his Jesus is an anti-Jesus, one who denies his own divinity. In stories like "The philanthropist," "The great Baro," and "The dummy," (*Cold Tales*), another aspect of things, the back side of the weave, manifests itself through inversion.

The necessary confrontations must also be established with two English novels which Piñera greatly admired. *The Picture of Dorian Gray*, as with other Wilde stories, presents the protagonist's obsession with portraits. The very same obsession appears in Piñera's novel, but inverted: it is not, as in Wilde, the portraits that depict the moral decay of their subjects, but rather, that René experiences in the flesh the images offered by the portraits: the album of the human body which Mrs. Pérez shows René in order to excite him; the painting of St. Sebastian which his father shows him as a warning, and on which he has drawn the adolescent face of his son. In this case, the Piñerian inversion is abundantly clear: this St. Sebastian is not a victim of arrows being shot at him, but rather his own victimizer: he sinks the arrows in his flesh with his own hand.

The other novel is Samuel Butler's *The Way of All Flesh*. Piñera read this work several years before beginning *René's Flesh*. On several occasions, I heard him mention that book with admiration. In that English novel the word "flesh" is used with the same biblical meaning as it is in Piñera's work. Its relation to Butler's novel is in the end a Piñerian one: that is to say, a response. René's flesh is the way of all flesh, not *á la* Butler, but *á la* Piñera. Like Butler's protagonist, René will have the young person's full range of experiences. However, they won't be experiences of the spirit, but of the human body.

The criticism that has so far appeared of Piñera's writing usually emphasized its affinity with the writing of Franz Kafka. Their mental affinity is clear and shouldn't be minimized. But it is also useful to point out the substantial and essential distances between the two writers. It is only necessary here to indicate one which, however, I consider decisive: Piñera's body of writing lacks any religious undertone whatsoever. *René's Flesh* is an obvious example. There are few texts as irreverent and sarcastic as this novel. Personally, Virgilio Piñera mistrusted the religious dogmas of salvation and even of the existence of the soul. For him, as the protagonist of his play *Electra Garrigó* states, the gods have died and immortality is no longer. Alone in the universe, Man must learn to manage by himself. No less so of course when confronted by the mystery of his own body. One might wonder, as René does, about the destiny of his flesh in life, and not after death. In that respect, we must emphasize Piñera's mockery throughout *René's Flesh* of mystical concepts of the soul and its opposition to the body, and his intrepid parody of Christian metaphors and terminology. Or rather, of Catholicism. Biblical phrases are turned on their head. "Let there be light" becomes "Let there be flesh." Similes such as "The beef was being offered to her like the sacred Host," appear frequently. The cult of the flesh replaces the cult of the spirit. The school René enters, sent there by his father, is a violent caricature of Catholic schools. Every classroom is presided over by a crucifix. But in this inverted crucifixion, rather than writhing and suffering, a victim of the spear in his side, the nail, and the crown of thorns, Christ smiles contentedly down at the students from the timber's height.

In the last of three impressive chapters dedicated to René's carnal education, an education that ends in failure because of his obstinate refusal to be initiated, the author deploys his full irreverence. The ceremony in which the students are initiated is held in a sort of nave, similar to the nave of a church, "a church of the body," with an illuminated pulpit, flowers, and multi-colored lights, and an altar in the back. The walls of the nave are decorated, not with the images of saints, but with enormous tapestries portraying famous cases of torture, realized, however, in the style of animated cartoons, of comic books. Laughter can be heard, resonant chuckling. It is the parents who have been invited to witness the ceremony and who fill the nave of this singular locale. The students are all naked, and at the close of the ceremony, instead of being offered the Host, they are branded on the backside like cattle with a red-hot branding iron. In this aspect alone, Piñera is closer to the black masses of Sade and Huysmans than to the infinite waiting and postponements of Franz Kafka.

Just now, I claimed that the action of *René's Flesh* appears to occur in empty space. I should be more precise. The novel does not unfold in any specific country, land, or city. Suggestions of locale or geography are scarce or lack relief. There are few props on the stages where the action takes place: neither furniture nor domestic objects abound. We are often unaware of how the characters dress, how old they are, and what they eat. Given the double meaning of the word *carne*, which means both flesh and meat, and which Piñera puts to great use in his text, we might suppose that his characters eat beef and—as Mrs. Pérez wishes René would do, seeing him so pallid— drink glasses of blood every now and then. Nevertheless, despite the space of the novel being stripped bare, despite the neutral tone of the narration, which is rather indifferent to the visible world and to any psychological development of its characters, the atmosphere is so precise and well designed that the *reader sees everything*. Virgilio Piñera, appealing to apparently simple recourses, achieves the participation of the reader. I think *René's Flesh* occurs in a practically empty space because it is entirely the space of the mind. (And this may be key to the effect it has on the reader.) That is why everything in the book seems essential: one is within a subjective space, constructed by the synthesis—more recollected than seen—of objective living space. If we accept the novel from its first lines and agree to its mental space, nothing then appears illogical. Its two great opposing principles between which its protagonist struggles, the flesh as pleasure and the flesh as pain, as represented by Mrs. Peréz's world and that of René's father, fit together as a single possibility, although they throw off sparks at the slightest contact. When one accepts the work, that is, that it is artistically possible to personify the invisible conflict between man and his body and that such a conflict is not presented in the style of a naturalistic chronicle but as *grand guignolle*, *René's Flesh* develops with an inexorable logic.

In his brief study of this book, the critic José Rodriguez Feo, referring to the kind of reaction its reading elicits, turns to words like disturbing and bewildering, to expressions like trembling in horror, an enigma to be deciphered... In his study, he states that when the reader, (or critic) believes the narration is bordering on the supernatural or the fantastic as often occurs in Poe and Wells, or that the threads binding the story to the everyday world have been severed, *René's Flesh* imperturbably maintains its "charges of reality," as Piñera himself would ironically say. Rodriguez Feo offers an explanation for this: style. And it's too bad that he didn't expand on this analysis. Piñera's style, which Rodriguez Feo terms "colloquial," returns the reader (or the critic), flabbergasted by the storyline, to the familiar, everyday world. Piñera wrote all of his stories in a style forged in overt and declared opposition to the baroque style of Lezama, his contemporary. At a very young age, he understood that the world he had to relate could only be expressed in the style of domestic small talk, parody, and frankness, if it were to be made "credible." Although a poet, he renounced metaphor and allusion: his style, which may seem unpleasant at first, has a certain rough, metallic quality, a physical proximity to objects and events that is nonetheless startling. He rejected the "lyrical" mode of description, which he called "adorning" a story. He searched for set phrases and popular expressions in Spanish, above all in his Creole versions in which he achieves irresistible moments of humor. The way Piñera has negotiated this contradiction is significant: by making his unusual narrative subjects commonplace. The events in *René's Flesh* border on the implausible, to use a term employed by Rodriguez Feo, and are rendered credible for the reader. The structure of the novel is simple and the narrative time is linear, practically Balzacian. When *René's Flesh* was published in Buenos Aires in 1952, it must have seemed old-fashioned, anachronistic: it had far too orderly a structure for its day. It now looks like a pioneer of the current postmodern tendencies in Latin American literature: less experimental action, a linear time flow... If we add to this Piñera's preoccupation with the human body, prevalent in these closing years of the century, *René's Flesh* is doubly novel.

Finally, the English-speaking reader is holding a work that will, by the catharsis its reading provokes, help him or her along in the modern process of accepting, beyond idealistic notions and the fetishism of the intellect, a primary truth: that we are made of flesh.

Translator's Note

Starting with the title page of *René's Flesh*, I have had to push around rather than pick up the gauntlet Virgilio Piñera throws down to the translator of this work. Whereas English distinguishes between "flesh" and "meat," Spanish fuses the two concepts in the single word *carne*, which is used in phrases like "flesh of my flesh" and "flesh and blood" as readily as in "meat pie." In *René's Flesh*, Piñera seizes on this linguistic duality to express one of his central axioms: that life is one big, existential slaughterhouse in which we are at once the butchers and the butchered. From the opening scene of the novel, the volatile ambivalence of the word *carne* constantly undermines any moral or conceptual boundaries the reader might draw between the characters and the physical continuum they share with the bloody side of beef.

I have tried to suggest this ambiguity at times by using the word "meat" where human bodies are being discussed and "flesh" in reference to food. However, I beg the English-speaking reader to, as it were, help flesh out Piñera's vision by recognizing that wherever the word "flesh" appears, it may be understood as "meat," and vice versa.

René's Flesh

Encounter in the Butcher Shop

The Equitable Butcher Shop, like any other shop in this line of business, is no fancy establishment; but today, in contrast to the prevailing placid afternoon, it looked like a fortress under siege. Though all is calm in the immediate vicinity, the shop itself is a hub of anxiety. The human tide continues to advance without truce. It now forms a line more than a block long.

The excitement—bordering on hysteria—is due to the unrestricted sale of meat. The public will be able to buy as much brisket, hocks, pot roast, steak, and ribs as they desire; those with a more demanding taste will purchase handsome quantities of pork or delicate legs of lamb. In effect, *carte blanche* has been announced for the duration of the afternoon and everyone is prepared to obtain the meat they need.

In times of rationing, people need not manifest their sanity when, as is now the case, meat is being sold on the free market. The act of abstaining from meat day after day has led them to the false belief that they will soon become victims of starvation. "What will become of us?" they say. And thus they spend their lives devising ways to obtain meat.

So one can understand their hysteria. At the sight of such quantities of flesh (which they will buy after standing in a line formed of anxieties and shoving) they now see it transformed into a terrifying void. The ones closest to the counter lay their eyes on the enormous sides of beef hanging from the meat hooks and inhale with pleasure the smell of coagulated blood. It is, as it were, a national holiday.

The female element predominates in the line: elegant ladies and women from the villages, maids, young girls. They all cut boldly into the line where it is the tightest. One of these ladies, Mrs. de Pérez, has by dint of smiles and hips managed to insert herself mere inches from the meat. Dressed as if for a party, she is chattering incessantly with her maid. Suddenly she cries out in surprise.

"Why, it's actually René! Look, Adela. Isn't that René there in the middle of the line? He looks hypnotized. Look, Adela," and she points him out. "Look how pale he is. If he were my child, I'd give him a glass of blood every morning. My God, what times these are!"

René, whose face is practically rubbing up against a quarter ox suspended from a meat hook, displays a frightening pallor. Butchered, throbbing flesh horrifies him. A corpse doesn't make the least impression on him, but the sight of a dead steer provokes him to nausea, then vomiting, and finally leaves him bedridden for days on end. Why then, despite such terrors, is he in line at the Equitable?

René is the son of Ramón, who has a pronounced taste for the flesh, a preference so passionate as to

4

constitute a veritable priesthood and even a dynasty, something that is passed on from father to son, that is jealously bequeathed to keep the enthusiasm alive.

This explains his presence in the butcher shop. For a young man about to inherit his father's crown, there's nothing like visiting the slaughterhouse on a regular basis. Men armed with large knives and picks assault the beef, splitting it from top to bottom. René has been brought here to witness this slaughter. It made such a frightening impression on him that he fell gravely ill. Consequently, Ramón judged that the matter should be approached gradually: first, systematic visits to butchers shops, then to the slaughterhouses, then later, to the great human hecatombs.

Emerging from his state of self-absorption, he took a look at the people there. His eyes ran into those of Mrs. Pérez, who hadn't taken her own eyes off him. She lived in unrequited love with René's flesh. According to this lady's very arbitrary canon, he was the living incarnation of a Greek demigod. Although there may be some historical confusion here, one can't deny that René is a splendid creature. While he doesn't possess the muscles of an athlete, his beauty resides in the quality of his skin. But more than this, what makes him irresistible is the seductiveness of his face. Its dominant quality is the appearance that it is appealing for protection against the furies of the world. And something curious: that appearance manifests itself in his sacrificial victim's flesh. Mrs. Pérez imagined his flesh wounded by a knife or punctured by a bullet, or she thought about it being used for pleasure or pain. When she set eyes on René's flesh for the first time, she experienced the unpleasant and distressing sensation that it was mere inches from being crushed by a truck, that it was a sheer miracle it remained intact, that it would only be a few minutes before something demolishing fell on top of him, annihilating his flesh. Countering all that, she saw it abandoned in divine ecstasy. Flesh this "vulnerable" (as she called it) promised unsuspected delights for the flesh lucky enough to acquire it along the path of life.

About to celebrate his twentieth birthday, René knew only his own flesh. Ramón had restricted him to such a solitary life that René had never even seen the naked flesh of boys his own age, much less knew the flesh of women. Ramón had striven to educate him in the most absolute of monasteries. He seemed to be striving to show to his son that there was only one man and one woman on earth: he and his mother.

This program of isolation was being realized with terrifying precision. Wherever this outlandish trio lived, people would always say the same thing: What school did they send their son to? What children does he play with? What girls does he look at? It would be pointless to try to answer such questions when others of a broader type remained unanswered as well: Who was Ramón? Where did he come from? What did he do...? Some people asserted he was a traveling businessman, others, an engineer, some, a smuggler, and there were even people who declared him an assassin. The truth is that the only thing certain about Ramón was that he was a man hopelessly in love with meat; so much so that he was making sure that his son's flesh thrived under the strictest vigilance possible in order to offer it up in holocaust to heaven-knows-what obscure divinities.

A rumor raced through the neighborhood concerning René's father's cult. Mr. Powlavski, an old Polish immigrant and an established jeweler, had heard from Ramón's lips this phrase spoken to an elderly man: "Don't get upset, while there's flesh, there's hope..."

6

René had set his eyes again on the hanging side of beef and was about to faint. Mrs. Pérez couldn't do a thing without risking her place on line. She was struggling between coming to René's aid and remaining in her spot. If she helped him, she'd lose her beef, but to let him faint would be intolerable as well. Then she saw her friend Laurita (her companion in *bel canto*,) who was standing right beside René. Signaling to her, she made her understand the situation. Laurita pulled a vial of smelling salts from her purse and handed it to René to sniff; he was revived and so was Mrs. Pérez.

And at that very moment, someone behind her spoke into her ear:

"I've witnessed everything."

"Good afternoon, Mr. Nieburg. You don't need a fifth sense to realize the condition that young man's in. Believe me, he inspires me with deep sadness."

"You know, madam, he doesn't affect me in the least. I don't like that kind of flesh. Rather, what I wish to say to you is that we still find that young man to be a profound mystery. I think he's a conspirator."

"You're always finding conspiracies, Mr. Nieburg. It's easy to imagine things and believe they're true. I..."

"Please, Mrs. Pérez, don't make yourself out to be discrete. Mr. Powlavski told me in confidence that you yourself had told him René has the face of a conspirator."

"How dare Mr. Powlavski put such slander in my mouth. It doesn't matter," she said plaintively. "There you have the very truth in front of you (and she pointed at René): look at him and tell me he looks like a conspirator. I'd say he looks like a sick person."

"A sick conspirator in any event, Mrs. Pérez. Look at that face: it inspires total mistrust."

"Scoundrel! Only an ill wind like you would dare call curses down on that poor head."

"They're already arranging—he and his family—for those curses to fall on other people. You're so naïve, madam. Excuse me, but I can't help but laugh. Don't you see that René's appearance is part and parcel of a farce?"

"Well, say what you will, but I will continue to believe René needs help."

"Why, of course, my dear friend; no need to worry. Certainly you can come to his aid. With your charms, the young man will be cheered up quite a bit. Well, it's my turn. Long live meat!—" and he said into her ear: "In all seriousness: be very careful with adventurers like him."

Mr. Nieburg's words threw Mrs. Pérez into a state of confusion. She began to imagine horrible situations: she saw René entering her house to rob her blind; she saw him in her bedroom caressing her with one hand while plunging a dagger into her heart with the other. So vivid were her terrors that she shouted out loud and went weak in the knees. She couldn't faint: the beef was being offered to her like the sacred Host. She found one more ounce of strength, picked out this and that, paid, and left. But before walking out, she went over to where René stood on line and held her hand out to him. In this way, she let Mr. Nieburg see that his words hadn't made her the least bit uneasy.

René was confused and turned his eyes back to the side of beef. People had commented when Laurita gave him the smelling salts to sniff. And now this woman was approaching to offer him her hand. René knew her by sight. (How could one help but notice the insistent and picturesque Mrs. Pérez?) Wherever he went, he would always bump into her, but she never dared say hello.

René didn't find her greeting unpleasant, but at the same time he remembered that his father had absolutely forbidden him from entering into friendly relations with anyone at all. What recanting and punishment awaited him if Ramón saw him exchanging greetings with Mrs. Pérez.

To top it all, they would talk in the neighborhood about how he'd grown faint on line (damn meat), and it would reach his father's ears. That is, his father was sending him to the butchers shop with the aim of familiarizing him with meat, and he had permitted himself a fainting spell. Instead of taking advantage of this profusion of butchered flesh, he partially closed his eyes and let his mind wander. He remembered how his father had told him that his "flesh was lean," and that on the verge of turning twenty, the promise it showed was frankly discouraging. That memory led him to the most torturous meditation of all: what was to be the fate of his flesh?

The years he had lived with his father threw no light on this question. Ramón, like those wizards who wrap themselves in mist to hide from other mortals, jealously kept all aspects of his life hidden. He sensed the abnormality of that life, but lacked proof. On the face of it, all was normal: eating, sleeping, taking a shower, going on a trip, returning, going to see a movie, reading. But at the same time—what perpetual excitement, moving from one city to another, from one country to another, from one continent to another even more distant. And his father's long, eternal homilies on the value of the flesh, on the meaning of the meat factor in the progress of nations. In truth it was an awfully complicated language, for meat was present in all topics of conversation. Now he remembered the gloss Ramón had made on Archimedes' celebrated apothegm: "Give me meat and I will move the world." Wherever René looked, he found overwhelming quantities of meat.

He once asked Ramón if he was thinking of making him learn the butchers trade, and his father answered that grapes will ripen on the vine... He added: "In any case, don't take this business about being a butcher literally. I believe you've never seen me butcher a head of cattle, nor am I a member of the butchers' and beef vendors' union. Just because I require your participation in the cult of meat doesn't necessarily mean you're going to be a butcher. You're destined for something infinitely more noble."

What was his father proposing? What was he proposing with those phrases always left half in the dark, his speaking in proverbs, with those phrases of double and even quintuple meaning? Why refuse to speak straight and to the point? But was a man who disguised each and every one of his actions capable of doing so? One had to see him walk: he did so as if fearing an act of aggression, always turning around in fear of a surprise attack, his eyes exploring the terrain before venturing outside. Without a doubt, someone was after his father, or he himself was after someone. René only had to review his brief life to confirm his presumption. Hadn't the life the three of them lived been one constant exodus? He couldn't recall having spent more than a year in the same country. They settled into this one or that one as if for the rest of their lives and then one day Ramón would pull up the stakes to move hundreds of miles away where everything was different—people, customs, language. A few months would pass and once again the exodus. They wouldn't leave cities pursued by threatening mobs, nor escorted by squads of soldiers, but there was such violence, anguish, and irritation in those precipitous dislocations. Now he remembered the last city where they "spent the night" in Europe before the great leap to North America. They arrived in the city during the winter and they abandoned it that same winter. The snow didn't have time to melt. He wasn't to blame if because of these dislocations his impression of the city became so narrow, so unilateral as to picture it as "eternally white."

Their arrival at the country of choice would also be peculiar: no sooner would they arrive than someone would approach them, quickly put them in a car, and take them to a new house. There, René would experience the same uneasiness as in the previous houses. He would have to peek through the window to see the transformed landscape and convince himself that he hadn't taken a step backwards. In these temporary lodgings there was always the eternal "office" of Ramón, an additional room in the house, but constantly kept closed. What did his father do in such an "office," what purpose did it serve? Ramón would spend his time there and Alicia herself would not have dared to bother him. The rare times René saw him leave the "office," he observed the signs on his face of exhausting fatigue, the drunk's unsteady gait. Moved, he expressed to his father his desire to help him with his work. Ramón responded with a stentorian cry.

In this last European city, they had beaten their record for staying in one place: they resided there for just eight months. All of a sudden they flew to North America. René started laughing like a fool when he got home, weighed down by several pounds of meat, and saw his parents packing their suitcases. Ramón told him they would be leaving for North America within the hour. The package of meat fell from René's hands and with his mouth wide open, he looked like astonishment incarnate. It wasn't the announcement of the trip that

11

left his mouth agape (he had been raised on such surprises), but rather the uselessness of his purchase. This
sent him into such a fit of laughter that Ramón repri-
manded him; but René, rolling around on the floor,
shouted amidst convulsive bursts of laughter that the
cats were going to have a field day.

Such a picturesque "moment" made him roll his eyes
back in his head. The scene could even be repeated
today. When he arrived home, burdened with meat and
shame, would he find his parents feverishly making
their travel preparations? So wasn't it more prudent to
call and ask whether they were suddenly about to disap-
pear? But this idea—which in essence was nothing more
than his supreme goal of seeing his suffering in the
butchers shops come to an end—departed as fast as it
had arrived. And in its place this idea took shape: we will
leave this city to arrive at another one, and I will go
afternoon after afternoon to buy meat.

His future would always be the dead weight of his
past. It was enough to make him rebel against the rules
of conduct his father imposed on him, leave the meat
he'd purchased right there, and tell Ramón what's
what...

Just then the customer behind him said:

"Come on! Wake up!..."

René gave a start and stood before the butcher, who,
pointing his knife at him, asked him what kind and how
much meat he wanted to buy.

And once more, with the cry of a wounded animal,
he asked for two pounds of this and eight of that... Then,
to make his shame and frustration all the more obvious, the butcher offered him some scraps for the cat.

Pro Meat

After drinking his coffee, Ramón said to Alicia:
"You have to treat my wound."

René, who was still drinking his coffee, dropped his cup upon hearing the word "wound." He bent down to pick up the pieces. Could he have heard wrong? He heard Ramón's voice again.

"Come on, Alicia, get a move on, the wound won't wait..."

René's hands began to tremble, the pieces of cup leapt from his fingers. He heard Ramón's voice again:

"Come here, René, I need you by my side. It's time you start learning about these things."

René lifted his head and remained in that position, as if stuck onto a pole. For years he had followed the program of contemplating beef flesh. Suddenly, without prior warning, he was being invited to contemplate human wounds. Then he remembered that he would be turning twenty the following day and connected his birthday with his father's unexpected revelation. While proceeding with the cult of beef flesh, he would have a new task imposed upon him: to attend the treatment of his father's wound.

Ramón took off his shirt. René saw he had a chest wound.

"Wouldn't you want to have a wound like this?"

René turned livid, stood up, began to back away.

"No, don't do that," Ramón's voice intercepted him. "You must be present for the treatment."

"Please, papa, it makes me want to throw up!"

"You hear that, Alicia? So he wants to throw up... Then you don't want to have your very own wound?"

"No, no, I don't. It's horrible."

Ramón and Alicia looked at each other. René began to cry. He saw Ramón coming toward him; he thought he was going to wound him in the chest. He let out a cry and fell to his knees.

"Papa, I'll obey you completely; just don't kill me!"

"I won't be the one to stick the knife in your chest, son. But consider that there are millions of hands and millions of knives in this world..."

He grabbed René by the shoulders and sat him down in a chair.

"Look: your body, mine, your mother's body—everyone's body is made of meat. This is very important, and because it is often forgotten, many people fall victim to the knife. You already know that I practice the cult of meat—not of intact, athletic flesh, but of slain meat, truly alive and throbbing like this wound. Or like this—" and he rolled up the leg of his pants. "Look at that wound, the size of your fist. It's fresh. Even after it heals, the skin will be translucent and violet. Or if you prefer, I can show you my first injury, an injury forty years old that nevertheless continues to conserve its scar. Look at it—" He took off his shoe and sock with great calm and standing on one foot showed the sole of the other. "Don't you see how it runs from heel to toe? And it's same on the other foot. These two injuries represent my first battle with the flesh and from which, if I'm not mistaken, I emerged victorious. I won't relate that adventure to you, but you can be sure it was no bird's feather pressed against those soles for hours upon hours. So you see, my body has a lot of meat from which to cut... Want another example? Look at my right shoulder. You know that this part of the body is called the collarbone. All right then, it has been transformed into a grotesque protuberance. What is the cause of such a violent dislocation? And why aren't there any toenails on my toes and that in their place one can observe blackened breaches? Yes, look; don't tire of looking, of examining, and if you wish you can even touch me. Come on! Courage! You're seeing me as I really am. But there's more, this isn't all... Look here. What is responsible for the fact that the skin of my stomach—" and he showed his deformed stomach—"is covered with large seams? Not to mention other signs—tiny, but not therefore any less refined. Look at this perforation in my ear. It's the size of a dime. I confess to you I feel a certain tenderness towards that one. It's given me the sensation of being an observation post for all that is held within my body—." He let out a booming burst of laughter and threw himself on the floor. "What a body I have! What do you think of it? And listen, it's been forty years of struggle against the flesh, but always spirited, always collecting trophies, beating records; in a word, resisting, son, resisting..."

"Resisting, papa? Resisting what?" René said through his tears.

"All right, calm down, I don't see any reason for crying. I don't believe I'm dead yet... Calm down."

He was pensive for a moment and then went on:

"Do you think that all these blows, wounds, fractures are due to me having been an acrobat or a boxer? To what trade or profession do you attribute such anomalies? Fine, grapes will ripen on the vine... I believe yours have already begun to ripen. Tell me: haven't you thought that your body might become the same as mine?"

"No, no, papa!" René implored. "I don't like wounds. I'd rather keep my body whole."

"What nonsense! What does that mean, your body whole? So, if you don't want it damaged, what are you keeping it for?"

He took René by the arm and stood him on his feet.

"If your chest doesn't have a wound like mine, what good is it to you? If your stomach is free of seams, what do you want it for? If those arms make it to old age without injury, what good will they have been to you? If your legs don't bear a thousand and one injuries, for what pleasurable use are you reserving them? Tell me, you romantic hero—" and he shook him violently "—you young man-in-the-moon with a dreamy look in his eye, what do you think of life? Whole body, smooth skin, turgidities... Tell me son, your own father is asking you: Don't you love butchered flesh?"

"It's ugly," was all René could say. He let his head slump against his chest.

"Ah! Now our hero faints! Quick, call a doctor, bring the smelling salts... The king's son has died, the scepter passes to other hands! No, no, young dreamer, you haven't died and you aren't about to faint."

He put his shoe on, crossed his arms, and examined René very carefully. A fly that had fallen into a glass was

16

beating its wings in vain in an effort to escape. With consummate delicacy, Ramón caught the fly and placed it on a rose. He slowly began to put on his shirt. At last, lifting up René's head, he said:

"You know what my father's comrades called him?"

And as if calculating the effect, he began circumspectly to tie his tie. At last he said:

"My father, who died two years before you were born, went to the grave accompanied by more than two hundred injuries. Without a doubt he had been educated in the great traditions. Even I, I, who inspire such horror in you, I, who seem like a monster of deformity, couldn't even remotely compare to your grandfather. Do you know he had a wound that began at his right nipple, transversed the breadth of his back, and ended back at the same nipple? And that he kept this same wound— compared to which mine is nothing but a mosquito bite—open and festering to his dying day? Are you unaware that your grandfather, comrade of comrades, victoriously withstood twenty-five needles under his fingernails?"

René didn't let him continue. He embraced his father, and amidst heaving sobs, asked:

"Why, papa? Why was my grandfather the Human Pincushion?"

"Tell me, René, don't you turn twenty tomorrow?"

"Yes, tomorrow's my birthday. But tell me, why was my grandfather the Human Pincushion?"

"My dear child, tomorrow, the day you turn twenty, I will put you in possession of the secret of the flesh."

With these words a long silence ensued which Ramón found pleasing. René had flung himself into Alicia's arms, the two of them forming a homely Pietá at the mercy of an implacable Caesar. As if this improvised, aesthetic picture of mother with child irritated him, Ramón said:

"And tomorrow the battle for the flesh will also start for you. So now you know..."

He was interrupted by the loud ringing of the door-bell. René ran to open the door. He drew back in fright. Walking in with great self-assurance was Mrs. Pérez, saying:

"I'm not going to eat you up, my little treasure... I've just come to find out how your precious health is doing. I saw you in the butchers shop on the verge of fainting away."

She curtsied deeply for Alicia and Ramón:

"You two have a very sensitive child."

"We thank you, madam, for the interest you take in René," Ramón responded, "but I assure you his flesh will be properly tempered."

"The necessary tempering... " Mrs. Pérez repeated in ecstasy before a René whose flesh was tastily tempered for love. "I congratulate both of you," she added. "You brought into this world a being who will make a brilliant career of his body."

Hearing these words, René acknowledged Mrs. Pérez and prepared to leave the dining room. Mrs. Pérez grabbed him by the arm.

"You're not going to deprive me of your charming presence. I'll only be a few minutes. I neglected to introduce myself. My name is Dalia de Pérez. It's a great pleasure."

"A great pleasure," Alicia and Ramón said mechanically. "Well, the fact is," Dalia went on, "that this young man was about to faint on line at the butchers shop. Thanks to my friend Laurita, his pretty body did not tumble to the ground."

"Be assured that that scene will not be repeated, madam. Starting tomorrow..."

"Why, of course," Dalia said, "starting tomorrow, starting tomorrow... But a treatment of the nerves wouldn't be out of place. One can see that René's nerves are very sensitive fibers. You're not going to deny that nerves are also made of flesh, and that if we alter them, the whole body is altered."

For a moment she found herself muddled in her reflections, and then added all at once:

"What I mean to say is that René's flesh isn't made for pain. That is," and she bolstered the phrase with a giggle, "no pain whatsoever for that flesh."

"Exactly how I feel," said Ramón. "So much so that that's why I send him to the butchers shop. Tell me, Mrs. Pérez, isn't it a pleasure to see all that butchered flesh?"

Now Dalia was the one about to faint.

"What! My God, what are you saying! Butchered flesh! The torture rack! No, no, remove that infernal vision from my sight, and from your son's sight as well. Look at his body: it's trembling like a leaf. It's a body built for pleasure. Make life pleasurable for your son's body."

"My enchanting Mrs. Pérez," Ramón responded ironically, "I see you take a tremendous interest in René's destiny. Don't worry; my son's flesh will flower in its own time.

"I'm enchanted to hear you say that, sir. When I hear the word flower, my soul returns to my body. And if I can be of any help in that flowering, I am at the disposal of your son."

René turned red. Dalia was making him blush. The blood rose to Ramón's head. Should he throw the woman headfirst into the street?

But Dalia didn't give him the chance. She was walking toward the door as she expressed her regards. Once there, she unfurled a seductive smile, expressed her regards again and said:

"Make his flesh flower."

The Cause

The next day, René's birthday, Alicia woke him up
very early. She told him Ramón would be waiting for
him at seven o'clock in the "office," that he should
hurry up, that it was quarter to seven, that he should go
without having eaten. She tickled him as she said this to
get him out of bed. René resisted, not so much out of
laziness as from the stupor in which his father's order
had left him. What was the meaning of going to see him
"without having eaten"? He eventually got up, went into
the bathroom, washed summarily, and at seven o' clock
knocked on the door to the "office."

"Enter," he heard Ramón's somewhat muffled voice
say.

René pushed the door open and went in. He thought
he was in a dentist's reception room. The walls were
painted white and from the ceiling hung one of those
lamps used in operating rooms. In the middle of the

room was a kind of dentist's chair, between yellow and cream-colored. In a glass cabinet, clamps, forceps, scalpels... Hanging from the ceiling at the back of the room, pulleys, ropes, and slings... René could see several oxyacetylene blowtorches on an iron table. Finally, his eyes came to rest on a very large painting, an oil painting of the Martyrdom of St. Sebastian, or at least the painter had taken this martyrdom as his point of departure, since one couldn't exactly say in the case of this painting that it was a martyrdom. The painting presented a beautiful youth, as Sebastian had been, in a relaxed position with a wandering gaze and an enigmatic smile on his face. Thus far, the painting presented nothing out of the ordinary, but it was in reference to the arrows that this oil departed from the traditional model. This St. Sebastian was drawing arrows from a quiver and sticking them into his body. The painter had shown him in the moment of sticking the last one into his forehead. His arm was still raised, his fingers now removed from the end of the arrow and seeming to fear that this arrow hadn't sunk definitively into his flesh.

He came still closer to the painting. At that moment the light from a reflector fell on the painting, which until then had only enjoyed a slight illumination. René stepped back in fright: Wasn't that his face? Wasn't this St. Sebastian René: his hair, his mouth, and his forehead? As if in a dream, he heard Ramón's voice:

"It looks like you, doesn't it?"

René didn't answer. His eyes remained fixed on the young Sebastian's face like one of the arrows. Ramón asked him again about the resemblance. René was surprised anew. His father was sitting in his armchair, his fingers horribly constricted by several tourniquets. Ramón insisted again on the resemblance.

"The face is the same," mused René. "Yes, father, that's me; but I don't understand..."

"Tell me, son. Do you like it?"

René felt all his strength abandoning him. His emotions were very intense. Living with his father had been strange, but things such as what was happening right now affected him immediately. It was slowly dawning on him that Ramón was also going to count on him for "the service of pain." His father's voice, repeating the question, pulled him suddenly from that childish plane on which he had been moving until then, and placed him in the reality of violence. He found himself obliged to respond. Ramón asked him for the third time.

"Yes, father. I like it."

"That's not saying anything! Obviously I know you like it! You're talking about the painting as such... And that's not what I'm talking about. I know it's a good canvas because the painter who executed it is one of us, and we never do things poorly. What I want to know is whether you feel like the René in the picture."

"Pierced with arrows?"

"Pierced with arrows and everything in this room. It's all so little in support of the cause!"

He removed his fingers from the tourniquets. They were bruised from the compression.

"I've never spoken to you of the Cause?"

"The Cause?..."

"The Cause is world revolution. As long as it remains unrealized, we must serve it with arms. There's a chief. This chief, who betrayed the Cause, controls our country. He pursues us because we pursue him. His pursuit takes place in and out of that country. Your grandfather, who had the privilege of serving the chief who crushed the old chief, spent the last ten years of his life pursuing his chief, who, in turn, was pursuing him. The end result was the death of your grandfather."

"And the chief is also pursuing you, father?"

"I'm not done telling you yet! Yes, he's pursuing me. I received your grandfather's inheritance. I am chief of those who are pursued, who pursue those who pursue us. Nevertheless, the two chiefs are very far apart. In other times we were so close that we shook hands every day. Then we began to separate. At first we thought that it would only be a few hours before we finished him off. We soon realized the truth. We abandoned the country; we found ourselves face to face, as they say... But he initiated the pursuit. What else could he do knowing he was being pursued? We began putting land and sea between us. Over the course of thirty years the possibilities of settling anywhere were reduced; hell, the earth isn't boundless. And now you see us reduced to this city."

He got up from the armchair and turned his back to René. "Do you know how many times partisans of the chief have placed me in mortal danger?"

"Mortal?..." René exclaimed. "Father, do you mean attempts on your life?"

"That's right, René, attempts against my person. Well, eighteen attempts of the first magnitude, not to mention others of lesser importance. For example, an attempt of the first magnitude is one in which the pursuers corner you, you see their faces, you see their weapons, their arms bind you, you're gravely injured, you escape by the skin of your teeth... As for those of lesser importance, for example, they would send you a time bomb. You're endangered, but since you are suspicious of all packages, you don't take it in your hands. At one point, the chief and I were tied for the number of attempts of the first magnitude. Then he began gaining an advantage over me; he had greater resources. Many of our people, tired of waiting for the worldwide revolution to triumph, either went over to the side of the enemy or simply withdrew from the struggle. This produced a kind of window on my person which, I confess, he has known how to use to his advantage. On the other hand, the fluctuations of international politics has been so propitious for him that as I speak to you, he has almost every government at his disposal; they are almost all friendly to him. So as not to bore you, until very recently we were seven attempts even. From then on, we haven't been able to deal him a single blow. He, however, beat his own record, doubled it, added another two attempts. He now has eighteen to his credit. If he still feels pursued, it is because he fervently desires to lose his flesh. The truth is that only in theory does he await an attempt on my part."

"But father," René exclaimed keenly, "I don't see why you have to die. Everything can be worked out. Write that chief a letter explaining to him that you are retiring from the pursuit."

"Retire from the pursuit!... The pursuit never ends, it is infinite; not even death would bring it to a close; you'll be there to carry it on. Haven't you seen runners in relay races? When one of them lets the torch fall, the next runner immediately picks it up. Your grandfather handed me the torch, I'll pass it on to you, you'll put it in the hands of your child or in his absence, in the hands of the most outstanding member of the party. The cause can't be left idle even for an instant."

"What are you fighting over?" René asked, extremely agitated.

"Over a piece of chocolate," his father responded solemnly. "It's all caused by a piece of chocolate. The chief now pursuing me succeeded many years ago, through hard and bloody struggle, in crushing the powerful and fierce chief who had prohibited under penalty of death the use of chocolate in his states. The latter rigorously maintained this century-old prohibition. His ancestors—founders of that monarchy—had prohibited the use of chocolate in their kingdoms. They said that chocolate could undermine the security of the throne. Imagine the efforts, the struggles that took place for centuries to prevent the use of the aforementioned foodstuff. Millions of people died, others were deported; there were civil wars. No cost was too high to prevent chocolate from "getting through"! Finally the chief who now pursues me obtained a crushing victory over the last sovereign and we experienced the joy—oh, so short-lived!—of flooding our various territories with chocolate."

"Tell me, father. How did chocolate undermine the security of the throne?"

"It's very simple: the founder of the dynasty claimed that chocolate is a powerful foodstuff, that the masses should be kept in a perpetual state of semihunger, that this was the best means of assuring the perpetuity of the throne. So imagine our joy when, after centuries of horrendous battles, we could flood the country with chocolate. The masses, who had been bequeathed that pathetic predisposition to drinking chocolate, went about consuming it like crazy. Everything ran smoothly at first. But one awful day, the chief began to restrict its use. Your grandfather, who had seen his father and his grandfather perish over the implantation of chocolate, was categorically opposed to this restriction. And so the first friction with the chief took place. As in all struggles to the death, there were the indispensable trial balloons, the apparent settlements. One day we would wake up filled with hope: the chief was giving *carte blanche* in the use of chocolate; another day he would limit its use to three times a week. Meanwhile, the discussions were heating up. Your grandfather, the most influential figure close to the chief, would reproach him for such fatal policies, going so far as to call him "reactionary." There was a bitter dispute, resulting the next day in my father's secretary in the War Ministry being found in his home in the throes of death: someone had forced him to drink a gallon of hot, bitter chocolate. That was the last straw. My father openly opposed the government; the group of chocolatophiles was formed. I was very young at the time, but I remember very vividly a march under the balconies of the House of Government by people eating chocolate bars. In reprisal, the chief seized all the chocolate extant in the country. We didn't back down but instead wore chocolate-colored clothing. The chief, considering that all this could very well incite the masses to rise up against him, declared us guilty of high treason against the state and ordered a huge trial. With great difficulty, my father was able to cross the border and seek refuge in the neighboring country. Did you know that the trials resulted in the death of thousands of our people?"

"But if they weren't guilty, why did that chief have them executed?" René cried out, beside himself.

"Why?... Ask him," and Ramón guffawed. "Meanwhile, my father and his supporters kept up the holy cause of chocolate; consequently, he would have to die. He knew this and furthermore, he knew that the masses, who wouldn't have openly protested the prohibition were it not for the campaign carried out by the opposition, would now engage in a struggle to the death over the right to eat and drink chocolate when and wherever they might desire. Events soon confirmed the chief's suspicions. The peasants revolted. This resulted in their death by the thousands and the deportation of many thousands more to the frozen regions of the country. Almost all of them died. Then your grandfather made the first assassination attempt. The chief's secretary-in-chief was one of us. I won't spend time on the details of this arduous commission. Suffice it to say that the cup of chocolate that the chief was going to drink one morning was poisoned."

"You mean the chief drank chocolate?" René exclaimed in surprise.

"How can you be so naïve! Of course he used chocolate—and my God, in what quantities! He and his sympathizers knew this drink to be highly stimulating, not to mention that if they prohibited the masses from enjoying it, it was precisely because if the masses and the government were to drink it on equal footing it would have politically weakened the latter. Don't forget that the chief and his sympathizers aspired—by means of the secret bonds of chocolate—to world domination."

"Father," René interrupted, "Now that I think of it, I've never seen you drink chocolate. As for me, I don't know what it tastes like..."

"You're still ingenuous... So we would lower ourselves to drinking chocolate? You think we're so foolish as to be seen with a cup of chocolate in our hand? What we're defending is the cause of chocolate. Would it make any sense for us to drink it like a bunch of desperadoes thousands of leagues from the battle over chocolate? And to finish illustrating the point: I must confess that we're sick of it. Your grandfather himself would smile slyly when they spoke to him of chocolate, which didn't prevent him from giving his life defending it tooth and nail."

René walked over to the painting and, placing one finger over the hand holding the arrow stuck in St. Sebastian's forehead, he asked Ramón innocently:

"Why didn't you tell the painter that, instead of an arrow, to put a cup of chocolate in my hand?"

Ramón grew suddenly agitated.

"We leave that for propaganda!"

He went over to the table, rummaged around in a drawer, pulled out a photograph.

"Look. Here you see us at the anniversary banquet of the prohibition of chocolate. Do you notice that we're each holding a cup? Nevertheless, we never held such a banquet and by no means did we drink chocolate. But this didn't prevent us from printing millions of copies of the photo to be circulated throughout the world. But let's leave your naïve notions to one side and return to the chief. He had discovered the conspiracy. The morning I'm telling you about, he appeared in the Chancellery carrying a steaming cup of chocolate in his right hand. Seeing him, his secretary was frozen stiff with fear. Then, without wasting any words, the chief told him to drink the chocolate... You can imagine how the scene ended: the secretary was forced to drink down his own hemlock. Within minutes, he was a corpse. That very day the government of the country in which we were spending our exile declared us pernicious foreigners. A lot of water has passed under the bridge since then. Your grandfather was assassinated; I'm about to perish. The ring is growing tighter and tighter. That's why, and on the occasion of your birthday, I've called you here to inform you of the disposition of the party and of my own disposition."

"The disposition of the party?..." René could barely stammer.

"It's the party's disposition that you be my successor, in my role as the pursued as well as of the pursuer. They are two diametrically opposed functions. Each requires different tactics. You will learn both, but since luck has been against us of late, you will have to prepare yourself for being the great pursued of our Cause. My advice is that without expressly resigning the office of pursuer, you place an accent on the extremely complicated technique of being pursued. Don't forget that for the moment the perpetuity of the Cause depends on flight... A good fleer can cause great damage to the enemy. He who flees does so from two things: from another man like him, and from confession. The first is defined as an attempt on one's life; the second, torture."

"Torture?..." stammered René.

"Absolutely," his father answered coldly. "If I had the painting made, it was for the sole purpose of making you come to an aesthetic understanding of your destiny."

"But father, I'm the one torturing myself."

"Effectively, you're the one torturing yourself. It's a way of inviting others to torture you. Who, faced with so many arrows, could resist the temptation to stick one more into you? I, for example." And quick as lightning, he stuck a needle in René's arm. René let out a horrible cry and fell at Ramón's feet, who, lifting him up, said with immense tenderness:

"There's your birthday present."

He sat down in the armchair, applied the tourniquets, and jovially exclaimed:

"Go have your breakfast."

The Human Body

Mrs. Pérez had pretensions of being a writer. Two volumes of verse and the fact that she was the widow of a famous journalist conferred on her a certain notoriety among her friends. Still young and possessing a fortune, she wished to achieve prominence. And after a certain fashion, she was succeeding. Although she could never fill her home with "the best," and not even with much of "the mediocre," she was considered a triumphant woman. She burst with pride to say that her "Thursday musicales" were one of the attractions of the city.

On these Thursdays—as anachronistic as Mrs. Pérez herself (to whom her no less anachronistic husband had bequeathed the atmosphere of the provincial soirée)—three things took place: the recitation of poetry, piano playing, and singing. All of it wrapped in a cloud of absurd conversation. Dalia recited her own poetry, sang her own songs, and accompanied herself on the piano. Furthermore, she helped enlarge this "absurd cloud" with incessant prattle mixed with stupid laughter. She was one of those people who, seated at the piano and absorbed in whatever they're performing, suddenly gets up to take part in the *sotto voce* conversation of her guests, who, bored with the "piece" that Mrs. Pérez is interpreting, are critiquing it scathingly. Letting out her famous laugh here and there, she asks them what they're talking about *sotto voce*. The guests feign innocence. Dalia goes back to the piano. And thus, every Thursday Mrs. Pérez's life is (it couldn't be otherwise) a bed of roses...

But on the Thursday of our story, Dalia had withdrawn into a deep silence. Her nerves were at the bursting point: she would get up, sit down again, walk around the salon, arrange some flowers here, give orders to the servant there... She was scarcely attending to her guests. She left Mr. Powlavski in midsentence; she didn't kiss the enchanting Laura; she forgot to compliment Blanco, the critic. They were beginning to comment on her strange behavior.

What was happening to Dalia? In a word, she was awaiting the arrival of René. In presenting him to her friends that Thursday, she wished to enjoy a resounding triumph. Her feminine vanity could not bear to lose this triumph. Nieburg and Powlavski would become green with envy. Laurita, who had also had her eye on René, would chew on her fingernails out of sheer peevishness; Blanco, who boasted of knowing all the young people in the city, wouldn't forgive her this introduction. So impatient was Dalia to "harvest" this triumph that she was all ready to announce René's visit, but restrained herself in anticipation of a fiasco.

Mercedes (her rival in *bel canto*) arrived to distract her from her restlessness. She begged, in the name of the guests, that Dalia deign to open the poetic-musical session with the pretty ballad "I Await You Day and Night." Recovering her habitual vivacity, Dalia sat down at the piano. She ran her fingers up and down the scales, and shortly her voice "flooded" the salon. Midway through the ballad the guests were commenting *sotto voce* on the melancholy with which Mrs. Pérez was singing.

Suddenly, this very melancholy interpretation was interrupted by the energetic sound of the doorbell ringing. As if shot from a gun, Dalia got up and ran to the front door, leaving the salon. She returned in an instant, but this time with the look on her face of a winner running her victory lap. She reappeared leading René by the hand. Mr. Nieburg dropped his cigarette on the rug out of sheer surprise, and Mr. Powlavski rose to his feet throwing the whole weight of his body forward. Then Dalia went from group to group making the formal introductions.

By the grace of the recently arrived guest, Dalia was again Dalia. The faces of Nieburg and Powlavski were burning questions devouring Dalia's face, which burst with vanity. René, timid as always, said very little and even blushed when Laurita extolled his splendid gray eyes.

"How the hell did you become friends with René, Mrs. Pérez?" asked Powlavski.

"You remember that afternoon in the butchers shop?" Dalia answered. "And you remember how pale René was? Well, I went to his house that very afternoon. We've been great friends ever since."

Hearing the word "house," Nieburg and Powlavski said in chorus: "Describe the house."

"It was like any old house: living room, front hall, bedrooms, dining room, kitchen, bathroom..."

It suddenly occurred to her to mention the "office." If she supplied Nieburg and Powlavski with this morsel, her triumph that night would be magnificent. But just as she was about to give free rein to her proverbial rumorography, she stopped dead and her expression suddenly changed. She noticed that their two faces revealed an anticipation that went beyond simple curiosity.

"What's wrong, Mrs. Pérez? Is there something you can't tell?"

"Oh, no, not at all! It's a very domestic-looking house. There's nothing you can't see, and furthermore, René's parents showed me all around."

Taking drastic measures, she began to speak of the fanfare over the discovery of a new drug to calm the nerves. Nevertheless, the implacable Nieburg and Powlavski kept returning to the earlier topic: they asked for details, specifications, heights and widths, feet and even sixteenths of an inch... To get them off her back, Dalia took advantage of the servant who was passing by with a tray; she grabbed two cocktails, placed them in the two men's hands, and left them in midsentence.

She hung on René's arm as she took him to see a glass cabinet crammed full of fans and pieces of ivory. Nieburg and Powlavski followed them. Standing in front of the cabinet, Dalia was now pointing out this and that ivory to René, speaking nonstop all the while. Standing about a yard away, Nieburg and Powlavski were—without René being able to see them—making mysterious signals to Dalia and giving her looks that asked many more questions, and even with their fingers were expressing their desire for a private interview. Dalia responded by casting a murderous glance at them, but Powlavski, ignoring the threat, approached her and asked her with utter insolence to play the Emperor's Waltz... Mrs. Pérez had no choice but to play it. As she didn't know it by heart, Powlavski offered to turn the pages; as he did so, he leaned over the performer and asked *ad eternum* whether anything out of the ordinary was going on in René's house. Dalia was nearly swooning as she finished the cheerful waltz.

At that moment, the servant announced that dinner was served. Dalia found herself obliged to accept the arm Powlavski offered her. With hesitant steps, she crossed the salon and collapsed into the chair that Powlavski himself slipped under her behind with mock solicitousness. Making a superhuman effort, Dalia, who was seated to the left of Blanco the critic, responded with a smile to the question the latter was asking about the consommé:

"No, my friend, it isn't chicken, it's beef."

And she hastily added:

"Tonight's dinner is composed exclusively of...carnal...dishes."

She let out one of her laughs and said again:

"Carnal dishes... A beef consommé, a mutton stew, pork chops..."

"My dear friend," Blanco said, "you aren't going to complete the menu by telling us that the fourth course is a stew made of human flesh...?"

"As for that, no. Although cannibalism..."

And she shut up, totally confused and beginning to blush. Damn Nieburg and Powlavski for causing her to make stupid remarks! There's always a party pooper, and they had decided to torture her. Plucking up her courage, she said amidst boisterous laughter:

"Well, my friends, if anyone at this dinner is a vegetarian or abstains from meat on religious principles, you can fast..."

"I don't think any of the guests fall under either of the two categories, Dalia," said Mercedes. "I don't see anything but sharpened incisors... Unless the guest of honor..." and she cast a penetrating glance at René.

Everyone looked at him; he felt their gazes like needles in his flesh. Furthermore, the flesh was being alluded to once again; it wouldn't just be the "main course" of that meal, it was also the topic of conversation, and who could say what dangers he would be exposed to, what traps, what depths...

"No," said René in a tiny voice, "I eat meat as well."

These words, uttered as if by a victim facing his executioner, were received with a general outburst of laughter. So René ate meat *as well*. But how did he eat it? With his jaw trembling, his teeth unsteady, with the mouth of a dying man, with the confusion of a sinner...

"*Caramba*, Dalia," exclaimed Blanco. "Your little friend's statement constitutes a downright reproach. He considers himself and us to be sinners."

"What are you saying!..." cried Dalia. "Can't you see you're scaring him? His flesh isn't yet like ours; it faints away at the slightest thing... Why, the other day at the butchers shop..."

"I can attest to that," Laurita shouted mockingly, raising her hand. "The other day at the butchers shop..." and she saw Dalia chastely lowering her eyes.

"So," said Blanco, "what happened at the butchers shop?"

"Nothing so important as to make a mountain out of a molehill..." answered Dalia. "Just a predisposition of the spirit when faced with the flesh."

"Human flesh?" asked Blanco.

"No, faced with beef flesh. To make a long story short: the other day René was on the verge of experiencing a fainting spell when he saw the sides of beef hanging from meat hooks."

"Okay, okay..." said Blanco. "And now you serve him a dinner composed exclusively of meat dishes. Well, it's going to give your little friend a fainting spell tonight."

And he roared thunderously.

At that moment the mutton stew was served. René thought he too was a lamb and that Dalia and her friends were going to pick him to pieces. He thought of saying something—he was about to say it—but Dalia was faster, asking him:

"Are you going to eat the stew?"

"Of course I'll eat the stew," René answered, with such precipitation that the words jumbled up in his mouth. "I'm going to eat stew and pork chops and if they're served, roast beef and baked veal as well, and even pig's feet and tripe..."

"Bravo!" Dalia applauded. "Long live meat!"

"To meat!" shouted Blanco. And he served himself a big helping of stew.

Everyone followed his example except René, who barely tasted the stew, as well as the rest of the menu. Dalia left off encouraging him. He could take it or leave it... As if René's anguish when faced with meat weighed on everyone's heart and shut everyone's mouth, the dinner transpired in deadly silence.

Until at last Dalia broke the silence, exclaiming:

"Such is life..."

And, getting up from her seat, she gave the signal to leave the table. The enchanting soirée had been decisively transformed by René's presence into a wake. Dalia didn't sing anymore, nor did any of the guests ask her to do so. There were no more bursts of laughter, nor did anyone revive their displays of frivolity. René, appearing to be made of marble and seemingly stripped of his flesh, was able to freeze all those throbbing pieces of flesh made of appetite and excess. In the four or five small groups that formed after dinner, all that anyone talked about was him: to "flay" him, to smash that funereal character to little bits. Who did he think he was? Wasn't he made of flesh? Was he some superior soul? May it never occur to that killjoy to return to Dalia's soirées!

And as if by common agreement, a general exodus took place. Desolate, Dalia was repeating: "But it's still so early!... But it's still so early!..." *Vox clamavit in deserto...* They all withdrew sporting airs of offended ambassadors, barely saying goodbye to Dalia and with ostensible discourtesy, failing to acknowledge René.

Reclining against the chimney, he waited for everyone to leave. He wasn't reclining against the chimney in order to adopt a romantic pose *á la* Chateaubriand, but rather because he felt he was about to collapse. Those friends of Dalia had let him know very clearly that he was an antisocial element. Only by the carnal path did human beings realize themselves; he, on the other hand, in his denial of the flesh and of his own flesh, was a loner, a mystic, an anchorite, a cenobite. To dare to be or pass as being thus in such eminently carnal times?

Furthermore, Dalia would say all this to him and much more. And he, still in this house to which he would never again be invited. At that moment, he heard Dalia's voice, saw her coming toward him.

"What? You haven't left?"

René jabbered:

"Well... I... Dalia... right away..."

Dalia was now by his side, taking his hands in hers.

"You're so charming! My God, what a pleasant surprise! I thought you'd left without saying goodbye—with complete justification, of course: those people are unbearable. It's just as well they've gone. This way we can be alone. The night is young..."

And she stood there looking at him amorously.

"It's very late, Dalia. Besides, it was my fault that..."

"You're at fault for my sins? Don't talk nonsense. You're adorable. Come here. We'll be more comfortable on the couch."

She sat him down. She went around turning off the lamps, leaving one lit next to the sofa. She returned with two glasses of cognac.

"A toast to our eternal friendship. We're going to be friends for all eternity, aren't we?"

René answered in monosyllables. He was beginning to get tipsy, for he had drunk the cognac in one shot. Furthermore, Dalia's perfume was like an invitation to relax, to sink into oblivion. Suddenly he remembered Ramón and stood up.

"Oh," said Dalia. "What an ill-bred boy! What are you doing... Now that we're here, truly among family; now there's true intimacy."

She got up and picked up a large-format book from the table in front of them. She sat down, pressing herself against René in his fright, and said:

"You do like painting, don't you? Well, we're going to distract ourselves..."

The book was an album of paintings. The title page said: "The Human Body." She held the book closed for several minutes in order to observe René's reaction, who squirmed in his seat out of extreme nervousness. Then all of a sudden Dalia opened the book and showed him the first print. The figure represented a completely nude young man in the classic posture of anatomy manuals. René felt cold. It seemed to him the figure was shivering. As if in a dream, he heard Dalia's voice posing the same question Ramón had asked him in front of the painting of St. Sebastian: "Do you like it?" He was assaulted by the idea that she was in cahoots with his father, and that all of this was a scene prepared by the two of them, that the album would be a horrible succession of tortured figures, and finally that Dalia herself would burn the soles of his feet or would stick him to the wall with an arrow... He leaned back and dried his forehead which was bathed in a cold sweat. He begged Dalia to leave the album for another occasion; he didn't feel well at all after the cognac he had drunk. Without paying attention to him, Dalia flipped the page. This time the figure was female and, like the previous one, was presented in a typical anatomic position. The result was so aseptic that, fearing René would start to reflect on the miseries of the flesh, Dalia began to eroticize the "frigidity" of the figure. She said that no woman could conveniently display her natural charms without the concurrence of an appropriate frame, and that in her humble opinion the one that would best serve that figure was a couch on which to stretch out her body in elegant indolence. René was revived a little: Dalia's description had succeeded in pulling him out of his stupor. Dalia, judging that the process of eroticization was progressing by leaps and bounds, put words into action: she stretched out on the sofa in the famous position of the Nude Maja.

"Do you understand what I'm trying to explain? The arms, brought toward the back, allow the breasts to manifest their autonomy, which otherwise are reduced to being mere dependencies of the chest. As for the hips, one can't speak of rounded contours if not in this position..."

She let out a stupid laugh and asked him point-blank:

"Do you know what rounded contours are?"

René, seated at one end of the sofa, was contemplating Dalia's position in such abstraction that he didn't hear the question. She asked him again and still René remained silent. Dalia abandoned her pose and shook him; he mumbled a few words. She took him by the arm as she said:

"You're not going to believe this... We women aren't the only ones who look good on a Recamier. What a misconception! You men, too..."

And as she spoke, she obliged René to stretch out on the sofa. The album slid onto the carpet. René sat up in order to grab it but Dalia, the faster of the two, caught it, and with her other hand on René's chest, obliged him to remain lying down. Then she stretched out beside him and opening the album at random, showed him the figure of another naked man, but this one with his muscles taut. The artist, to add to the realism of the scene, had presented the figure in the moment of lifting an iron bar. His legs, planted firmly on the floor, bore all that tremendous weight by virtue of which veins, tendons, and muscles were rendered visible. René sat up energetically, remained pensive for a moment, and exclaimed:

"And why didn't they draw him with an arrow in his hands?"

Dalia let out one of her famous laughs.

"An arrow?... My goodness, I don't understand what you mean!"

"Yes, an arrow instead of that rod," he said impetuously. He got up as if possessed and adopted the figure's pose. He repeated with infinite anguish: "An arrow! Yes, Dalia! An arrow!"

She could only laugh and felt deliciously excited. This prelude to what she imagined would be René's sexual initiation savagely excited her. So, staring into his eyes, she said:

"No one is contradicting you, darling... Of course an arrow...Cupid's arrow..."

"No, Dalia," René shouted. "I'm not talking about the arrow of Love. I'm talking about the arrow of Pain."

And no one knows how it all would have ended up—whether purely and simply in bed or in a philosophic disquisition—had the telephone not rung at the very moment Dalia was opening her mouth to answer René. Dalia answered the phone. It was Ramón calling to say that it was already late and that René would have to get up very early since they were going on a trip the next day. For an instant, Dalia thought about not saying anything to René, but she restrained herself. If the son continued to delay, his father would come looking for him. She decided on a *mezzo termine* : she would tell him that Ramón had called to remind her not to keep René up to all hours of the night.

And that's what she told him, in the hope that René, now as eroticized as she, would not obey the parental order. But hearing Dalia, René leapt to his feet, smoothed his suit, ran his hand through his hair, mumbled a few excuses, said goodbye, and dashed off. Dalia barely had time to place the album in his hands.

"It's my gift to you to remind you of this enchanting *téte-á-téte*. And please return."

That is: "Come back to Paradise." But René was in pursuit of his habitual hell. And of this "paradise lost," all that remained was the album. But would it in fact remain? Might not his father—that modern Midas of Pain—burn it before his eyes in an expiatory *auto-da-fé*?

In the Service of Pain

René got up at five in the morning to get ready for the trip. He had spent the night wondering where his father would take him. He asked Alicia who said she had no idea, but judging by the baggage, it wasn't a trip around the block. She also thought Ramón would be back that same day or the next.

Once he had packed his suitcase, René went into the living room to look for the album. He didn't see it on the table where he'd left it, although he was sure he had put it there. Alicia had probably placed it on the bookshelf. He went back into his room; the album wasn't in the bookshelf, either. He asked Alicia, but she hadn't seen it.

On the way to the train station, he was thinking of only one thing: where could that damn album have gotten to? He didn't dare ask Ramón. Whenever he did, the answer was always unpleasant. He looked at Ramón's briefcase; perhaps the album was actually in there. Finally they arrived at the station.

There were very few people riding the train. The first class car contained only ten passengers. Ramón took a seat near the door. The seat facing him was unoccupied. René placed his raincoat and suitcase there. As he did, his thoughts returned to the album. He looked at the briefcase resting on Ramón's lap. He leaned his elbow against the window, let the air blow on his face, tried to think of nothing in particular. He began to feel a little more relaxed. Suddenly he felt a weight on his knees. He heard his father's voice, as if in a dream:

"It was a magnificent present from our friend. I was looking it over last night and thought it might come in handy to distract yourself from the tedium of the trip."

René looked down and froze in the image of a victim waiting for the axe to fall...

"You're no longer interested in Mrs. Pérez's fine present? Well then, you can just be bored stiff... As for me, I'm going to have a smoke."

René continued struggling with himself for several moments. He squeezed the album cover as if wishing to strangle it. He expected an unpleasant surprise. Ramón never did anything gratuitously. Finally, he decided to open the album. He let out a throttled cry of horror. The passengers closest to him looked at him in surprise. He held his head up to the window so the air would blow on his face. He remained in that position for several minutes. He felt the album burning his legs and his soul as well, but his curiosity proved stronger than this inferno. He opened the album and like a man going to his own execution, without terror or resistance, fixed his eyes on the first figure. Someone had modified it. The man appeared in the same posture, but hundreds of arrows were stuck in his flesh, while his face was none other than René's. His hands, resting on his thighs, held an arrow pointed at his body. But there was more. The person who had modified the figure judged it opportune to furnish it with a background: a field planted with arrows so close together that one couldn't even have walked among them. Automatically, René drew his feet in, having the sensation that he couldn't have gotten up from his seat, that the arrows would prevent him from walking down the passageway of the train, that he wouldn't be able to get off at the station, that the arrows would bar his way and pinning him to the ground, would turn him into yet another arrow. He had a fit of rebellion. He was about to grab a pencil and scribble all over the album until not a trace remained of those horrible figures. All he did was turn the page, resigned to confront new horrors. This one would be the pleasant female figure, presented as a new St. Catherine on the rack. To his surprise, the page corresponding to that figure had been ripped out. Of the twelve figures in the album, all that remained were the six male figures transformed into as many Renés. His mouth was filled with a single word; he experienced the distressing sensation that he was suffocating. Yes, that word was: REPETITION! They wished to convince him through repetition and adapt him through repetition. He saw himself turning the pages of an infinite number of albums in which were exhibited an infinite number of Renés. He contemplated the following figure: it was the one of the man holding up the bar, the last one he had seen that accursed evening at Dalia's house. The person retouching it had limited himself to making two modifications: one, of the face, which was now René's face; the other, of the rod, transformed into a burning hot arrow whose terrible fire on the figure's hands made one wonder whether it wasn't the arrow that was holding up his hands, burning them to the quick and leaving them weightless.

He turned to the third figure: It was he, skinned alive. At his side was the figure of a man displaying a sharpened scalpel in his right hand and in his left, several strips of human skin. The flayer had a white oval with a question mark on it where his face should have been. René felt himself seized with profound disgust; he stuck his head out the window and threw up. All of a sudden he had a hallucination: the train had derailed and he saw his father horribly mangled. As for himself, he left the wreckage of the car with just a few scratches. Something peculiar: Dalia was offering him her hand to help him over his father's corpse.

At that moment, Ramón returned and seeing René so pensive, pinched him on the nape of his neck. René, as if hypnotized, raised his right arm. Ramón lowered it and said:

"That's what happens from thinking too much."

René said:

"I thought you had killed yourself..." Ramón laughed boisterously.

"Killed myself, eh?" He slapped his thigh. "I'm not the kind of man who kills himself. Other people kill me..."

He pointed at the album.

"You finally decided to look at it. What do you think?"

René placed his finger on the flayer.

"What does this question mark mean?"

"It's a beautiful symbol that occurred to me last night," Ramón exclaimed. "First, let me say that it was my duty to acquaint myself with the nature of Mrs. Pérez's present. How curious! Mrs. Pérez sums her whole life up in terms of pleasure. I would like to see her for just a minute in the tourniquets... But let's leave Mrs. Pérez to her pleasures. As I was saying, I examined the figures one by one and confirmed that in the state Mrs. Pérez presented them to you, they would be absolutely useless; they wouldn't facilitate our plans in the least. So, as in days gone by I had a passion for drawing. I thought that by sacrificing art slightly for the sake of the Cause, I could—with the best of intentions in any case—retouch the aforementioned figures in order to render them serviceable. This album is, without a doubt, a handsome gift. I couldn't tell you its price, but it certainly cost Mrs. Pérez a pretty penny. There was no reason to throw it out just because of its pleasurable figures when with a little bit of effort they could be ready for the service of pain. I went diligently to work, and indeed I was up all night, but there you have it, retouched from cover to cover, filled with the spirit of our Cause. Not to mention that it will be of great use to you at school."

Hearing the word "school," René displayed a look of surprise. But Ramón, overlooking his son's curiosity, continued:

"So, as I was saying... When the time came to retouch this pretty little figure," and he placed his index finger on the flayed man, "I had two felicitous ideas: to accompany that figure with another, that obviously is the flayer holding up the skin of the flayed man; secondly, to paint his face white and put the question mark there. I don't understand why you haven't hit upon the meaning of it all right away. The faceless man with a question mark means that we don't know who your flayer is. It could be H, it could be X, could be Z..."

To this, René posed an ingenuous argument:

"How do you know unless you're one of the other guys that I'm going to be flayed?"

Ramón ran his hand through René's hair, shaking his head:

"There's no doubt about it, you need to go to school. Obviously I'm not one of the other guys. Painting you skinned alive is just one of a thousand examples. You understand? Look—" and he turned the page. "Here's another version. I liked the idea of your executioner displaying the question mark so much that I repeated it in the remaining prints. In this one we see a man with a blowtorch in his hand. The man at his side displays a totally roasted behind. You can't say that the man with the blowtorch is the flayer; no, certainly not: he's the roaster..., which doesn't prevent them from having the blanked-out face and the question mark in common. They're just variations on a theme. Now then, don't go ingenuously figuring that the number of variations is limited to those in this album. That would be a grievous mistake. You could spend ten years thinking up figures and tortures, just to be surprised one fine day by a gentleman who proposes to you a game you'd never before imagined. On the other hand, all I've tried to do by crudely retouching six pictures is to offer you a bit of pedagogy—of our pedagogy. But of this you can be sure: realized in six outstanding chapters. You see this man injecting something like liquid fire into your veins, a fire that causes the patient to dash madly about, but restrained by the ropes that tie him down, he writhes like someone possessed? Well, this relates to a trial for accomplished initiates, true masters of resistance. I advise you to examine this print, and at greater length, the last one. This one—" and with a dry flick of his thumb, he turned the page over. "Through strenuous contemplation, you will learn a great deal."

René leaned over to see the figure and fell back against the seat, clamping his legs together.

"Yes, of course, I understand your scruples. That's every man's Achilles' heel. There has been great discussion among experts on the question of whether the man being tortured is more afraid of the physical pain or the moral aspect of castration."

He closed the album and placed it on top of the suitcase. He looked at his watch.

"Let's leave off consideration of these subtleties for the time being... You're going to be on pins and needles in a few moments."

Hearing the word "needle," René felt himself jabbed as he repeated the word. Ramón began to laugh. He said maliciously:

"What I mean is that we're approaching the station. Don't forget to put the album in your suitcase."

René began to do so, but he couldn't figure out the latch.

"Bring it over here; I'll put it in. As for the latch, it's simple: turn it once to the left, and *voilá*."

He put the album in the suitcase and placed it on René's lap.

"Let's go: smooth your hair a little. I don't want Albo to imagine anything..."

René was going to ask him who this Albo was when he was interrupted by the conductor asking for their tickets. The car began to take on the unique appearance of when its passengers are in a rush. Some staggered drowsily after having traveled for three hours, others grabbed their baggage, and the most diligent were already on their feet. The train began to slow down, blew its whistle at length, and finally released its last billows of smoke.

They had arrived at a tiny station; there were few people on the platform. Ramón was speaking with the porter on the platform while he looked all around for Albo. Finally he saw him. He signaled to René and went over to meet him.

Albo was a man in his fifties, with a jet black beard and dark glasses. He had a circumspect look about him. He greeted Ramón and René. The latter couldn't avoid feeling disgust as he held out his hand. Ramón asked Albo whether everything was in order and added that he was leaving on the return train in just a few minutes. He told René that Albo was in charge of bringing him to the school. René would stay there for a year, but he as well as Alicia would come to visit him. Albo judged it opportune to make a comment. He said that the director would be pleased to see the pupils' parents attend the initiation ceremony, which would take place two months after the commencement of classes. Ramón assured him they would be there, and considering the interview over, he hugged René and told Albo to get on the road.

They walked toward the car, which was parked on the only street in town. René waited for Albo to start the car up and then asked him about the school. All he would say was that he didn't know anything about it, that he was following orders, that the headmaster, Mr. Marblo, was in charge of everything. And he retreated into absolute silence. Dumfounded by such reserve, René had no choice but to watch the landscape as it quickly slid by. He hadn't realized that the town was located on a hill and that the highway on which they were driving zigzagged back and forth, searching for the turn that would lead it into the valley. After a few minutes he could see it, but rather than a valley, it was more a large hollow full of trees. He caught sight through the trees of a two-story house and a little further in the distance, another smaller house. Which of these was the school? Or neither of them? René could barely proceed with these conjectures, for the speed of the car was faster than his thoughts. Suddenly he found himself in front of a large house. Albo jammed on the brakes. René bounced in his seat. Albo said they had arrived, that he should get out; but René, who once again was suffering from the nightmare he had experienced in the train, sat there stock-still. Albo took him by the arm and forced him out of the car.

His eyes were stinging and they would sting even more if he remained standing in the sun. He expected Albo to call at the house, but at that very moment he found himself enveloped in a cloud of dust: Albo's car was taking off. The sun was getting hotter and hotter. René took off his jacket. The house remained obstinately shut and silent. The ground floor was composed of a façade that lacked a single window. The upper floor had two, but although they were open, the curtains were drawn.

He had a notion that someone was spying on him from behind one of the windows. As if caught in error, he put on his jacket. He looked at his watch. He had been there for ten minutes so far and no one was coming out to receive him. He thought about knocking on the door. He didn't do it: someone would probably take offense. However, the heat—and even more than the heat, his anxiety—was becoming unbearable. The shade of the trees was a few steps away but he didn't dare leave the spot where he stood. The irritating sensation that he was being spied on prevented him from doing so. It was as if he were about to be called by a whistle or a doorbell...

Mastering such childishness, he began to take a few steps toward the trees when he heard his name. He stood with his back to the house, his heart beating rapidly. Perhaps they hadn't called him. But yes, he heard it again, spoken this time in a higher pitch and an imperious tone of voice as well. He turned around and saw a sort of giant in the doorway. The man saying his name was heavyset and of an unusual stature. He looked about fifty and was bald as a billiard ball. A few paces separated him from René. The man stretched out his arms as if to trap him, while at the same time calling out his name again. It seemed to René that those enormous arms were going to grab him and he instinctively backed away. The man reached his side, took him by the arm, and brought him into the house.

His first impression was a pleasant one. Displayed on the walls of a long corridor that divided the floor into two wings were photos of famous athletes, beautiful women, and big game. Here and there were comfortable seats and small tables with packs of cigarettes. Halfway down the corridor was a jukebox, and at the end was a refrigerator. The man pushed open a door and they entered the study.

It turned out to be pleasant as well. In the windows were cheerful, multicolored curtains; vases full of flowers were on the tables. The man offered René a cigarette and invited him to take a seat.

"I assume you've already figured out that I'm the Headmaster."

"Mr. Marblo!" René exclaimed.

"Yes, my name is Marblo. The driver told you, didn't he?" He uncorked a bottle and poured two drinks.

"It's a superb cognac. You should drink it without apprehension."

René took the glass and thought how very curious it was that the headmaster of a school offered alcoholic beverages to his students.

"I was observing you from the top floor. I always like to take a quick look at the neophytes (and he put stress on the word) at my own expense. You see, if the newly arrived student knows he is being observed, he pumps up his muscles and then one can't truly tell the, let us say, specific tone of his body. I don't know whether you're aware that our objective is the body and nothing but the body. That's the reason why you had to be exposed to the rays of the sun for ten minutes."

He remained silent for a moment, then added:

"I can't tell you in advance, but the general impression I have of your body is that it will have to sustain a great struggle before it may achieve victory."

René experienced the same terror as when confronted with the figures in the album. He tried to get a grip on himself, he swallowed a little cognac, grimaced sadly several times, cleared his throat, coughed, set the glass on the table...

"Come, come," Mr. Marblo said. "Come... In your case, young man, you'll have to start from scratch. Too nervous... We'll soon have to cut a good number of those nerves."

He poured himself a glass of cognac, putting it away in one shot.

"By the way, have you seen the motto of our institution?" And he pointed with his finger, stiff as a lance, at a banner hanging on the wall, which displayed the following inscription: "Suffer in silence."

René looked up.

"Suffer in silence," he said. "But why? I assume this is a school. Must one suffer in order to learn?"

"You said it, young man: 'One must suffer in order to learn...'" and Mr. Marblo slammed his fist on the table. "Knowledge must be beaten into a person... But in silence. We've almost completely transcended every kind of lamentation, moan, death rattle, ouch, and all the rest. Unlike other schools, we cultivate the golden rule of silence."

He sat there pensively.

"And if silence doesn't occur spontaneously, then we produce it..."

René experienced a fit of rebellion. He stood up and harangued Mr. Marblo:

"But what kind of knowledge am I going to receive at this school? I don't see why I have to suffer in order to learn. I'm no genius, but I assure you, Mr. Marblo, that neither am I so dullwitted as to require punishment for being unable to solve a math problem or memorize a history lesson."

"A perfect speech, young man, perfect," Marblo exclaimed, rubbing his hefty hands together. "That's about the thousandth time I've heard it. You're not the first to unload a long-winded speech on me. Everyone says the same thing when they enter, and in the end they leave transformed into champions of suffering...in silence. You'll soon have the opportunity to meet Roger. You don't know who Roger is? Well, Roger—in the very seat you're sitting in now—created a scene of the kind that marks a new plane. He began by insulting me and ended by demanding that I take him home. Then, he jumped on top of me, prepared to strangle me."

He parodied being strangled, bringing his hands to his throat and making them tremble like jelly. He held his hands like that for a few seconds and then proceeded:

"The fact is that Roger was like a thoroughbred bull refusing to be sacrificed. And take note, young man: today, he is champion of the upper level and will graduate with the highest grades. We often converse, and one has to see how he laughs about that fit of rebellion the year he entered. That's why you see me so indifferent when faced with your song and dance; yes, for one can't describe it as anything but a song and dance, a kicking fit pure and simple. I bet that after a few months you won't want to leave this place, and that you'll even put in extra hours of study in order to do brilliantly on your exams. Remember, young man, that I've been at this for twenty years, that hundreds of students have passed through my hands, and that I've had extremely few failures."

He got up, rang a bell.

"I consider this interview over. Now you'll go to your cell; later on, you'll be called to lunch. A light lunch, just like dinner. Too much food is inconvenient on the eve of the commencement of classes. Yes, tomorrow the school year begins. Obviously, you'll be wearing a uniform. Any questions? No?"

Someone knocked on the door. Marblo said to come in and a man entered.

"Pedro, please take this student to his cell."

Pedro nodded his head, took René by the arm, and they left the Headmaster's office. They climbed a set of stairs at the end of the corridor which led to another corridor. On each side of the hallway were rooms with metal doors, each with an oval peephole made of glass.

"Mr. Marblo sure exaggerates," René exclaimed when he was in the room. "To call this a cell!..."

The bedroom was actually the complete opposite of a cell. The bed—in the latest style—had a spring cushion, linen sheets, and feather pillows. Next to the bed was a dresser; in one corner of the room was a worktable. The color of the walls turned out to be very pleasant: a light green that went well with the large yellow squares of the curtains. Wasn't it all truly comforting? René had to admit that his room was expressed in the modern lingo of interior decoration by the word "invigorating." So invigorating that he was already beginning to feel at home.

He sat down in an armchair next to the table. He saw his baggage on a chair. He found the sight of the suitcase disagreeable: the album was in there. But it all was so invigorating that he soon forgot about the suitcase and the album and even his father. The academy wasn't his family but it had the advantage of keeping him far from it. At this boarding school, he would not be under Ramón's constant vigilance. This was a tremendous advantage, but at the same time, Ramón never did anything gratuitously. For example, he had said that the album would be extremely useful at school. How so? Would it serve unspeakable ends? Furthermore, his father's affairs would never be entrusted to the indiscretion of a public place like a school. Nevertheless, the placard Marblo had showed him was in a certain sense related to the album: "Suffer in silence..." The album could also be defined as the suffering of the body. And hadn't the headmaster told him that the school's objective was the body and nothing but the body? But everything he saw at the school was altogether inclined toward pleasure: the corridor with its photos of women and athletes; Marblo's very own study, so cozy; his invitation to smoke and drink. And his room—didn't it represent the ultimate in comfort? How could one suffer between these four walls? Unconsciously, he ran his hand over the upholstery of the armchair and confirmed that it was silk. He felt relaxed. He got up and went to see what was behind the door at the back of the room. He pushed it open and before his eyes were all the fixtures of a deluxe bathroom: tiles, bronze faucets, mirrors, etc. Nor did it lack what the most refined person would have demanded in a well-stocked toilette: scented soaps, eau de cologne, toothpaste, shaving cream, bath salts...

He felt like taking a bath. He opened the door and began to undress. As he went over to the bathtub he caught sight of a black curtain hanging in the back of the bathroom. Why that gloomy note amidst all these cheerful colors? A closer examination convinced him that the curtain wasn't the strangest part, but rather, whatever was hidden behind it that gave it such an extremely disturbing shape. René could have sworn someone was behind the curtain, someone who was neither moving a muscle nor breathing. His curiosity grew so intense that he yanked the curtain back at once. Before his eyes was a perfect reproduction of René himself in the moment of crucifixion. It drew its inspiration from the crucifixion of Christ but the sculptor had made a most important modification: in place of Christ's face, full of pathos and anguish, René's face, sculpted in plaster, was held high rather than slumped against his chest and his mouth displayed the laughter of a contented man. One could even say that that face had just heard a joke and was unable to keep from laughing; or also—and why not?—the face of an athlete in his prime who has run triumphantly around the track.

René, dripping wet and shivering, looked at it in fascination. Suddenly he remembered the theory of repetition. This school also employed the mechanisms of repetition! He had to yield before the evidence. Despite the curtains, the soft bed, in spite of the music, the cigarette, and the cognac, something sinister—that could well be defined as "the service of pain"—nullified those pleasant moments of life one by one. There was no longer any room for doubt: this school was the school of suffering...in silence—just as Marblo had accurately described it. But in that case, (and here René's total ignorance of the human soul again revealed itself), what was the point of that dubious combination of pain and pleasure? If the objective was none other than the annihilation of the body, of what use is a feather pillow to a crushed head? And what good are fleeced slippers when one's feet are live wounds? Either total suffering or total pleasure, René said to himself. This false line of logic brought him to the problem of contrasts. Contrast, indicating difference, would reveal the nature of suffering in its true light. How ingenuous René turned out to be, abandoning himself to the voices of his demon! No, at this school directed by Marblo, he would soon have an opportunity to listen to the Preacher, who would, among other things, resolve this seeming contradiction. He would then find out from the Preacher's mouth that they no longer proposed the ancient dispute over contrasts; that on the contrary, pleasure and pain marched hand in hand, without hampering each other in the least. It was precisely at this school (the Preacher would say) that pain is taken up as one of many objectives by which man makes and destroys his life..., just as in a factory, when the day's work is over, our pained workers go in search of pleasure.

But being completely unaware of these new theories, René felt a profound disgust as he faced the comfort that surrounded him. If his destiny was pain then all the more so: headfirst into pain... But he would never accede to placing his bloody feet in fleeced slippers. He immediately refused to take the bath he'd planned on, he wouldn't shave, and by no means would he put on clean clothes. And so, still somewhat wet, he flung himself into the armchair and sat there like someone on death row.

At that moment, Pedro entered the room. Seeing René so disheartened, he started to laugh. At the same time, he tickled him on the belly. René didn't even smile, and told him he was sad, to which Pedro responded amidst bursts of laughter that he was sure his sadness had been caused by his discovery of the double.

"The double?..." asked René, repeating the word, for that figure of Christ was none other than his double.

"Yes, man, the double... I bet the double's got you scared. It happens to everyone."

He peeked into the bathroom and took a quick look at the sculpture:

"And you didn't even destroy it!"

"What!..." shouted René. "Has someone actually dared to...?"

"Well, don't you dare!" Pedro told him. "Last year, Carlos smashed his double to bits, and when Mr. Marblo arrived, he was greeted by a shower of plaster shards. No one likes to meet his double. Well, I'd like to see all of you if you were to meet your doubles at the end of classes..."

"At the end of classes?" cried René. "What do you mean by that?"

"What I'm saying is that now the double is just painted white, but by the end of classes, you'll see it covered with red marks. Haven't you seen a red pencil around here somewhere?"

And he took a big, red crayon from the work desk.

"You'll be using this crayon to mark on the double everything you learn down there..."

René snatched the crayon from him and began to roll it between his fingers as he scrutinized his own body. He looked like he was searching for a spot to test the quality of the crayon. At last he found it at the center of his chest. Then he marked the spot with a cross.

"What are you doing!..." Pedro shouted at him. "You're not the double. It's the double you're going to have to mark when the time comes."

"I thought," René said, "that it would be more convenient to play the double. I wouldn't be obliged to go to classes at this school. Furthermore, I wouldn't be offended if at the end of the course my classmates took me for a redskin. But tell me: what kind of knowledge are we going to acquire here?"

"Mr. Marblo will tell you that," Pedro said in alarm. "I'm a servant. I've come to ask you if you need anything. Nothing?"

"Nothing, Pedro. I don't need a thing." And René smiled sadly.

"Well then, I'm leaving. If Mr. Marblo gets wind of this conversation, I'm going to get it. Sure you don't want anything? All right then, see you later. And good luck!"

Let There Be Flesh

Following one of Marblo's orders, René got up at seven. He had to make a great effort; he felt dizzy, there was a film on his tongue, and he was about to vomit. At the accursed dinner the night before ("in confraternity," as Marblo had called it), the students got drunk. Strictly speaking, it was hardly a dinner: very little to eat and lots to drink. All kinds of hot condiments: cucumbers, pickled fruits and vegetables, sauces... At the dinner, René noticed the school's singular type of tyranny: those remiss in eating these stimulants were seduced—through covert violence—to devour them. Marblo and the faculty pinched those remiss, tapped them on the head, introduced the condiments into their mouths—always gently and sweetly, but firmly. René had left the whole affair hopelessly drunk. He danced on a table and fell face down in a tray of pickled fruits and vegetables.

At this "confraternal dinner," he had met his classmates for the first time. In the large hall profusely adorned with flowers and plants, the neophytes were brought together. And René had counted them. There were exactly fifty young men, ranging from fifteen to eighteen years old, almost all of them well proportioned and physically vigorous. By all appearances, everyone was in an excellent frame of mind. No matter how hard René scrutinized them, he couldn't find any signs of worry reflected on their faces. They looked like un-preoccupied pupils. As always occurs among young people, some of them had started up animated conversations. Of course the common topic was their discovery of the double in their room. Certainly they were extremely intrigued by the reproductions of Christ exhibiting each of their faces. He had asked one boy if he liked the school. The latter answered that he didn't know if he was going to like it or not, but that he was pleased by what he'd seen so far, although he couldn't understand the business of the double. René expounded at length upon the strangeness of the situation. Juan— for that was the neophyte's name—cut short René's explanation, saying that the most prudent thing to do was to wait for Mr. Marblo to explain it to them, that he wasn't particularly bothered, that his mother had matriculated him into this school because out in the provinces they spoke of what a very fine school it was, that he was very content, that his mother had told him that he would hardly study, that the greatest importance was placed on physical exercise. René asked him whether he had spoken with Marblo. Juan repeated point by point everything Marblo had said to René, and added that he didn't attach any importance to the business about "suffering in silence," since it wasn't for nothing that he had a mouth and was able to open it and shout; that that's what he had said to Marblo, and that he had laughed a great deal.

And at that moment, over an intercom installed in the hall, a forceful voice told them to get into line. Hardly were they in formation when the second-year students arrived: fifty boys who, like hunting dogs, flung themselves at the neophytes and began sniffing them zealously. And it all looked like a dance step: with their arms held back, they only touched the neophytes' bodies with their noses. One could hear the characteristic snuffling of dogs as they run through the countryside in search of prey, which, once retrieved, is sniffed from head to toe. And what precision of movement these "dogs" displayed! They passed one another in search of new prey; they looked at each other, sharing their olfactory impressions. As for the neophytes, they were laughing at such a farcical scene. Some of them, feeling the sniffer's nose on their stomachs, nearly split their sides with laughter. Once all of the neophytes had been sniffed, the second-year students fell back—still in silence—to one corner.

Right away the intercom announced the third-year students. And so they appeared, but taking such slow steps that René would have thought their limbs hurt them terribly or that having been woken from deep sleep, they were still not completely awake; or possibly that they were suffering the effects of some drug—they appeared so slow and limp! In contrast to the rest of their bodies, their faces reflected such intense vivacity that they seemed to go ahead of the rest of their bodies and walk autonomously. These faces were the faces of the doubles (there was no doubt about it) and also the faces of athletes who have roundly triumphed on the track. Halfway to the neophytes, René experienced the sensation that their faces had *already* reached the body of each neophyte and were awaiting the slow and belabored arrival of their respective bodies. At last they reached their intended goal. Then, with hands like tentacles, they began to probe the bodies of the neophytes. René thought of doctors when they palpate the patient's anatomy. These hands were knowledgeably exploring the flesh. Without a doubt, they were experiencing an enormous pleasure in this contact; they looked at one another, sharing their impressions, and their glances expressed what could be done with these still-intact bodies. At last they put an end to such passionate handling and assembled their crowd of smiling faces in front of the crowd of second-year noses. Marblo, followed by the faculty, had made his entrance. Ten professors in all. Looking at them, René thought that they were ten truly wretched bodies. How could one speak of the cultivation of the body with human rags like those? One saw at a glance that these bodies were prematurely aged. They looked as if they had just left a dungeon where they had spent half their life. It had been a long time since their flesh had been in contact with the rays of the sun or fresh air.

They all wore glasses. It was a terrible moment when Marblo, with affected fervor, told the neophytes that he had the pleasure of presenting to them the people who would be their professors for three years. They rested their eyes on the neophytes, and it was as if some joker had put glasses on a bunch of octopi.

Marblo expounded upon the intimate knowledge these professors possessed of the human body. René recalled that Marblo said the word "body" endlessly, adding that if the neophytes placed their blind faith in the teaching body, they would come to make of their own bodies whatever they desired. That he didn't understand a word when people spoke of the spirit. What do they mean by spirit? Does anyone know? Has anyone touched it? He said that if by spirit one understood the body, then the school he directed was highly spiritual. He also made it clear that the only book they would study in his institution was the book of the human body, that the body contained everything a man needs to "forge his way into the flesh of another man..." He immediately followed this by elaborating on the nature of suffering, declaring purely and simply that a body deprived of pain isn't a body but a rock; that the greater the capacity for pain, the greater the vitality; that he was convinced of the efficacy of his teaching method in achieving that prodigious vitality. In continuation, he said that he was very satisfied with the results obtained, of which the living proof was the third-year students. He emphasized the triumphant expression on their faces. Some them had come to surpass the healthy joy on the faces of their doubles. The maximum exponent of such a feat was Roger, who without a doubt would receive the Highest Honors of his course.

Marblo signaled to him. Roger left the line and walked past each neophyte, showing him his face. René trembled when he found that face before him; it seemed to him that that face had reached such extremes that it could never retrace its path...

And now, on the threshold of the first class, René wondered amidst these confused evocations of the confraternal dinner, whether "facial cultivation" would begin with the first lecture. Yes, without a doubt it would begin with the first lecture. Marblo had clearly said that the cultivation of the body would give the face a triumphant expression. René entered the bathroom and yanked back the curtain that concealed the double. He absolutely had to look it in the face: it would be his own after the three years of apprenticeship.

He was rudely awakened from these reflections by Pedro's voice. In just a few minutes, the veil of mystery would be drawn back... He went into the corridor and took his place in the line of neophytes. Pedro told them to walk by the office at the end of the hallway, where Mr. López would hand them their school supplies.

Hardly had the first student come back out supplied with his materials than the group burst into boisterous laughter. But since René was one of the last ones (several neophytes had thrown themselves on top of the student), it was impossible for him to figure out the cause of this explosion of hilarity. There was more laughter and jeering. René tried to make his way toward the student, whom his classmates had literally crushed.

Pedro called them to order and René found out the reason for the pig pile: The student had been fit with a muzzle, making him look like a trapped animal. The passage of men into the condition of beasts was soon generalized. As the neophytes were muzzled, the silence became oppressive.

It was René's turn. He entered the office and saw a very cheerful man being handed a shiny muzzle made of black leather by a subordinate. He told René to approach. As he put the muzzle on him, he said with extreme courtesy: "Don't be afraid. You'll soon get used to wearing it."

And it would have been impossible to respond or even to thank him. He already had the muzzle over his mouth and Mr. López put a bracelet on his wrist and slapped him on the shoulder to make room for another neophyte.

As he walked down the corridor, he felt his ears were going to burst from the pounding of his blood. There was no doubt about it: they were dogs from here on in... He thought: "Does this mean we're going to live as if in a kennel? Will it be my mission to sleep during the day and bark at night? Then why this muzzle? He suddenly remembered Mr. Marblo's expression: "Suffer in silence..." It was obvious that the muzzle would prevent clamorous suffering, public, shouted out loud... He touched his muzzle; it so constrained his mouth that any attempt to part his lips would have been useless. Mr. Marblo had already told them: if silence wasn't achieved naturally, it would be "fabricated."

It was fabricated by those shiny muzzles. Who could have cried out? No matter what happened, he would stand fast—or with his mouth fastened... His anguish grew so intense that he felt the need to cry out but all he could manage was a strangled sound like the rasp of a dying man.

As if in horrible contrast, at that moment he heard Mr. López shout out at the top of his lungs: "Material handed out: fifty muzzles!" There was silence and the stentorian voice shouted once again: "Pedro, you now can take them downstairs!"

Pedro was rushing around. The order of the line had been profoundly altered and it looked like the convulsive body of an epileptic. The imposition of the muzzles had the effect of bringing out all kinds of mischief in the neophytes. The same Juan who had chatted with René during the confraternal dinner now took pleasure in viciously pinching the ears of the classmate preceding him in line, who, so as not to be surpassed by his classmate, was hitting the neophyte ahead of him on the head. Pinching and knocks on the head quickly spread throughout the group. The whole line was swaying, contracting, and stumbling in deadly silence. It could be characterized as the caricature of suffering in silence.

Since Pedro could not control the mutineers, he needed the help of Mr. López. The latter left his office followed by his assistant. He extolled the "fiery, gay spirit" that the neophytes were exhibiting at that moment as a very beautiful demonstration, but lamented the fact that he was forced to clarify for them that this was not the occasion for its manifestation.

This short but eloquent speech was sufficient to re-store order. Mr. López asked the neophytes to please follow him. They did so docilely and soon came to a freight elevator situated at the end of the corridor. They saw on its display the numbers one, two, and three. That explained Mr. López's phrase: "take them downstairs..."

The ride down lasted only a few seconds. Suddenly a slight jolt indicated that they had arrived "downstairs," at the first floor. When the elevator door opened, the neophytes entered a corridor whose ceiling was so low one could touch it with one's hand; here and there were red position lights. At that moment an alarm siren went off. Its blast was so oppressive that René thought it was a call for help from a city threatened by disaster. Soon new sirens began to sound the alarm. The din was so awful that the neophytes' bodies were vibrating. It was more than their ears could take; if the noise continued, their eardrums would burst.

Suddenly the sirens fell silent, the gallery was lit up, and the neophytes saw a man standing next to the door to a room. He signaled for them to approach. Two strapping young men who popped up as if by magic were pushing them toward the man, who was armed with rods brandishing spikes at one end. René felt something touch him and jumped. The spike didn't penetrate his flesh—it was blunt—but it was an un-pleasant and humiliating sensation when it touched him.

The man, who was none other than the professor, was rubbing his hands together as he invited them into the classroom:

"This is an honor for me... Welcome to my humble retreat... But what a charming bunch of boys!... We're going to do great things in this Course..."

His glasses were constantly slipping down, requiring him to push them up first with one hand and then the other. He was skinny and sallow like all his colleagues. He walked over to a table set on top of a very high dais and sat down with great pomp. Meanwhile, the two young men were actively engaged in seating each of the neophytes in their assigned seats. René saw that the seats were in every way identical to that sort of dentist's chair in Ramón's room. In addition, they had a number on the back, like theater seats. René looked at the bracelet Mr. López had put on his wrist and saw that his number corresponded to his seat number. It was number ten.

He was unable to expand on the unavoidable thought that this school treated its students like convicts. One of the young men tied him by the feet and hands to the seat with various straps. To what extent would they turn a human being into a package? First the muzzle, now the ropes. Soon they would be blindfolded and shot against a wall...

How ingenuous those students were who imagined themselves executed by a firing squad! No, that school was neither a tribunal nor a court-martial; the teaching body wasn't a firing squad. On the contrary: at this school the body was something precious and wondrous that had to be saved at all times. Everything would be lost at that school...except the body. The famous statement by the gallant Francis I was a veritable treatise on ethics; but here the body demanded every kind of sacrifice, even that of honor... At this school no one spoke of honor corps, but rather of honoring the *corpus*... They would have to sacrifice everything to the body. It was out of honor that these boys were now downstairs, seated in something like dentist's chairs, bound hand and foot, and muzzled so as to prevent them from expressing their doubts and their useless theories on honor.

The eyes of all the neophytes turned to a small door at one end of the classroom. On the door hung a sign: "First Aid." What did it mean? They didn't have to wait for an answer. The small door opened and a man dressed in a white frock came out. A stethoscope was hanging from his neck. He reached the dais and whispered to the professor. The latter nodded his head. The doctor—for that's what the man was: a doctor—walked over to the neophytes and began to auscultate them. Meanwhile, the professor lit a cigar and put a record on.

At last the doctor finished his exam and returned to the dais. The professor started nodding his head again. The neophytes were trembling: now and then the doctor would look at them and point first to one, then to another, and shake his head as if expressing his doubts about the proper functioning of their hearts. But he pointed with his outstretched arm to one student in particular, explaining that he possessed a heart of steel. The professor said that more likely than not this student had a heart of butter. The doctor protested strenuously, saying that science never erred in its judgment, and that he, the professor, was speaking such rubbish because his heart was made of butter. The professor replied that his heart was made of granite, that he was very sorry the doctor's was made of turd...

They squabbled like a pair of youngsters. In the face of such childishness, the neophytes seemed like wise old men obliged to attend a comedy sketch. Now the professor showed the doctor a pocket watch, and the latter showed him his wristwatch. Then a discussion began about a difference of two minutes. The doctor told the professor that his time lag was due to the poor quality of his chronometer; that everyone knows that a device purchased for a few pennies may speed up or slow down. That his was a Swiss chronometer. The professor got lost in a confused explanation about the bad luck one can have when buying a bargain-basement watch, but that in any case, cheap watches are better than calibrated Swiss chronometers.

The discussion got lively when they started to tell with an abundance of details of the watches they had owned up until then. The tension of the neophytes had reached its peak, but the doctor and the professor, as if nothing were amiss, were becoming increasingly involved in their chronometers... The doctor said rather ugly things to the professor; the latter, considering himself mortally offended, began to stare at the ceiling. Once the doctor had fallen silent, the professor lowered his gaze, turned off the record player, pulled out a bottle and took a long swig, clicked his tongue, said: "Ah! Ah!", placed his feet on the table, and forgot about the rest of the world.

The neophytes, terribly excited, began to low, squirming around in their seats. Then the professor said:

"Uncomfortable, right?... It's a matter of adapting yourselves. Right now you hate the muzzle, but within a week you'll be begging me for it on bended knees. You won't be able to live without it."

He took his feet off the table and leaned forward as far as he could:

"Today we'll have the first lecture. Actually, it isn't a lecture. Rather, it's a test."

He shook his head as if in doubt:

"Well, as we'll see, it's a little of each: it's a lecture and a test. The former, because our Course on Electricity begins with the exercise that we're going to do right away; the latter, because this exercise will tell us the degree of nervousness of each one of you. To tell the absolute truth, it's the only exercise that amuses me. I've given it a name in keeping with its objective: "the electric seat." Yes, you don't have to look at me like men on death row. The Americans have the "Chair" with a capital "c," the great Chair that takes them quickly *ad penates*; but since our mission is the cultivation of the body and not its suppression, we have the "seat." You are all seated in your respective seats. No matter how much your brains have tried to think of what the "seat" is capable of doing, you won't have a precise idea until I push this button (and he indicated a device placed on top of the table).

Whether, as he was saying that he would push the button he actually put his finger on it, or he pushed it intentionally, the electric current flowed to the seats and the boys arched in pain.

"Oh! Pardon me, my finger slipped!..." he said very contritely. He pointed again at the button. The neophytes began to tremble.

"This is button A. The two that follow are buttons B and C. You can well imagine that B allows a higher current than A, and C than B. No, we don't have a button D. If we did, this school would automatically become a prison and we would be compromising the safety of your bodies. We don't belong to the phalanx of final consequences!"

As if to emphasize such an impossible thought, he energetically shook his head, placed his right hand on his chest, and made a sign of denial with his left.

"My dear boys, a moment ago I said that this first exercise is our first lesson in the Course on Electricity. Its theoretical component could be summed up as follows: a body is subjected during x amount of time to the alternating flow of three electric currents. The point is to see whether the sufferer will or will not be overcome by the shock. Now then, note that I just used the term "sufferer." The *quid* of our problem is rooted in suffering. The exercise ought to be assimilated on the basis of pain. Completing it by any other route will prove absolutely false. You hear? False. We aren't fakirs who master pain; it is pain that masters us. Don't lose sight of the fact that it is wholly a moral problem. We've had very brilliant students whom we've found it necessary to expel. For what reason? Because they were insentience incarnate... They would solve any exercise, no matter how complicated, in a masterful way. But how would they solve it? Mechanically, my dear boys, mechanically! How dreadful! They were beings without souls—without the soul of pain. Looking at them, one thought of certain pianists who execute their techniques mechanically: a perfect touch, without even thinking about whether one note had been played instead of another; hands flying from right to left and from left to right... Altogether perfect, but... Oh! How horribly painful it is to verify that pain is a stranger to them! Not a shred of emotion throughout the entire concert! Now I remember Arturo. He was my favorite. An exquisite body. He had me fooled for a long time. His body solved any problem, no matter how complicated. For him, I ended up inventing a few. All right then, Arturo wasn't suffering; he lacked the consciousness of pain. I could tell this from his face. You've already seen each of your doubles. Arturo's face was always the same. He was now in his second year. The wholesome joy that every face ought to display as it experiences pain wouldn't appear on Arturo's countenance; all that it reflected was the most absolute stupidity. I found myself with the painful necessity of communicating the situation to Mr. Marblo, who, *ipso facto*, threw Arturo out onto the street. So, pain is our star and it will guide us over this tempestuous sea. You'll say to me: but why do they put muzzles on us when one is supposed to give free rein to pain? We put them on because we stand for pain that is contained, concentrated, and reconcentrated. The mouth that opens in order to cry out automatically displaces a precious amount of pain. If I were to express myself in psychological terminology, I would call it a discharge. And we are wholly and completely against discharges. You will use the muzzles throughout this Course. It is necessary at all costs to prevent you from being defeated by discharges. The muzzle will end up molding a convulsive grin, which will eventually be transformed like a miraculous lily into the stereotypical smile of the second Course, and the petrified smile of the third Course."

He set his mouth in a convulsive grin and held it that way for several seconds, which to the neophytes seemed like centuries. He took a long swig from the bottle, wiped his mouth with his hand, and went on:

"But enough of niceties. Let's get to work. However, one last warning of a strictly pedagogical nature: as our beloved Headmaster says: with this exercise begins the service of pain. So, make an effort to suffer as much as you're able. Don't grab the wrong end of the stick, foolishly thinking you're going to prove your virility. No; I've already mentioned that here honor is superfluous. To know one is suffering, that the pain is awful, that one is that close to begging for mercy, and yet, not to give in, constitutes the sufferer's *abc*'s. And now let us begin. The test will take exactly fifteen minutes. Well, when I say 'test,' the word has to be understood as relative, because essentially we're not testing anything, unless one considers that after fifteen minutes it has

been proved that you have suffered effectively. Finally—
and this is just routine—I will break the silence by
reading several passages on celebrated cases of torture."

He pulled a large, threadbare book from a drawer,
opened it at random, and holding it open with one
hand, pressed button A with the other.

The fifty bodies then began a kind of St. Vitus' dance
in their seats. Their buttocks and head were the points
that formed the axis of their movement. The entire
weight of their bodies gravitated around the former
point such that their heads were keeping time—a time no
metronome could measure. Their thoraxes convulsively
pressed forward and their backs knocked violently
against the backs of their seats. Accompanying this grotesque dance, the professor could be heard reading the
following passage:

*In the days of the LXVI Olympics (513 B.C.), there lived
in Athens the courtesan Lena. Her body, repeatedly sung by
the poets, her body, envy of women and the tabernacle of its
worshippers, found itself involved in the famous conspiracy
hatched by Harmodious and Aristogiton against the tyrant,
Hiparch.*

*Betrayed by a slave, Lena was brought before Hipias,
brother of Hiparch. Hipias wished to hear the names of the
conspirators from Lena's own lips, but she kept them obstinately sealed. Neither promises nor flattery could convince
her to part her lips, on which floated the smile of the chosen
people. So Hipias, impatient and bloodthirsty, had her tortured.*

Here the professor pressed slowly down on button B,
spit to his right and left, and proceeded in a nasal voice:

*Her clothes were rent. At the sight of her divine flesh,
Hipias exclaimed: "Oh, Lena, your flesh has been your nour-*

ishment until now! Show it your gratitude by confessing all. Your flesh does not deserve the torment."

But Lena clenched her jaws even tighter. Then Hipias clapped his hands twice and the executioners stepped forward. Lena was seated on an iron chair under which was a brazier. Hipias said to her: "Listen, Lena, I'm not going to tie you down. When your flesh can no longer resist the heat of the brazier, you will rise from the chair and that will mean you are resigned to make your confession."

And Lena was seated in the chair. The executioners lit the brazier. Within a few moments, Lena began to squirm in her seat. From his table, Hipias contemplated her in silence. A little later Lena's flesh began to roast. The smell was unbearable; Lena was being suffocated by her own fumes. Hipias held his arms out to her but Lena, in atrocious pain, clung to the chair. Hipias made a sign and the executioners threw more wood on the fire. Then Lena, whose hands were fusing with the chair but whose feet were flung out toward Hipias, Lena, on the verge of being overcome by pain, stuck her tongue between her ivory teeth, squeezing it with such fury that the enemy left her mouth, mortally wounded.

The professor closed the book, released the button.

"The regulations establish a recess between buttons B and C."

The neophytes, suddenly arrested in their mad seated dance, looked like dolls with their heads slumped on their chests.

"All right, all right!" the professor exclaimed, tapping the table. "So we feel pain, eh? That means we're suffering... I wish that Mr. Marblo could contemplate you, but that's not possible: he is very busy with the sacred, unpostponable performance of his duty. Well, now you've heard the passionate account of Lena, the sufferer. You should overlook the picturesque style of the chronicler and that ending that speaks of the enemy leaving her mouth mortally wounded... It means simply that Lena spit her tongue out. Lena didn't have the rare privilege of a school like this one. She was just a primitive in pain, and on the verge of being overcome by suffering, acted as does a savage. If Lena had come through our school, the story would have turned out quite differently. Her beautiful tongue would have gone with the rest of her body into the bosom of the earth."

The small door opened again and the doctor appeared, followed by a nurse with paraphernalia for giving injections. The doctor, who held a hypodermic syringe in his right hand, looked over at the professor; the latter winked at the former and the doctor began walking toward the neophytes.

"Don't get scared," he said, "this isn't part of the exercise. It's just a simple subcutaneous injection for those who have collapsed."

He walked back and forth among the neophytes. His exclamations of surprise could be heard with every step:

"Admirable, my dear colleague, admirable! Magnificent debut, magnificent! Only two boys collapsed; of no great significance!"

He pulled the needle from the arm of one neophyte and rubbed his skin with a cotton swab:

"There you go! Fresh as a head of lettuce and with double the vigor for button C."

He passed down the line of chairs and suddenly let out a cry of surprise:

"Could it be possible!... No, I can't believe my eyes. Run over here, professor. This is quite a case... Blessed be the Lord. Run. Could we be in the presence of one of the chosen ones?"

The doctor held René's face, bathed in tears, between his hands. The professor came running from the dais. The neophytes who hadn't collapsed set their eyes on that face coursed by a river of tears. The doctor was smiling the cocksure smile of doctors, but the professor, turning to him, froze it on his lips:

"Tell me, Mister Doctor, is he really one of the chosen ones or are we actually in the presence of a new Arturo?"

At this, the doctor became flustered; the syringe slipped from his fingers, shattering into a thousand pieces.

"Pardon me, professor, I've been hasty in my judgment. You are foresight incarnate... In fact, he could be a new Arturo. Oh, what bitter disillusionment if your presumption proves correct!"

"That's what I say," shrieked the professor, convulsivey clasping René's face. "Are you crying because the pain hurts you physically or are you crying because the pain hurts you morally?"

Confused, totally forgetting that René was muzzled, he assailed him with questions:

"How did it hurt? Did it hurt on a scale of one to ten or one to a thousand? Have you suffered with your whole body or with just one part?"

The doctor burst into loud laughter. The professor, finding himself caught in error, stepped on the doctor's foot, who then began to groan. Meanwhile, tears continued issuing from René's face. The professor, faced with such abundance, asked the doctor whether it wouldn't be appropriate to give him an injection, since he felt the emotion caused by his weeping might bring René to the point of collapse. Along with the rest of the neophytes, René had to experience the discharge of button C. The doctor said that in cases such as this, the school statutes categorically prohibit the lachrymose manifestation of suffering from being "terminated," be it by oral injunction or by means of a cordial or injection; that it also should not be forgotten that said lachrymose manifestation was the only discharge permitted (permitted, of course, only during the first semester.) If the neophyte was crying, one could presume that his flesh hurts, and if his flesh hurts, one must believe he is apt for the service of pain.

"Admirable reasoning, my colleague, admirable reasoning!" the professor said. "But you forget that experience has taught us that in nine cases out of ten, they cry physical pain with their right eye and moral pain with their left. And what result does such sobbing yield but impurities? Remember that our goal is sobbing in its pure state."

He turned brusquely to René and stuck his index finger between his eyes like a sword.

"Does the human power exist on the face of the earth that is capable of saying whether this sobbing is reflexive or automatic?"

But René had stopped crying. The professor felt himself screeching to a halt. Now, instead of the river, it was the desert that was forestalling him. René's face looked like a parched river bed. His earlier tears had dried up and their trails were still visible.

Irritated, the professor spun around on his heels.

"Come on, Mister Doctor, get moving. We still have button C to go."

"I'll do it just as a routine measure," the doctor responded, "but we don't have anyone else who's collapsed. See for yourself whether all those heads aren't straighter than spears..."

It was true: the neophytes' heads looked like spearheads. Even René held his high at the mere announcement of button C. What would happen now? Would the flow of the current allow them to understand even a single word of the professor's horrible readings? René was sure that none of the neophytes had been able to attend to the reading of the torment of Lena. Of all that wretched gibberish, her name was all he remembered. What kind of absurd school was this where they mixed culture with torture? He was now resigned, but just let them keep from telling stories in the middle of the sad convulsions, of the ugly electrical epilepsy.

He couldn't follow up such bitter reflections. The professor opened the large threadbare book, rapidly flipped several pages, and finally stopped at the one he wanted. He pressed button C and began to read in a drone:

Cuauhtémoc, king of the Aztecs, in order that he reveal the site where the gold was hidden, was...

He was unable to continue. His voice had cracked in his throat, and there it lay like a corpse. His finger was hysterically pressing down on the button, threatening to rip it apart altogether.

What had happened? Well, a break in the current, or perhaps a short circuit, or perhaps there had been a calamity in the electrical power plant. Whatever it may have been, it was certain that the current wasn't flowing. Muzzled laughter—no less mocking for being muzzled— pricked the professor's dignity, causing him to lose his composure altogether.

"Silence!" He bellowed, having already lost all self-control.

But since the silence hadn't been broken, due to the efficiency of the muzzles, he again felt himself ridiculed. He put his hands on his head, climbed down from the dais, and walked over to the small door. The fact that the ceiling lamps were still lit succeeded in making him even more furious. So what was wrong with the buttons? They had never failed. And the flaw was undeniably having a deplorable effect on the student body. He pushed open the small door and a flood of light fell directly on his face. The doctor, who was asleep in an armchair, jumped up and asked if someone new had collapsed.

"What the devil are you talking about?... The only thing that's collapsed in this class is the damn button C. Go and give it an injection of Coramine."

The doctor, laughing to split his sides, responded:

"My dear professor, the first aid service here is conceived of in terms of the flesh, not of mica. But I'll try, I'll try... Will you give me a cigar if I revive the little button?"

The professor grabbed him by the neck and dragged him over to the table.

"Quit kidding around and help me."

"But help you how?" the doctor said. "I'm not a thaumaturge who could touch this collapsed button, exclaiming: *Fiat Lux!* No; look: I touch it and nothing."

Doing as he said, he pressed the button and the whole class received a discharge. Like fetuses in the womb, they touched their feet to their head.

"Bravo!" cried the professor. "Now we can resume the exercise."

He touched the button but the current didn't flow. He touched it again with the same result. He put his hands to his head, bewailing his misfortune. He said that Marblo would blame the flaw on the professor's faulty handling; that it was always the same: in the end, he had to pay the price...; that instead of blaming the breakage on the inexperience of the electrician, it was easier to attribute it to the wretched professor. He began to whine. The doctor whispered something into his ear while pointing at the time.

The professor's face reflected the deepest surprise:

"In nothingness?... What do you mean in nothingness?... I don't understand."

"Obviously in nothingness; submerge them in it."

"You mean to say, take them *ad patres*? That isn't anticipated in Marblo's regulations..."

"Don't be alarmed. In nothingness means in the darkness. Submerge the neophytes in darkness. Let's turn out the lights and retire to our shelter—" and he indicated the small door. "In half an hour someone will come to release them. For that half hour our little cherubim will believe they're receiving the electric current and listening to the background music of your readings."

"You've saved my life, my dear Mr. Doctor. It's an inspired solution: our cherubim won't complain about the change. The darkness doesn't bite or jab... Let's go, colleague," and he took the doctor by the arm.

They climbed down from the dais. The professor put one finger on the switch to the ceiling lights. Suddenly he withdrew it:

"I'm afraid. What if it doesn't work?"

"Don't be so fatalistic. Come on, flip the switch."

"No; no, I can't," the professor whined. "They'll make fun of me if the switch doesn't work."

"You're such a baby, professor! All right then, I'll turn the lights out. Don't you want to say a few words to your flock first?"

"No. What for? We're leaving *a la inglesa*... Please, just turn out the lights!"

The doctor flipped the switch and the classroom was thrown into darkness. The intangible muzzle fell over the neophytes' eyes, and its soft imposition made them think that their noses too would be muzzled and it would all be over in a matter of seconds. Nevertheless, they had made a crass error: at this school they would never be done with the body. On the contrary, they would always be starting with it, and if anything was coming to an end at that moment it wasn't the body of any of the neophytes, but rather the class they were now taking, although—it must be admitted—in darkness.

René's Flesh

The record contained the following text:

"*Attention, René! René! Attention, René! René! René! One more time: Attention! Can we begin? All right then, attention!* (A long pause.) *Why do you not want? Do you not want because wanting, you do not want or do you want because you want not to want? Do you want wanting or do you want not wanting? How do you want?* (Noise.) *Do you want the noise to stop? No, you are unable to want; you've said it yourself: you don't want. Say along with us: I want, you want, he wants, we want, you want, they want. Now say them without the pronouns: want, want, wants, want, want, want. Repeat. René, repeat faster. Like this* (The voice conjugates the verb at an amazing speed.) *Attention, René! 'I want' is calling you. 'I want' wants to speak to you. Repeat after us: I want. Now, letter by letter: I.W.A.N.T.* (The voice murmurs "I want" dozens of times.) *René, are you there? Are you listening? Yes,*

René is listening. No, René, don't think; don't ever think; just want, want, want..." (The voice shouts "want" over and over again accompanied by a gong.)

And that's how the record ended. But was it actually over? No, for it started up again an instant later. Slouched in the armchair, lying on the bed, or face down on the rug, René could always hear it. This horror had been going on for three days. The record was turned off at night when the preacher made his appearance to cross-examine him on the word "want." On that word alone! The record would start up again at six in the morning and wouldn't stop until six in the evening. One speaker was installed in the bedroom and another in the bathroom, so that if René should leap from the frying pan he'd fall into the fire. Dear God! Three days on coffee and that record were enough to drive even the most stable person mad. And when he managed briefly to fall asleep, he would wake up shouting: in his dreams he saw himself transformed into a record that talked to him nonstop.

Was this all part of the school's curriculum? Not exactly, though as time went on, René came to understand that the "cultivation of the body" was achieved by two methods: physical and mental. This school was a double-edged sword: its blade cut on both sides. In this regard, the students of "the third course" could relate marvels... In this case it was a special matter—that of "René's case," as it was called among the faculty.

In fact, René was a case and a half, but not that case the professor and the doctor thought they were confronting during the first class. No, those tears—as the headmaster had expressed so well—were of the crocodile variety. He was obviously suffering—no one claimed he didn't suffer intensely during the various exercises— but coexisting with the indisputable nature of the sufferer was another, infinitely more dangerous nature: that of a rebel, the kind that "shrinks from all contact with the agent of pain," according to Adolfo, professor of the second course and a great connoisseur of the flesh. On two or three occasions over the course of the first trimester (which now was coming to a close with the initiation ceremony), René had overtly refused to receive the holy bread of instruction. One morning he told Pedro he didn't *want* to get out of bed and certainly didn't *want* to show up at class. Pulled bodily from his room and carried to class, he flatly refused to carry out the indicated exercise and even had the audacity to harangue his classmates. Brought before Marblo, he was given a dressing down. Marblo told him that his mistake was all the more serious since the Archimedes' lever of this school was precisely the very word René was refusing to put into action. He added that everything, absolutely everything, depended and rested on the word "want"; that not to want did not exist in the school's vocabulary.

They held a special staff meeting that evening. Mr. Marblo told the faculty of the real danger that the presence of an agent provocateur like René presented to the institution. "Arturo's case" was trivial compared to René's, and if he, the Headmaster, wasn't taking drastic action, it was out of remaining consideration for Ramón with whom, furthermore, he had spoken at length on the telephone. Ramón had said to him: "By all means, my dear Marblo; if necessary, tighten his strings until they snap..." The professors laughed at such a graphic description.

"That's right," Marblo said. "No one like Ramón to say in a few words exactly what's on his mind: until his strings snap!... That is: if the violin refuses to be tuned, its strings must break."

Of course the strings screeched horribly as the pegs were tightened so. But René possessed a will of iron. A few days later the incident took place again. René's attitude was inciting a lack of discipline, and this could not be tolerated for another second. As Marblo would say so well in a second staff meeting, the institution would not allow itself to be shaken to its foundations by that little brat. Above all, his school was a business; yes sir, a business run by the book, and although he held Ramón in high esteem and owed him a great deal, he was not for that reason about to endanger the smooth functioning of his establishment. As would be expected, he blamed the professor of the first course, the one who had been in disgrace since the button incident. He insulted the professor harshly and let him know that his mission was not simply to transmit knowledge but more importantly, to make the student "a chemically apt being for the service of pain."

Less than a week before the initiation ceremony, René was already a lost cause. This business of "chemically apt" didn't hold water with him. In desperation, the professor had irrevocably submitted his resignation on two occasions.

The great dilemma was whether to inform Ramón that his son was being expelled from the school, or to allow his illiterate flesh to appear in the ceremony. The latter was impossible: the object of this ceremony consisted precisely in demonstrating to the parents and professors that the bodies of the neophytes were perfectly suited for the service of pain. How, among a group of bodies carrying out brilliant exercises, could they allow that rebel, that hedonist René, to be present? Such a thing would have caused a perceptible drop in the students' morale, thus compromising the institution's good name.

The faculty took measures commensurate with the gravity of the situation. For many reasons—the school's reputation, the self-respect of the professors, and above all, the consideration due Ramón—it was necessary to attempt the impossible in order to subdue René. Although as Marblo privately suspected, the situation was absolutely desperate. Comparing him to Roger's case, one could not help but be convinced that René's rebelliousness was taking a different route. Whereas Roger had rebelled out of pure fear—fear in the face of physical pain—René was rebelling out of pure contradiction. This then was the crux of the matter: it was no coincidence that René was the son of Ramón, a dyed-in-the-wool revolutionary. Despite the fact that René may have been undeniably skilled for the service of pain (and without a doubt, had he been interested in the craft, he would have left his father in the dust), his revolutionary nature overshadowed his other skills and aptitudes. With Roger, Marblo was to suffer horrors, but he knew from the first moment they met that he was in the presence of material apt for suffering and that once set in its groove, it would roll peacefully along by itself.

René was a different matter altogether. Here was the case of someone who didn't commiserate with his flesh as such but rather, protested the outrages inflicted upon it. If out of consideration for his father, the school had to bear the dead weight of his son, better to turn it into a gymnasium or a brothel... Confronted with such grim prospects, the sallow bodies of the professors scrambled about, protesting strenuously. Entire lives dedicated to the service of pain would not now—because of the scruples and hysterics of this young man—be thrown in the gutter. If René wanted pleasure, if he aspired to having his flesh caressed, if it gave him pleasure to be tickled, or if he sought to make his body into an instrument of eroticism, then he should get out for none of that was practiced here. Plain and simple: he should get out. And fast.

But Marblo, a true pedagogue and an even greater diplomat, nipped the protests in the bud with two judicious reflections. He said that on the one hand, it was in the highest spirit of the school, in accordance with its most ancient traditions, to exhaust all resources when faced with situations like the one they were now confronting. The professors knew there were still certain methods that had yet to be tested.

Then, placing his right hand over his heart, he solemnly swore that if the "resources" failed, he himself would throw René out onto the street. On the other hand, he said that he couldn't overlook the exceptional destiny of this neophyte. Nothing less was expected of him than that he carry the torch of the holy Cause of chocolate. The professors opened their eyes wide and burst out laughing. Marblo said very coolly that he saw no reason for their laughter, that millions of men had died for the aforementioned Cause and many millions more were prepared to sacrifice their lives; that René, future chief of the chocolatists, could not be treated the same as one of those students destined to enlist as a mercenary for whichever chief paid him the most for his services; that in conclusion, as headmaster and director responsible for the establishment, he was asking the professors to exhaust all resources. He added that there was nothing at risk, for if the institution succeeded in making René effectively torturable, its reputation would grow, and if it was defeated in the attempt, the very act of throwing him out onto the street would send a strong message that the school was no place for reprobates or fugitives.

What was the resolution of this whole affair? To suspend René between the record and the preacher. He had to define himself. Either he sided with God or with the devil... Of course, Marblo was putting all his eggs in one basket. If René decided in favor of the suffering flesh—fine, there would be no problem. But if he chose the path of the flesh as pleasure, all was lost. Even if the school expelled him from its bosom, it would still be considered a defeat. The rival institutions would say that its teaching methods were obsolete. Marblo quivered with fear. In addition to the reasons already outlined, Marblo's own family pride was engaged in this battle—his great stature as the high priest of pain. The times they lived in were so "efficient," the world was driven by such an unfeeling mechanism because of this very "efficiency" that the poor wretch who failed in his mission was irremissibly condemned to the worst of punishments: oblivion. In no way whatsoever did Marblo wish to be forgotten among the men of his age.

He shut himself up in his study with the intention of finding the instrument that would cause René's resistance to yield. After deep reflection, he came to the conclusion that only repetition could work miracles. Repetition would soften even iron: hour after hour, minute after minute, it would be repeated to the obstinate young man that he accept the service of pain.

That was when Marblo thought up the diabolical combination of Record Preacher. During the day, the mechanical component would repeat *ad eternum* his invitation to suffer, always in the same monotonous tone, while at night the human component would argue in the person of the Preacher. Thus, the systematic alternation of the mechanical voice with the human voice aided by his weakness from lack of food would force the rebel to take up the parliament flag. But what would happen if René weren't "softened" by the furies of repetition? Here, Marblo rubbed his hands together in great contentment. If the rebel was defeated by the furies of repetition, it would be automatically demonstrated that he was effectively torturable. The whole world would be moved by the sight of a student who elegantly completed a test designed for experts in the field. Marblo's satisfaction was so great that he let out a belly laugh and cried: "No, René, there's no escape for you!" Then, pen in hand, he proceeded to draw up the text of the record.

The sun was casting its final rays, its dying light enveloping people and objects and starting to dissolve the outlines of both, when the record vomited up its final, lacerating "I want" of the day. This day (the third of his captivity), René had been on the verge of capitulating. He rang the bell three times, and three times Pedro appeared, polite and smiling. He had been entrusted with the job of conveying René's possible surrender to Marblo. This would mean a reward in cold hard cash and a day off. Over the course of those three days, and on the silliest of pretexts, Pedro would enter the room and ask René if he could announce the good news to Mr. Marblo. Without a doubt, René's ringing of the bell smelled strongly of surrender. If he was ringing—not once but three times— it was because he was on the verge of surrendering. As with sick people *in extremis,* Pedro could feel that René was about to hand his soul over to his Creator, which, translated into the language of the school, meant that he was about to surrender his flesh to Marblo.

"Well?" cried Pedro.

René shook his head "no."

"You've got to be crazy," Pedro told him. He held René's hands and whispered to him: "Why are you being so obstinate? Should I notify Mr. Marblo?"

"No! No!" René exclaimed. "You'll never convince me!"

"We'll convince you, son, we'll convince you... Repetition is capable of softening even stone. Greater miracles have been witnessed in the vineyard of Mr. Marblo."

The Preacher was standing there. Pedro took off like a shot. A kind of chubby dwarf—whose nightgown made him more closely resemble a package—had entered the room. He was barely three feet tall. His face, hardened by the years and by excess, was nevertheless that of a child. This dwarf's greatest ambition had been to serve God, but his slight stature had been an insurmountable obstacle between him and the Church. Not even the Jesuits would admit him into their Order. One morning (very many years ago), Marblo discovered him in a market, stuck in a pigsty, lamenting his unlucky fate. Marblo struck up a conversation with him and was astonished at the profound knowledge the dwarf possessed of the sacred and the profane. Marblo decided on those grounds that this dwarf was just the thing his school of pain needed. In accordance with one of the institution's most notable mottos—"Ever lower"— this dwarf was a real find. They quickly came to an agreement. The dwarf, with tears in his eyes, scaled Marblo's imposing height and kissed him on the forehead.

He was a true find. The spirit of lowliness—what the school lacked up until then—was marvelously served by that dwarf rejected by the Church. It must be said that his revenge was something that surpassed all intellectual cruelty in its cruelty. For example, he interpreted the crucifixion of Christ in the spirit of the school. This is how he told it: Christ was interesting insofar as he was made of flesh. In accordance with this, Christ was son of the flesh, of the flesh apt for the service of pain. He added that his interpretation of the Passion, though less elevated than that of the Church Fathers, was in its lowliness infinitely more human. According to him, Christ was a sufferer, son of a sufferer, and even grandson of a sufferer, who had perished on the cross for the cause of the flesh. The dwarf presented the following argument: "I was not present at the crucifixion. *Ergo*: I can falsify the facts. *Ergo*: my falsification is thus: Christ should have thrown pieces of pain to the dogs of his flesh; the crucifixion was his supreme satiation. *Ergo*: Christ didn't die on the cross for the love of men. *Ergo*: Christ died on the cross for the love of his own flesh."

Marblo was enchanted by such a carnal interpretation. He said it fit the school's spirit like a glove. At last the students would have a mirror in which to see themselves. And what a mirror! Marblo was bursting with vanity. None of the rival institutions possessed such a treasure. To see oneself in the flesh of Christ was something truly innovative. Now the business would run at full tilt. It isn't every day one finds someone like this dwarf with such a lowly interpretation of Christ right around the corner. Suddenly, thanks to this find, everything took on a new light: the downstairs floors seemed farther down and the school's motto wallowed in the mud... Swyne (as Marblo baptized him) was without a doubt a bona fide pearl. It was Swyne who thought up the brilliant idea of the doubles. He maintained that Christ as he has been represented for centuries was a hindrance in times so foreign to piety as the present. That anguished countenance, that head fallen on its shoulder, those tears, and that mortal sweat seemed ridiculous for our sporty spirit. Our age fled from piety at top speed. Had the Church followed his advice (which is why he was excommunicated), millions of faithful would be flooding its naves to contemplate the modern face of Jesus.

But now Marblo's school offered them its congregation, and its students would all be modernized, crucified Christs, but...with beaming faces. Softened, mashed, ground down, squashed, but...modern, always modern. Nevertheless, there was one who refused to be modern; one who dared declare himself ancient in the old sense of the word: cultivated body, intact skin, polished fingernails, abundant, curly hair; flesh with cushions at its head and back, luxuriously stretched out on a chaise lounge, with drinks at arm's reach, one bonbon, two bonbons, three...and a strawberry on top, and then a sour cherry; lamb at nine, and another kind of meat at twelve, like his own flesh on a bed of feathers...

Blaah! It was enough to make one vomit. This picture corresponded in every detail to what René had said in a conversation he had with Swyne the night before. He had told him straight out that he was not prepared to place his body in the service of pain, that one's body was one's sacred property and no one had the right to profane it. What language! This unexpected speech made Swyne retch violently. My God, what airs! René was decidedly abnormal, or, if a worse qualifier were possible, eccentric. That is, he was off-kilter, striving to swim against the tide of suffering flesh. There was no other solution than a general retreat. Swyne was determined to lead it if that night the eccentric persisted in maintaining his position. Repetition is efficacious, works miracles, but it has no effect on a madman. Crazy people are found in an insane asylum and not in a school for absolutely normal children. The hell with him!

Swyne looked at the floor and said again:

"We'll convince you, my son, we'll convince you..."

"You won't convince me," René repeated.

And the pitched battle was underway for the night. Like a cat lunging at a scrap of meat, Swyne lunged at René. Gripping René's waist between his knees and holding his face in his hands, he brought his mouth so close to René's that the two of them looked as if they were stuck together.

"You are an urchin. So, blockhead, while the Savior of the flesh died on the cross for his own flesh, you persist in trying to save yours. Whom the devil have you dedicated your flesh to? Tell me, snot-nose! To some filthy bitch, perhaps? What's going on? You're not satisfied with your own hide? Listen: you're shameless, you're indecent. But even worse, you're the laughingstock of the school."

"That's a lie," replied René. "They're all lies. Besides, I don't care."

"Fine, it's a lie," Swyne whined. "Don't you see they're going to make a monkey out of me if I fail with you? You can't allow that to happen. Does my body mean so little to you? It's certain death if I fail. No, you wouldn't let... You're going to want very soon. Let's notify Marblo that you finally want... No? You don't want; I can see you don't want..."

He burst into tears like a child. He ended up laying his face against René's, who, feeling the tears on his skin, roughly pushed the dwarf away.

"No, don't separate my face from yours. I'll cry for all eternity on your face. If you're so cruel to your teacher,

96

it must be bewailed with tears. Look: I'm a dog that's licking you. There's nothing else for me to do. You've defeated me. My tongue is yours. I will lick you for all eternity."

He ran his tongue in a frenzy over René's face. René pushed him off and leapt from the bed. So Swyne was resorting to his tongue... Up until that night, he had developed his subtle lines of argument for hours, while René, sitting in an armchair, looked straight into the beam of a lamp. At least during those sleepless nights there was a certain distance, a few feet separating the two bodies; but now the dwarf was digging in to lick him.

Swyne leapt from the bed, pricked up his ears, looked at René, and barked like a dog. Crawling on his hands and knees, he reached the armchair, raised his arms as if they were paws, and placed them on René's chest.

"Now I am a dog. I'm going to soften you up faster than you can say 'cock-a-doodle-doo.' If I haven't managed to soften you up as Swyne, as a dog my tongue will work miracles."

He jumped cheerfully and curled up on René chest. His large, thick tongue, pasty and red, leapt out like a flame. The clock in the hallway struck seven. Swyne began to "work over" René's face with the caresses of his tongue. He selected one area—René's right cheekbone—and began to work like a trenching spade.

"This takes time," Swyne said, "but we have the whole night ahead of us. You know very well that this is the decisive moment. Don't imagine we're going to let our prey go just like that..."

He stuck his tongue out again and started on René's nose. After two or three passes, his tongue began to swell and get redder. Swyne was licking from top to bottom, which made René sneeze violently and experience the peculiar sensation that the tip of his sinus cavity was touching the ceiling. He tried to turn his face away, but Swyne was holding it firmly between his hands.

"Are you beginning to soften up? An excellent remedy, the tongue... But fewer words and more action. Let's proceed now with that eye. You're looking at me defiantly; that's not good in a pupil."

Once again his tongue went to work. René's face was covered with beads of cold sweat, which, mixed with Swyne's saliva, was beginning to form a filthy poultice so fetid that it made him horribly nauseous.

Now Swyne had imparted a livelier rhythm to his tongue; it no longer limited itself to René's right eye, but traveled back and forth between his right and left eye. At moments, it ignored his eyes and flung itself at his mouth with the sizzling sound of burning beeswax dripping on paper.

"What do you think? Do we need to throw more coal on the fire?... They can't say you have leathery skin. At your age, it's just a matter of minutes. Should I pull you from the pot? Tell me, are you ready yet for us to serve your flesh to Mr. Marblo?"

René opened one eye like Polyphemus. Apparently his gaze was not pleasing to Swyne, for the latter immediately flung himself like a madman at that fierce and melancholy eye.

"Curse you! You still haven't softened up; there are only a few hours left and your skin is as leathery..."

This thought caused him such horrible consternation that he burst into tears.

"Yes," he said between sobs, "all that remains is retreat. Where will they take me in, covered in ignominy? The pigsty is my destiny."

He was lost in far-off worlds. He saw his future life so clearly that he exclaimed:

"Oh no, Lord of the heavens, you won't allow—you'll want René to want, and if he wants, all is saved."

He got back to work with redoubled vigor. His tongue passed frenetically over René's face with such momentum that now it was lost in his hair, now it was introducing itself into his ears or descending to his Adam's apple. The clock could be heard striking eight. Swyne pricked up his ears.

"Still tough," he mumbled.

Suddenly he cupped his hands to his mouth and shouted:

"Help! Help!"

Pedro, always on guard in the corridor, hearing Swyne's shouts, pushed the door open and burst into the room.

"Has he collapsed, sir?"

"Worse," responded Swyne. "He's hardened from head to toe. There isn't a second to lose. Run and find Mr. Marblo. He makes the big decisions; I'm only a subordinate. Run, get him out of bed, tell him that the flesh is getting cold... As for me, I won't let my tongue rest."

And Swyne's tongue again fell—now violet and hysterical—on René's face: the very image of inertia.

Pedro flew off in search of Marblo. He had had a few drinks too many and was dead as a dormouse. Pedro had a hard time waking him up. When Marblo opened his eyes and saw Pedro, he automatically stuck his hand in the drawer of the night table and pulled out a handful of bills.

"No, sir," said Pedro. "The flesh is getting cold..."

"What flesh? What are you talking about?"

The revelation came to him like a hammer blow to the head. He slammed his hand down on the night table; the vase, pitcher, and bottle flew into the air. He got out of bed and put on a *robe de chambre*.

"It's getting cold," he repeated like a madman. "But has all of it gotten cold, or is some of it still warm?..."

"I don't know, sir," Pedro answered. "Swyne isn't allowing anyone to touch it. He's afraid."

"So he's afraid... Afraid... Let's go."

They set out on a mad dash through rooms and corridors. When they reached the corridor, they could clearly hear renewed calls for help. Marblo came to a dead halt.

"It certainly is getting cold..."

At last he pushed the door open and rushed into the room. Swyne was still straddling René. In the silence of the night, the squelching of his tongue could be heard clearly.

"Definitely cold?" Marblo asked.

Swyne, looking at Marblo with the eyes of a defeated general, answered:

"On the verge of..." and sticking out his tongue again, he proceeded with the softening. Like the vanes of a fan just turned off, he passed his tongue weakly over René's face, at last letting it fall on his lower lip. Panting like a dog, he lay down on the rug and looked at Marblo. Then, as if he were yards away from Marblo, he shouted in a thundering voice:

"Help!"

"Please, my admirable Swyne! Please! I'm prepared to offer you all my assistance."

"Help!" Swyne shouted again, staring at René.

Marblo understood. With one leap he was on top of René, who creaked like a dry branch. He stuck out his enormous tongue and began to lick René's face clean.

"Listen, my dear headmaster. The hours remaining are decisive. Perhaps many tongues can work the miracle. We need, we require, we clamor for, we demand twelve dozen tongues."

"That many?..."

"...That many. We're going to organize an emergency team. It will be my final attempt at softening him up. It's necessary that René's flesh be licked systematically. What I mean is, licked from the top of his head to the tips of his toes."

"Understand, my dear Swyne, that the 'second-year dogs'... They've been working intensively all day."

"That doesn't interest me," Swyne said coldly. "It's the same to me whether they're first- or second-year dogs. Tongues are what we need." He observed his own in the bureau mirror.

"Swollen. My tongue is swollen. But even though it falls to pieces on me, I will continue to lick this snotty little brat. Make room for me, Marblo."

He fell upon René and began to lick his chin. Marblo in turn was licking René's nose clean. They remained in this position for several minutes until Swyne, definitively defeated by his flesh, said to Marblo:

"Let Pedro call the second-year students."

"Will it work?"

"We'll know the answer to that by six in the morning. How many tongues can we have ready?"

"At the moment, fifty. I'll have fifty 'dogs' come from the third-year course. They're the freshest and don't have to do anything in the initiation ceremony tomorrow."

He called Pedro over and gave him an order.

"All right then, tongues to the grindstone," Swyne said. "What do you think of that table?"

"*Ad hoc*," Marblo said, "*ad hoc*. It's long enough for the flesh of this... piece of iron," and he let one hand rest on René's stomach. René opened his eyes.

"What!..." exclaimed Marblo. "You deign to open your eyes?"

He picked René up as if he were light as a feather and laid him on the table.

"Do you want yet?"

René didn't utter a word.

"So, you still don't want..." and as he spoke, he stripped René naked. "Well listen to me: you're going to want, and soon."

"It's useless, my dear Marblo, absolutely useless. We've done everything humanly possible. Although a miracle... That is, I expect a miracle." He lifted his eyes to heaven. "A miracle, Lord God of the Armies!"

"Don't despair, Swyne. Victory will be ours in the end."

"In the end?..."

"Why, of course!" And Marblo let out a bellylaugh. "If I'm consenting to this business of the tongues, it's purely out of condescension. But I am convinced that it will be useless."

"Well then?..."

"I know what I feel..." He brought his mouth to Swyne's ear and whispered to him. "Let him employ his time now and get as cold as he pleases. Later..."

"More violent methods?"

Marblo left the question unanswered. All of a sudden the door opened and Pedro stuck his head in with a look of affected seriousness. He stepped to one side to let the third-year students enter.

Some of them had been pulled out of bed and others grabbed in the game room. This explained their badly matched assortment of clothes. While some were in their pajamas, some were properly dressed and others were in their underwear. The regulations of the school (very similar to a military code) anticipated the call to arms, so when Pedro blew his whistle it was the signal for them to follow him—like rats after the Pied Piper of Hamlin—though it be to their certain death.

When Marblo shut the door, the room resembled a suitcase packed with far too many objects than could fit. Swyne accommodated ten students on the bed, another ten clustered by the window, and the remaining students distributed themselves between the bureau and the rug.

Swyne warmly embraced Roger. He said that as the leader and outstanding student of the third-year course, the honor of initiating the softening up of the rebel was his.

"It's a question," Swyne said solemnly, "of softening up his flesh. It's hard—rather: leathery, recalcitrant in the face of the benevolent action of pain. This flesh—" he grabbed one of René's legs, holding it up—"is striving to harden, is getting colder by the minute. If it succeeds in freezing, we're all lost."

He let René's leg drop. He leaned over his body. He picked up another leg and considered it in great detail.

"Yes, if at least one part, just one part, dear Lord, wanted to soften up..."

He gave himself a fillip in the face.

"Listen to me, René: will you concede me one part, just one, for the initiation ceremony? This leg, maybe?"

The leg grew even colder. Trembling, Swyne let it drop back onto the table.

"Please, my dear Swyne! Please! What childishness! Just finish forming the first team. Time is running out," Marblo said in an urgent tone of voice.

Swyne turned to Roger.

"What part do you prefer, my admirable Roger? You may select the part you like best."

"I prefer the face," Roger answered, coating his words with the grease of his smile.

"Well there it is," Swyne said, "and may God find it pleasing that *Finis coronat Opus*..."

Then Roger, overflowing with rivers of tranquillity and waterfalls of confidence, Roger, the outstanding member of his class, archsuffering flesh, prepared to bring René's recalcitrant flesh to its senses.

Just as we test the point of a pen once or twice and, assured of its quality, move it from left to right over the sheet of paper, and now and then the hand pauses as the brain vacillates between one thought and another, so too Roger stuck out his tongue and taking one of René's toes, applied his tongue to it once or twice to assure himself of the quality of its point. Without a doubt, it would only have occurred to a master in such an art to have chosen that part of the body for his test. Roger resembled one of those calligraphers who makes a few strokes in the margin of the page with his pen. He let go of the toe and moved over to the face. He slipped one hand under René's head and leaned the other on his chest. Then he looked at Swyne.

He was indicating the tongues that were to second Roger's. One for each part of the body: two legs, two arms. As for the thoracic cage and the stomach, they were considered one single section.

"Roger, please open the session," he said.

Roger licked René's forehead profoundly. He shook his head in doubt. He passed his tongue over the rebel's lips. He shook his head again.

"What's wrong, Roger?" Swyne asked.

"Hard as a rock," was all he said.

Swyne made an imploring gesture. Marblo looked at him as if he were a freak. He slapped him on the back, showed him the time.

"My admirable Swyne, don't appeal to on high when it is from on low that you should be asking for help. It's ten o' clock. Time is flying."

"Oh, yes, absolutely. Excuse me, Headmaster, but I'm in despair. Frankly, I'm in despair."

He turned to Roger and his followers:

"To work, boys!"

The six tongues got to work. Due to the resistance offered by the "terrain," they advanced arduously. They would stop, get tricked up in the flesh, skate and bounce off it. Their faces were growing congested and their backs were covered with large beads of sweat, while their arms, resembling oars, rowed desperately in the vacuum of that recalcitrant flesh.

The rest of the assistants were engaged in animated discussion; their voices rose *in crescendo*. The cigarette smoke grew denser by the minute. It was useless for Swyne to attempt to maintain order, to look imploringly at Marblo.

Marblo, on the other hand, was taking it all with an eminently sporty spirit, and even in jest. No one knows how a bottle appeared in his hands, a bottle of gin that began to be passed around among the students. Swyne looked at him again imploringly. Marblo told him that during the great storms at sea, sailors are comforted by a double ration of alcohol. He rang a bell and within a few seconds Pedro appeared, disappearing forthwith and reappearing with a basket full of bottles.

"Please, Marblo," Swyne said, placing his hands over the basket in Marblo's hands. "Please. Gin will make their tongues pasty."

"So much the better, my admirable Swyne. Pasty versus hard; hard versus pasty. We'll see who wins."

"But Marblo, you're going to disorganize my people," Swyne wailed. "Don't you see that I have to organize the work crews? Have you forgotten that this flesh must be licked systematically?"

"It will be licked. I don't see why it shouldn't be. But allow me to give the lickers some encouragement."

Uncorking the bottle, Marblo handed it to the students.

"In that case, don't stop at saturating them with alcohol. Combine it with the flesh," said Swyne.

"A marvelous idea, my dear Swyne. You are always inspired. Meat should always be present in every one of our proceedings," and he rang the bell. "So, alcohol and meat... How's that, Swyne?"

"What can I do for you, sir?" Pedro said, entering the room.

"Run to the pantry. Bring meat—lots of meat. Come back with fresh meat, smoked meat, roasted meat, boiled meat, blood sausages..."

He gave Swyne a rough slap on the back.

"Flesh versus flesh! You said it, Swyne: one has to offer a lot of flesh to the flesh in order to defeat it. The road to heaven is paved with flesh."

Swyne pulled out his watch.

"One moment, Marblo. Hold up for just a minute. I have to relieve the crew."

He pointed to six boys at random who already were rather euphoric after the gin they'd swigged.

"Stop!" he shouted at Roger and company. "Lay down your tongues!"

He turned to Roger.

"What do you say, my Eminence?"

Roger, with a red smile due to his congested face, said:

"Very hard," and spit abundantly.

Hearing Roger's concise summary, Marblo burst out laughing. He handed him the bottle.

"Nothing, Roger, nothing. If a tongue as eminent as yours can do nothing..." He turned to Swyne. "So will we have to apply Draconian measures?"

Swyne answered with silence. He "sicked" the second crew on René's body. This crew, in order to work more freely, had stripped off its clothes. The effect was even stranger. The wounds, welts, contusions, pustules, dislocations, and hematomas on their flesh were all layed bare. It looked as if those six lickers had been waiting years for the chance they now had to openly exhibit their "gems" of suffering in silence.

They threw themselves on René's flesh like rabid dogs. This crew, whether in the spirit of emulation or from the effects of the alcohol, applied itself to the task of licking so aggressively that Marblo clapped his hands like a child.

"Have faith, Swyne. Have faith in alcohol to work miracles. Listen. Listen how rhythmically those tongues glide along the carnal path. Listen: hup, two, hup, two...! Onward, boys, onward!"

As if announcing the arrival of a brilliant idea, he hit himself on the forehead.

"What's wrong?" said Swyne. "Just found your head?..."

"Don't get sarcastic, Swyne. I'm not in the mood for impertinent remarks. I will, however, tell you what will soften it up."

"Soften up what?..."

"This little lad's flesh. We're going to soften it with alcohol. The most fundamental rules of every good kitchen prescribe its use in the seasoning of any kind of meat. And this—" he squeezed between the lickers and let his huge hand fall on René's stomach—"is no less meat than any other kind."

The six boys lifted their heads, displaying their hanging, throbbing tongues. Each resembled an animal that has been separated from its prey at the height of the feeding frenzy. Their eyes were bloodshot. It looked as if at any moment they might hurl themselves on Marblo.

"Down, boys!" Marblo said. "I'm soft, my flesh is melted. It's René who has to be softened up."

He held the bottle high above his head and covered René's body with gin.

Swyne came over with another bottle.

"Allow me, Marblo. Allow me, as Supreme Pontiff..."

And he let a stream of gin fall on René's face.

"In nomine Pater, Filiis et Espiritu Marmolus..."

The door whipped open, revealing two arms bearing an enormous tray with a roast pig on a bed of lettuce. The pig had entered headfirst and its toasted little eyes seemed astonished as it looked on that scene of liquefaction.

"The predicate!" Marblo cried happily at the sight of the pig.

"The predicate?..." asked Swyne.

"Why, of course!" answered Marblo. "Isn't the predicate that which is said of the subject? If I say: Man is made of flesh, the predicate of the subject 'Man' is his flesh."

"But Marblo, don't get confused. René is made of human flesh, and what just entered the room is pork flesh."

"Pure casuistry, Swyne! In the end, everything is flesh and nothing but flesh."

In the meantime, the pig had been followed by a platter of blood sausages. Had Pedro taken Marblo's order literally? A total of six servants were creeping into the room. The boys seated on the bureau got off to make room for the trays, but since space was limited, pig and blood sausages tumbled to the floor with a deafening crash. Small brooks of fat coursed this way and that over the floor tiles.

Who isn't hungry at midnight? Who could control oneself at the sight of a roast pig on a bed of lettuce?

boys closest to the pig stuck their hands in and, accommodating themselves as best they could, began to pull off pieces of pork flesh. Their greed was extraordinary; they exhibited a certain fury, wanting to stuff all that meat into their mouths at once. Hardly had the boys bit into a piece of pork than they threw it away to sink their teeth into a piece of lamb or a blood sausage.

Gulp and mouthful, mouthful and gulp... But the body protects itself against excess. So the boys soon began to vomit and urinate, and it all mixed with the spilled fat, and seemed as if all that was pulpy, soft, spongy, flaccid, and fungous were pressing against all that was hard, solid, firm, compact, and petrous in order to soften it up.

Suddenly Swyne cried out.

"Air, please. The flesh is suffocating!"

And he ran to open the window, trampling the bodies of the boys.

"Let the flesh suffocate, Swyne. Let it do whatever it pleases... He who laughs last, laughs best."

Marblo's voice was drowned out by the scandal a group of boys were causing in the bathroom. He looked that way. His eyes left him confused: cheering, the boys were taking René's double out of the bathroom. The disorder was so great that as they passed through the doorway, one of the arms of the cross was broken, causing Christ to arrive in the middle of the room with only one of his arms nailed down. The boys flung themselves on the double and began licking at it greedily. Marblo was wildly applauding, and Swyne, spilling gin over the plaster figure, said:

"Let's bet on who will soften up first."

"Enough childishness, Swyne," shouted Marblo. "The double will never soften up, and as for René, even less likely. Now he's the double of his double. And you well know... That means double the hardness. All the tongues on this planet wouldn't be sufficient."

One of the lickers, hopelessly drunk, persisted in softening the right leg of the double. Since he could have spent his entire life licking that leg without managing to soften it up, he kicked the leg in a fit of fury, smashing it to bits. That was the signal for them to break the mannequin into little pieces. The rest of the lickers set about smashing the remaining parts of the body. Within a few minutes, the figure had been broken into a pile of painted plaster. Then the boys urinated on the pieces.

Swyne burst into laughter.

"Doubles against doubles! What do you say, dear Headmaster? Now you see, if it doesn't soften, they break it..."

"So, should we break him?" Marblo said, pointing at René.

"No, Headmaster! Don't get the dogs too worked up."

The clock struck midnight.

"God Almighty, it's twelve o'clock! We only have six hours left of darkness..."

"But after the darkness comes the light, Preacher," Marblo cackled. "The beautiful, pure, and radiant light; the light that will illuminate the bodies of the new servants of suffering in silence."

"What?" Swyne exclaimed. "Are you going to hold the initiation outdoors in the sunlight this time?"

"It's just a manner of speaking, my dear Swyne. Don't get alarmed. Our initiations will always be held below the waterline..."

"Ah!" was all Swyne said.

He went over to the lickers. They had fallen asleep, their mouths pressed like bloodsuckers against René's flesh.

"Look, Marblo!" Swyne whined. "This is the disastrous result of your gin. The tongues have fallen asleep on me."

"What do you say about these?" Marblo spun around on his heels, pointing at a pile of bodies snoring peacefully on the bed. "I'm truly afraid those tongues won't 'wake up' on time."

As if possessed, Swyne threw himself on the bed, pulling the bodies apart, wrenching apart one leg from another leg or two arms that were grasping a stomach. A pointless task: hardly had he succeeded in completely separating one body, when a moment later it detached itself and fell like lead on another separated body. Suddenly a half dozen boys, threw themselves on the bed, falling on Swyne, who with great effort managed to emerge from the mountain of alcohol-soaked flesh. He staggered toward the sleeping lickers. One by one, he began to peel their stiff mouths from the hardened flesh. With his enormous tongue, he began to lick the sleepers without rhyme or reason.

"What are you doing, Swyne?" Marblo shouted at him. "Only René has to be softened up."

"Don't be fooled!" Swyne said, panting. "Things are getting more complicated: the lickers are also hardening up... Come quick. We have to plug the leak... We're being threatened by an ecumenical hardening."

But Marblo had collapsed on the bed and was staring stupidly at Swyne.

"I'm starting to harden up also, my dear Swyne. I feel like I'm made of rock."

"Curses! Curses a thousandfold!" Swyne cried. "His flesh will end up hardening us all. Please, Marblo! You make the big decisions. Kick his flesh out once and for all."

"I can't," whined Marblo. "I'd break my foot."

"But it's all right if I break my tongue, eh?" Swyne shouted. "Come on, Marblo. You're the supreme authority. Maintain a little order."

"I can't. I'm getting harder by the second," and as if possessed, he began to lick his own hands.

"Then sound the call to arms. Look alive! Off with all clothes! This is a drama of the flesh. This can only be resolved between naked flesh."

With a violent tug, he removed Marblo's *robe de chambre*. Then without delay, he rent his own nightshirt from top to bottom.

"Help me, Marblo. We'll reveal ourselves the way God brought us into the world: with malleable flesh, disposed and trembling..."

He set Marblo on his feet with tremendous difficulty. The students who hadn't fallen asleep crowded around the headmaster and preacher. Swyne made a bold gesture as he turned to them.

"I said off with all your clothes! What are you waiting for?"

"That's right," repeated Marblo like an echo. "I said off with all clothes! What are you waiting for?"

He stood there thinking. Suddenly he let one hand fall heavily on one of the boys.

"You. Yes, you. Why aren't you licking me? Don't you see that I'm getting hard?"

The boy didn't wait for him to repeat the order. He threw himself greedily on Marblo's naked flesh.

"Mutually," shouted Marblo. "Mutually! There's no time to lose. Our admirable preacher has already said it. You lick me and I lick you..."

"We all lick each other," and Swyne completed the final vertex of the carnal triangle.

But it was hopeless. Like flies to a fly strip, their tongues began sticking to the flesh. Marblo felt himself falling into a bottomless pit, his tongue was slipping all over the student's flesh until it came to rest, stuck to the rug. Swyne felt his limbs getting harder and his legs growing numb; his arms weighed like lead. He looked around. A dense and compact sea of flesh spread out at his feet. He stepped on one body after another with his slipper, and with each probe, his foot shrunk in his slipper out of profound disgust. He staggered over to René's body and embraced his hardened and hardening flesh. The clock struck one. With his automatic tongue, he licked René on the mouth, but it was such an unconvincing licking, such a hesitant, cowardly, and bored licking, that he immediately retracted the tip of his tongue.

"You've defeated us," he whispered. "That means back to the pigsty. A pretty ceremony it will be tomorrow morning with the hard flesh of the son and the recriminations of the father. There's no doubt about it: we're sunk. We can only retreat. Yes, retreat. And I'm going to retreat right now."

He couldn't. His flesh refused to move. On the contrary, it stuck to another piece of flesh and lay there, asleep.

Scorched Flesh

The first bus loaded with parents arrived at ten in the morning. The initiation ceremony would take place promptly at twelve. At one in the afternoon, Mr. Marblo would offer the visitors lunch. They would then take a tour through the various outbuildings of the school, including the famous "downstairs" floors.

The initiation would take place in what Swyne called "the church of the human body": a large hall on the third floor, located at the very center of the building. He went there twice a week to expound on the philosophy of the suffering body. He did so from a pulpit presided over by a large, beaming Christ. Yes, Swyne was a real priest—a priest through and through, regardless of his cult. Invested with a white gown, he climbed the stairs to the pulpit, pressed his hands together in fervent devotion, stared at the image of Christ, and began to enunciate the sufferings of the flesh.

Swyne had one advantage over priests of the soul. While the latter have to preach or insist upon the salvation of the soul, Swyne limited himself to such concrete matters as arms, legs, bones, blood... The individual wouldn't have to deal with that elusive, incorporeal, and problematic thing that is the soul, nor worry about its salvation. On the contrary, the entire secret of human life is lodged in the body. In truth, a very simple secret: it's all over when the body brings its machinery to a halt. Man's opportunity is only valid during his corporeal life. As for the next life—a life after death—there is none.

This captivating truth offered one great advantage: since there was neither salvation nor eternal damnation, no one would vacillate by "shutting himself off" from another body or from his own. The flesh is just another means of resolving any problem life puts in our path. If, for example, a bridge must be hung over a chasm, the logical thing to do is to get hold of flesh specializing in this type of construction. Whether ten arms are fractured, twenty heads bashed in, seven chests crushed, or fifteen eyes poked out during the course of construction is of little importance. Once again, the flesh is posed with a problem and the flesh must solve it. So, if the hanging of a bridge or working in the mines or the fabrication of explosives (to mention only dangerous jobs) involves a mortal risk to the flesh, why should one be surprised that a group of men might use their flesh in defense of an idea, whether it be out of their own conviction or because someone is paying for their services? The eternal throng of casuists allege that to risk one's flesh in the hanging of a bridge is not the same as the rack of a torture chamber. The argument they put forth is the following: any flesh employed in the hanging of a bridge is not inevitably condemned to being slain. On the other hand, flesh in the torture chamber is thus condemned. Like a safe, it contains a secret, and to open it, it must be broken. Flesh in bridge construction mustn't necessarily be destroyed in order for the bridge to be hung. That is to say, it is flesh that avoids suffering at all costs. The worker walks along that girder with utmost care; he wears thick boots on his feet to protect him from the hardness of the steel; his hands are well shielded by gloves... An enormous terror possesses him when, having stumbled, he grips a buttress in mortal anguish. Isn't this flesh that fights to keep itself intact?

But the flesh that stretches out on the rack, the flesh for which the hazard of an accident is a moot point (given that its final destiny is to be slain)—in a word: isn't that flesh, apt for the service of pain, an insane challenge to the instinct of self-preservation? Doesn't it constitute a dangerous invitation to collective suicide? Isn't it madness that a man might offer up his flesh in order to keep a secret and that to wrench it from him another might be willing to sacrifice this flesh?

At this point, Swyne spun carnally around in the pulpit shrieking like a vulture over carrion: "Pure fabrications!" he said. "In the slaughterhouse, our flesh is nothing more nor less than the flesh of cattle. It is food for people. It resolves one of their problems of subsistence. If we were suddenly to refuse to immolate our flesh, human life would come to a halt and the world would be transformed into a charnel house. No, my dearly beloved, it is flesh that makes the world go round, and the problems arising from all the flesh of the human species combined are greater than the individual flesh of any one person."

And at this point in his sermon (yes, it was a pro-meat sermon), the compact carnality of Swyne grew enormous. What a boarding call he shouted out: "Long live perishable flesh!"

One way of making the flesh flower, of giving it the position its dignity deserved, was through these beautiful initiation celebrations, which Marblo's academy held year after year. With this year's celebration they had achieved the impossible in order that it be particularly brilliant. There were two reasons for this: in part, the spirit of emulation among the schools. Another school was located not far from there, which, despite its recent establishment, rivaled Marblo's in every respect. They even went so far as to say that the flesh was "better crafted" at that school. Who could say whether Marblo's school wouldn't have been totally eclipsed had it not been for the opportune discovery of Swyne (it was his brilliant innovations that worked the miracle of relegating the rival institution to a lower plane). But even so, one had to keep one's eyes peeled in order not to concede a single inch of terrain—in a word, always to be improving so that the others would become worse. The other reason was the presence of Ramón. Counting René among its students unquestionably strengthened the school's reputation. How could they do anything short of offering the father an impressive ceremony on the day of his son's initiation?

Unfortunately, the mass hardening produced by René's resistance to being softened was a complete moral defeat. Nevertheless, the young man would not have his way. If we stared mute with horror at that sea of hardened flesh, and imagined that it would be impossible for that flesh to take a single step, utter a single word, or move a single arm, then it could only await the arrival of faithful servants—the living antithesis of all that is rock-hard—to pull Marblo, Swyne, and company out of their lethargy.

So, when the first guests arrived, Mr. Marblo appeared at the head of the professors, stuffed into his tailcoat, fresh as the morning itself. Among the guests were a fair number of people eager to get even a "fleeting glimpse"—as they put it—of that eighth wonder that was the school from which the suffering flesh emerged purified. Furthermore (and this related to the protocol of the institution), personalities from the high official levels and the accredited diplomatic corps were present as guests of honor. The corps, curious by nature, was there in greater force this year: they were going to see and hear Doctor Swyne for the first time ever.

Marblo stepped forward and began shaking hands all around. The mothers, particularly excited by Marblo's physical reputation, were so effusive as to hug and even kiss him. A new batch of mothers succeeded in making a veritable uproar in the foyer. Marblo was barely able to answer the thousands of questions being asked him by those maternal mouths. "No, my dear lady," he was heard to say, "at the moment you can't hug your baby. The regulations state that the neophytes may not be seen by anyone before the ceremony."

He laughed discretely and added:

"They're on tenterhooks..."

One mother wanted to know how her son "stood." Whether he showed promise or not...

"Naturally the boy shows promise," responded Marblo. "Here, ma'am, everyone shows promise."

"Could my little Fernando do two years in one?"

"What!" Marblo exclaimed, and observed the most profound look of astonishment on the faces of two professors standing next to him. "What do you mean, my dear lady?"

"I mean two years in one. My little Fernando's education is costing me an arm and a leg. All I have is my widow's pension. Don't you think, sir, that the boy is vigorous enough to do two years in one?"

"But my dear lady, that's impossible," Marblo told her, confused. "Here we proceed step by step. One mustn't fool around with the body."

He swallowed dryly and continued.

"Let me give you an example. Let's take the manual that's used for the dislocation of the lower limbs. If it indicates that a leg must be twisted over and over again for an entire month, don't attempt to limit the exercise to fifteen days; you won't gain a thing that way. On the contrary: the student will suffer a setback in his education. The entire effect will be forfeited. Instead of having a boy apt for the service of pain, we would have a boy apt for service..."

Marblo left the phrase hanging. At that moment the government representatives were arriving. But like a flock of swallows, the mothers covered him with their hands, menacing him so he would finish the phrase.

"Say it, Headmaster, say it!"

Realizing that all resistance was pointless with mothers as curious as these, he said:

"Nothing at all...—that we would have a boy apt for service in the circus. He would do nothing but clown around."

And breaking the mothers' charmed circle, he ran toward the government delegation, all smiles and adulation.

"Bravo!" the mothers cried. "Clown around!"

They broke into a crescent, making way for Marblo who was guiding the Chief of State by the arm. They entered a large hall where an orchestra hired for the occasion was playing dance music. A few mothers and fathers had already begun to dance. The servants were walking around the hall with large trays, distributing cocktails so prodigiously that some of the guests were beginning to show signs of intoxication. They were betting on whether little Ramón was more apt for the service of pain than little Jorge, or whether little Pedro would stand up under the electric current better than little Paco... Two mothers were feeling so "carnal" that Marblo himself had to call them to order. The good women—who had both already had several cocktails—were locked in one of those judo holds, each of them demanding that the other concede the unquestionable "resistance" of her respective kid.

So Marblo used the situation to clear up certain misconceptions about the flesh, which unfortunately were very much in vogue. He said that there existed the false criteria of the *tabula rasa* as applied to the flesh; that is, if the flesh is not "prime," it must be discarded. But the truth was very different. Cannon fodder comes in two categories: leader meat and mass meat. The former is that of teachers, those people who aren't just tortured, but who torture themselves and in turn torture others, inventing new models of torture. The latter—no less courageous—are those people who let themselves be tortured and who in turn have the aptitude and knowledge to torture their fellow human beings, but who don't contribute inspired inventions to the cause of the flesh. Pointing to Roger's portrait, he said that neither he, Marblo, nor the staff of professors found this living example of leader flesh to be "any better" than the mass flesh of the rest of the student body; that the fact that he was "the outstanding member of the class" did not in any way mean that the other flesh wasn't making a valiant contribution to the battle of the flesh. And to bring his long-winded speech to a close, he took the two quarreling mothers by the waist and joined them in a fraternal embrace. But the genteel spirit of his teaching profession manifested itself and his iron fingers gripped their delicate flesh like pincers so that the two women began to moan.

"Oh, my dear little women, my dear little women!..." Marblo exclaimed. "Always your eternal birth pangs!"

Suddenly he heard someone calling him. A loudspeaker was repeating his name over and over again. He rushed off to his study. His first thought was that René had hardened to the point of rigor mortis. In that case, all was lost. Something gravely serious was occurring for them to be calling him so insistently. He pushed open the door to his study. There was Ramón, seated in a chair.

"How's it going, Marblo! A beautiful day; worthy of our initiation ceremony."

Marblo scrutinized Ramón's face. He perceived a certain sarcasm in what he said. The colossus began to shake. He spoke through his teeth:

"Yes, a beautiful day, though..."

"Though..." Ramón repeated, staring at him.

"It could cloud over..." said Marblo.

"I'm here to prevent that from happening," and Ramón laughed.

"I must confess to you that we haven't been able to keep René from hardening up and clouding over..."

"I always had my doubts about René," Ramón said, "but I thought that at school, contact with the professors and students would work miracles. Furthermore, our family tree... You know, Marblo, what we're made of."

He thought for a moment, then added:

"No, no, René can't be the great throwback."

"I'm inclined to believe that René's case is one of stubbornness. Not—as one would think at first glance—a typical case of an allergy to the flesh."

"That's what I've always thought, Headmaster. René is a great sufferer. It's just that he has the demon of stubbornness in his body."

"Obviously!" said Marblo. "It's a whim of his not to yield to the flesh. Though I must say: in his very resistance lies his aptitude for being a typical case of leader flesh. If at the age of twenty his flesh has defeated the efforts of many tongues fighting to soften it up, what won't it do at thirty when cured of those late-night romantic notions. Yes, my friend, I have faith in René. The only thing is—I must confess—his flesh isn't meant to be molded in this school. Flesh like your son's requires a special treatment far from other flesh and its gaze. Yes, don't be surprised. René is made of chaste flesh that must be molded in the most absolute darkness. Don't misunderstand me: I'm speaking metaphorically when I say absolute darkness and to draw out the metaphor, I'll tell you that René's flesh, like a photographic negative, loses all of its properties when exposed to the light."

"I'd add something else," Marblo said. "His flesh isn't just flesh. The demon of thought still dances within it."

Swyne, who had entered as Marblo spoke those last words, added:

"It's flesh that permits itself to think about itself. In contrast to the flesh we have here, René's flesh thinks. This then is the Gordian knot. If anyone cuts this knot, the spell will be broken. Yes, Ramón, your son is under the spell of thought."

He pulled a watch out of the depths of his gown.

"It's twenty of twelve. What do we do, Marblo?"

"Yes, what do we do?" responded Marblo. "René can't attend the ceremony. He's nothing but an inert mass."

"Well, friends, all is not lost." Ramón's voice was now very calm; one could almost say it had a sporty quality to it. "If we can't present the truth, we'll present a farce. That way, neither the school's reputation nor my own will suffer any damage."

"That's exactly what I was thinking," cried Swyne, very excited. "We'll come up with some way of conveniently displaying René before the eyes of the public. What occurs to you, my dear Marblo?"

"I'm thinking of an exercise, but I'm so confused since last night that I can't hit upon a solution. On the other hand, I'm afraid that René will ruin the party with his shouting."

"He won't shout," said Ramón. "I authorize you to lead him to the pillory under anesthesia. You'll work out the business of the exercise. Discover, invent, calculate... See you at the ceremony."

"Say, Ramón," and Swyne caught him in mid-stride. "Before you leave, don't you want to take a peek at René's flesh?"

"No. What for? I know it like the palm of my hand. Besides, I'm going to have an awful lot of fun at the farce we're putting on."

And never was a truer word spoken, for the sight offered by "the church of the body" was that of a colossal farce. Resplendent with lights, clotted with flowers, the cathedral was disguised as a music hall. On its walls hung the famous tapestries that were the treasure of the school, tapestries woven with the subjects of celebrated cases of torture and employing the techniques of animated cartoons. The result was so comical that—as Swyne said—they would cure you of any malady...

The body of professors was already seated in its "chapter chairs," placed on both sides of the altar. There were various chairs in every shape and color, which Swyne in his nostalgia for the Catholic cult had ironically baptized "assembly chairs." One of them stood out: an armchair upholstered in a purplish red material whose function was to receive Marblo's humanity as supreme authority of the school and officiating member of the initiation ceremony.

Laughter in every tone of voice could be heard as the assembly filled the ample nave. The mothers laughed out loud every time their eyes fixed upon one of the methods of torture represented in the tapestries. But as they looked toward the altar, their laughter froze on their lips. The neophytes, kneeling there naked, were in a crescent formation. With their eyes shut and their hands crossed over their chests, they looked like the marble angels placed at the entrance to sanctuaries. The mothers, who never expected to see their little lambs in such a posture (Marblo had received them so cheerfully, everything had to be equally informal), felt their hearts contracting.

Suddenly, Marblo made his appearance through a small door located at the back of the altar. The audience received him with a murmur of astonishment. He had on a white shirt and pants, and an apron of the same color, but stained all over with blood. He wore a red cap on his head. His right hand gripped a branding iron of the kind one uses to brand cattle. The chorus sung *Salva Facta Regem.* As if it were a scepter, Marblo raised the branding iron then immediately walked over to his armchair and sat down like a monarch.

He looked over the crescent of kneeling neophytes, looking for René. The naked flesh of the boys and their identical postures made it difficult to tell them apart. Nevertheless, Marblo's expert eye leapt over each and every one of those morsels of flesh and at last, sure of itself, came to rest at the very center of the prostrate mass. Swyne had truly accomplished wonders. At the last minute, Marblo washed his hands of the matter and it

was Swyne who had to "gather together the flesh" without, of course, forgetting René's. Marblo again recognized the dwarf's fiendish cunning: the hardened body
of René was kneeling in the crescent—just one of many
neophytes—his eyes closed, and his hands placed over
his chest. Anesthetized? This he could not discern. He
was able to see how his calm breathing gently moved his
chest up and down. He tried to see whether René was
being held up by some kind of device. No matter how
he stretched his neck, he couldn't see a thing. Was it
possible that he had reconsidered at the last moment
and, unhardening, had accepted the initiation? It looked
as if this was the case. Such are miracles: what fifty eager
tongues were unable to achieve, whimsy made possible.
Just as whimsy had induced him to harden up, that same
whimsy had unhardened him. And the more he looked
at René, the more Marblo became convinced that he
was there of his own free will.

The appearance of Swyne, now slowly climbing the
stairs to the pulpit, pulled him from this train of thought.
The Pope himself couldn't have done it with as much
majesty. Despite his compact stature, Swyne had such an
imposing air about him that a murmur of admiration
raced through the audience. He was wearing an ankle-
length robe of white moiré. As the light hit the fabric, it
hurt and dazzled the eye. But the originality of his dress
centered around his hands that displayed a pair of red
velvet gloves. Were those gloves perhaps an allusion to
that which all flesh awaits at the hands of its torturer?
His gloves made one forget about the rest of his vest-
ment. They caused all eyes pointed at them to converge
and everyone to lose their breath. Conscious of their
effect, Swyne climbed the stairs slowly, lifting his gloves
aloft as if they were the blessed Host. Once in the pulpit,
he lowered his hands and crossed them over his chest.

The audience celebrated this pantomime by bursting into applause. Swyne indicated his appreciation with a sweet smile. Then closing his eyes, he was rapt in ecstasy like a mystic. Was he praying for a happy outcome to the ceremony? Was he asking the demon of the flesh to see that his human flock reached perfect bestiality? He remained in that position for several seconds. Suddenly he cried out:

"Ladies and gentlemen, the first head of cattle will now be branded! If its flesh endures the trial without letting out a cry or moan, we will recognize it as apt for the service of pain."

He immediately mentioned the name of the neophyte kneeling first on the right in the crescent. As if shot from a gun, the neophyte rose to his feet and went to Marblo's side, but instead of facing Marblo, he showed him his behind. The assembly burst into boisterous laughter, which doubled when the neophyte went down on all fours. To have maintained an angelic position for such a long time and then suddenly to adopt the stance of a beast was the height of ridiculousness.

Swyne said again:

"Ladies and gentlemen, the first head of cattle will now be branded!"

Marblo stood up, leaving the iron on the armchair. He pulled a red-hot branding iron from a brazier and began to bring it close to the neophyte's youthful behind.

To encourage him, his mother stood on her chair and shouted to him:

"Don't flinch, Jorgito!"

This inflamed appeal was followed by the harsh jolt of the neophyte's body. The odor of scorched flesh spread throughout the nave. Jorgito had just been branded by Marblo without emitting so much as a sigh. With the demeanor of a more mature person, he stood up and went to take his place in the crescent. He knelt down, crossed his hand over his chest and closed his eyes to the delirious applause of the assembly rewarding him for his courage.

And so the neophytes offered up their behinds to Marblo. And every time one was about to surrender himself to the branding iron, a cry of encouragement from his mother would be heard: "Bravo, Juan! Go, Paco! Steady, dear Oswaldo!..." They all passed the test elegantly as the odor of scorched flesh became increasingly pronounced, and was so exciting that the applause and cheers grew louder with each branding.

The ceremony was at its "apex" when René's turn came. Marblo hadn't taken his eye off that flesh. Awake? Anesthetized? He glanced discretely toward the pulpit, begging for a sign from Swyne to set him on the right track, but it looked as if Swyne was becoming increasingly self-absorbed. The last of the neophytes had already returned to the crescent. He was now kneeling, placing his hands on his chest, shutting his eyes. What would happen with René? A catastrophe? Or on the contrary, had he yielded to the demands of the flesh and would he thus offer his behind to the holocaust?

Soon the truth, the plain truth, hit Marblo in the head like a hammer. His confusion, anguish, and fear had been so great that they had hidden from him the simple logic of the facts: René was neither anesthetized nor asleep, for no one in either of those states is able to hear his name and begin to walk. Swyne would never make the mistake of anesthetizing flesh that couldn't go to get branded. "What an imbecile I've been!" Marblo thought. "There's René, ready to be branded."

And he almost smiled, and was listening for René's name like celestial music when his heart was once again seized with terror. Would René's behind offer itself meekly to the branding iron or hardening more and more, would it remain fixed to the spot where it kneeled? But if logic didn't deceive, his flesh was neither anesthetized nor asleep. Oh, joy! But given the very fact that he was not anesthetized, he could harden up, and hardened, would possess the fiendish ability to make the branding iron fall from Marblo's hand. His excitement reached its climax. Once again his eyes searched for those of Swyne, who at that exact instant was looking at René as he shouted out his name three times.

The assembly was flabbergasted, heads lifted. Like wild beasts smelling danger, the faces of the audience— plainly excited by the branding irons and the odor of scorched flesh—reflected the tension created by Swyne's anguished appeal.

But the dwarf's eyes shone and from his chest came a sigh of relief. René had risen to his feet, staring all around him. The mothers began to whisper. With this attitude, René was violating the strict norms of the ceremony. Marblo was trembling like a victim of mercury poisoning and Swyne began to bite the fingertips of his gloves. René turned his head toward Marblo, who signaled for him to step forward. Walking timidly, his face reflecting the panic that was already beginning to seize him, René went to be branded. Marblo and Swyne breathed again. Only a few minutes remained before the nightmare would be over. Marblo stretched out his hand and grabbed an iron from the brazier. Now René stood before him, but once again he was altering the ritual. He stood there dumfounded, staring at Marblo without showing him his behind and in no way whatsoever going down on all fours. With his free hand, Marblo grabbed him by the waist and spun him around. If he thought this would be enough, he was profoundly mistaken. René stood there with his back to Marblo, and repeatedly turned his head, his eyes popping out of their sockets, to look at the branding iron Marblo clutched in his hand. With dissimulation, Marblo touched René's buttocks with the tip of his shoe and even gave him a shove to help him into a quadrupedal position, but René, instead of resting his hands on the tiles, stood desperately fast on his feet. Marblo again touched his terrified behind but to no effect. All the mothers were looking at Alicia. Why wasn't she haranguing her little lamb? Obviously they weren't supposed to, but they certainly would join in should Alicia decide to encourage René. She was undoubtedly light years from any haranguing and had adopted the position of the Mother of Sorrows. As for Ramón, he seemed to be absent from this drama, just smiling as he looked at one of the famous tapestries.

So Marblo—like a ship captain faced with an imminent shipwreck, or a surgeon confronted with a desperate case—opted for the heroic solution. "We'll plunge in the iron," he said to himself. Like a lightening bolt, he lunged his arm toward René's stubborn behind. But René's behind dodged the brand. He started to run down the center of the nave and Marblo, losing his balance, fell flat on his face on the tiled floor.

Then the mothers started shouting: "Catch him!" René, seeing those furies rushing at him, jumped a row of pews and ran toward the altar. His classmates were waiting there to grab him.

Swyne was shouting furiously, Marblo was roaring, the mothers were screaming at the top of their lungs, the neophytes were shrieking. The two jaws of the pincers—the mothers and the neophytes—were closing in on René's body. He soon felt the claws of his pursuers in his flesh. Now some of them were grabbing him by the legs and others were bending him over to completely expose his behind. Marblo prepared to brand him, but Ramón said:

"Stop right there, Headmaster! Your ministry is now concluded and mine begins. Give me the branding iron. I will brand the restless beast."

Holding the iron in the air, he looked at Marblo as if requesting permission. Then he immediately branded his son's behind in deadly silence. But he hadn't counted on René's rebelliousness. A howl from his mouth broke the silence.

"According to school regulations, the brand is null and void," Marblo said. "The prey cried out."

"According to the regulations; but I've branded René and I will accept his cry. Crying out or not, I will make his flesh flower."

He picked René up in his arms. He signaled for Alicia to follow him. One of the mothers blocked their way.

"That flesh is no good, sir. Give it dolls to play with."

The mother's observation was received with general laughter.

Ramón gently brushed her to one side and walked toward the exit.

But the same mother, as if speaking in the name of everyone present, caught up with Alicia in the doorway and said:

"It's of no use, ma'am. Bring another chunk of meat into the world."

And she slammed the door behind them.

Perfumed Flesh

One December afternoon, René was walking along one of the narrow streets that led from the port, the cold weather nipping at his ears and turning his nose red. He had a look of satisfaction about him; it wasn't the same René who just a few months earlier had walked over to be branded on the behind. Ramón had left him alone after that repugnant episode and hadn't reminded him again of "the service of pain." He was undoubtedly awaiting a new provocation. His father had a design on him, but for the moment everything was calm. True, his branded behind informed him that he wasn't just anybody.

Nevertheless, there was a solution to everything. He had worked out a plan and was boldly thinking of presenting it to Ramón. The plan was very simple: to be of use to society and to his family. He would look for work, study at night. If his father possessed a fortune, that was his own business. René wanted to become independent, to be entirely his own boss. He had already seen what happens when the father is Caesar of his child. No, he was now twenty, and that was old enough for him, not his father, to be giving his flesh orders. Since he still had no trade, he would begin by earning a living waiting on tables or operating an elevator.

Lost in this line of reasoning and daydreaming, he was walking the remaining ten blocks to the subway. He only had two more to go when he spied a group of people at the end of the block. This would have mattered little to him, but he was intrigued by the way they were assembled. Several of them were kneeling, others were facing the people on their knees. René thought of a wound, of someone killed suddenly. They clearly weren't fighting. The people were all standing stock-still. He quickened his pace. He was just a few yards away when a woman emerged from the group and as she passed René, said: "It's not worth the trouble: it's the same as usual..." So it had nothing to do with either a wound or a death... But now he was reaching their sides. He stuck his head in, looked, and stepped back in horror.

An old man with his chest bared was lying on a stone. Kneeling before him, two men, each of them with a knife in his hand, were watching him attentively. The old man's chest was pierced by two knife wounds. Although René was unfamiliar with the pallor of cadavers, he was perfectly aware that the poor devil had only a few minutes left to live.

A voice spoke from a window:

"Julia, will you get in here?"

"Just a second, Mama. They're finishing him off."

"Who?"

"Old Pedro."

"Don't dilly-dally."

"No, Mama. The old man's almost gone."

At that very moment, the old man said to one of the men:

"Could you get this over with quickly?"

The two men looked at each other and said as one:

"Yes, right away."

They were already raising their arms, getting ready to give him the coup de grace when it occurred to one of them to switch knives.

"Take mine and give me yours."

"You and your crazy ideas," said the other one. "Look, it's damn cold out here. Let's get this over with right now."

"Humor me, Antonio."

"All right, but you pay for the beer."

"It's a deal."

René had managed to situate himself by Julia's window. She was a fifteen-year-old, with one of those faces that are part madonna, part whore. He was looking from one knife to the other.

"Pardon me," René said to her. "Why are they assassinating him?"

Julia looked at him strangely. The word "assassinate" sounded to her like something from another language.

"What did you say?..."

"No one's going to stop them? Doesn't he have relatives?"

"Relatives?... Why, of course he does. Those two—" and she pointed at the two men with knives. "They're his sons."

"His sons!..." René repeated in terror.

"That's right," said Julia, "his sons... Antonio and Alfredo."

A man standing next to them said to René:

"It's true."

"But they're murdering their father."

"That's the way it's got to be, young man," the man replied. "It's in their interest that their father dies; otherwise, they can't have his money."

Antonio heard what the man was saying. He stood up and said to René:

"A month ago, we told him to die, but he's the picture of health. Neither my brother nor I could wait any longer. We want to enjoy life."

"That's murder," René shouted at him with reckless indiscretion. "Besides, making him die right in the middle of the street..."

"He wanted it that way," responded Alfredo. "It's his express desire and his last wish."

"All right," said Antonio. "Let's get it over with."

With mathematic precision, they sunk their knives into his heart. The old man's body contracted violently. Rigor mortis began to take hold of his flesh.

"And now... To enjoy life!" Antonio shouted cheerfully.

"The old guy croaked?" Julia asked.

"Yes, darling," answered Alfredo.

Someone said:

"That was a good blow! But the old man shouldn't have needed more than a single stab."

"That's Alfredo's fault," explained Antonio. "He started playing with Papa's flesh."

"Let's celebrate his death with a few drinks," said Alfredo.

The two brothers walked off arm in arm. The rest of the crowd broke up. René was left standing alone at the scene of the crime, as if awaiting his turn to be murdered. All his promising plans were suddenly tinged by that spilled blood. If two sons would sacrifice their father in the middle of the street with the approval of a bunch of curious onlookers, one might imagine the life he wished to lead was in total contradiction to those violent methods; that such methods, from what he could discern, were common in the city and so it would be difficult for him to reconcile his projects with this legalized violence.

Legalized by whom? By one person or by everyone? This might be a neighborhood full of assassins while the rest of the city lived according to the norms of sanity. If an agent of the authorities were to pass by the scene of the crime at this very moment, he would certainly find it suspicious. Nevertheless, the crime was certainly committed with such assurance that more likely than not, the agent would pass by without making any admonition whatsoever and even go so far as to applaud the parricide.

He was so overcome with emotion that he wasn't aware that the snow had almost covered the old man's corpse. He was possessed by the idea of dying in such a sinister place. He tried to pull himself together. He lifted his feet above the snow; he made as if to walk, but something mysterious glued him to the spot. Perhaps the assassin designated to murder him?

A flashlight shone in his face. At the same time, someone said:

"At last, Samuel! I think this is the place."

The one responding to the name of Samuel was shining the flashlight in René's face and loudly confirming his companion's discovery.

"Ah!..." Samuel said, speaking to René. "Are you the young man who was asking so many questions?..."

"But how do you know?..." mumbled René. "How do you know so soon?..."

Samuel guffawed:

"From his own sons! We're from the municipal funeral parlor and they called us to handle their father's burial. We were delayed by the damn snow. We had to leave the car at the corner."

"Samuel, I found him," the other one said. "Give me a hand. Bring the shovel."

"I owe you a drink, Pipo. Is there a lot of snow covering him?"

"A dusting. Bring the shovel. Don't tell me you've up and died as well..."

"I'm still alive. But this damn cold. Would you give us a hand, young man?"

"You don't say, Samuel. So this is the one who's going to give us a hand..." Pipo said, laughing. "He's more dead than alive. And besides, we don't need him: the old guy was more bones than flesh."

"That's exactly why he weighs so much," said Samuel.

For several minutes the only sound that could be heard was the swish of the shovel in the snow until the corpse had been uncovered. Samuel, who was holding the flashlight, immediately placed it in René's hands and told him to light the way to where the car was parked. Like an automaton, René led the procession followed by Samuel and Pipo who hurled insults at the corpse for having had the damn notion—as they put it—to be killed on a night like this.

They threw the corpse into the car. René dropped the flashlight and backed away in horror. There was another dead person in the car: a young man with his head smashed in.

"What's your problem?" Pipo shouted at him. "You dropped the flashlight and we practically dropped the old man in the snow."

"There's a dead person in there!" René stammered.

"And what did you think there was going to be?"

"Fairies?" said Samuel. "What does this guy think life is all about?"

Life... The word rang in René's frozen ears. The flesh wasn't just molded in the school, but on the street as well... So sons do it to their parents... And surely parents... The generalized dance of the flesh! Or brothers against brothers, or the mother-in-law to the son-in-law...

He began to run with such haste that he bumped into a man crossing the street and they both rolled in the snow.

"Imbecile! Don't you look where you're walking? You could have fractured my hip."

Hearing the word "hip," René felt his terror intensify. With an imploring gesture, he said:

"I swear, sir, I wasn't trying to murder you."

The man guffawed and brushing the snow from his clothes, continued on his way.

But René stood there, fascinated by the sound of the word hip. All that concerned him was that for the rest of the walk home his flesh not run into anyone else's flesh again. He had to cover that distance without any part of his body—and by no means his hip—bumping into parts of other bodies. It seemed that the only way one could pass through life with flying colors was by avoiding the flesh of one's fellow men and women. But how? Was some people's flesh so dependent on the flesh of others that at a certain stage in life (yes, life) it caused one flesh to collide with another, or one flesh with two pieces of flesh, or four, or ten, a hundred, a thousand, a million?... What a nightmare! He saw his poor flesh running into an army of millions of pieces of flesh; he saw his flesh embedded in those pieces of flesh; he saw it in turn forming part of the army and running into other solitary pieces of flesh, and that solitary flesh embedding itself in his flesh army, becoming another flesh army...

And he found that he was standing in front of the subway entrance and that it was vomiting up an avalanche of flesh. His terror was so great, those pieces of flesh were, in his eyes, so bristling with malicious intentions that he stood there nailed to the spot. And those pieces of flesh didn't make way for his flesh, but instead closed ranks, trampling it. With great effort, he managed to lift it to its feet and, covered with contusions, press it against the wall of the passageway, innocently thinking that at last he had gotten his flesh to safety. But entering from the street, a new fleshy wave flooded the passageway, running into the wave that was on its way out. As if it were a feather, René's flesh was carried down to the platform and in the blink of an eye was pushed into and compressed in a subway car, trapped between the flaccid flesh of two old women.

When he surfaced again, he saw that it was eleven o'clock. Six hours in that nightmare... He went into a bar, looked at himself in a mirror. He looked sinister: there was a trickle of blood running down his face; one of his eyes was almost shut from being kicked. His overcoat had been ruined. Instead of going to the bathroom to clean himself up, he stood there staring at his face, as if refusing to admit that the image he found reflected in the mirror was his own. He stood like that for several minutes. Suddenly he realized the people were looking at him. He rushed out of the café.

He walked to a square half a block from his house. He leaned against a tree. He was numb from the cold, his teeth were chattering, and his head hurt. He couldn't stay there, but where could he find shelter? Though the more he thought about it, this was his chance to leave his family once and for all and begin his own life. But what life? Well, of course, Pipo's life... There didn't seem to be any other. He was so terrified that he was about to go straight home, but he controlled himself. "Life," according to Pipo, was, with slight variations, "life" according to Ramón. "Life" for one just as for the other could be summed up as "the battle for the flesh." So, where could he go?

His house was a hundred steps away and behind its door Ramón waited for him with that Exterminating Angel look on his face. He could "see" that face from the corner. Unconsciously, and as if in compensation, he saw Mrs. Pérez with her Eroticizing Angel mask. Might she receive him? He saw a light shining on her balcony. Wouldn't it be too late to knock on her door? But for a woman like Dalia, eleven is like any other hour of the day or night. And if she were receiving visitors? As on that fateful night! Would she still remember him? Yes, obviously she hadn't forgotten him. Dalia, who always received him kindly, who prevented him from suffering a fainting spell in the butchers shop; certainly she could help him. But how to get up there? The front door to the building was closed. He didn't have her phone number. He went back to the café, consulted the directory. There it was. He called. She answered in her shrill voice. Safe at last!

Dalia, swaddled in a pink peignoir, opened the door. Seeing René's lamentable condition, the "sensitive" woman was deeply disturbed, and could only say:

"You poor little thing!"

Once in the apartment, René collapsed into an armchair.

"But what's happened to you?"

"If you only knew, Mrs. Pérez."

"Never mind, you'll tell me later. The first thing is for you to recover your strength."

She thought for a moment.

"I didn't express myself well. The first thing is for you to take a bath; then I'll treat those ugly swellings. Finally, I'll prepare an excellent dinner for you. You must be starving to death, aren't you?"

And doing just as she said, she made him stand up and removed his overcoat. René went to sit down again in the armchair but Dalia, taking him by the arm, pointed him to the Recamier.

"You'll be more comfortable there. Besides, it's a piece of furniture you're already familiar with."

Even in his anguish, René got up. The flesh was also molded in the Recamier and...who knows, perhaps even slain there. He said hastily:

"Mrs. Pérez, I regret having bothered you. It was an impertinence on my part. I'm leaving."

"Oh!" Dalia exclaimed. "What do I hear? Impertinence... Regret... What kind of language is that? So, you don't think highly of me? Deep in your heart, you consider me a stranger?"

She whined exquisitely, having had ample practice from years of whining.

René begged her pardon. He promised to obey her in everything.

"As proof, love, follow me now to the bathroom. I'll give you a set of pajamas that belonged to my deceased husband. Yes, I keep all of his effects; I always believed they would come in handy one way or other. The only thing is that it will be a bit big on you. My husband was far meatier."

That word made René shiver. He stood nailed to the spot in the hallway leading to the bathroom.

"I only need to wash my face."

"Uh uh, darling! You just promised me absolute obedience. Besides, what's this business about Mrs. Pérez this and Mrs. Pérez that... You're making me feel ancient. Call me by my Christian name: Dalia. My name is Dalia."

They were now at the door to the bathroom.

"I'll go get the pajamas," Dalia said. "Come on! Why are you doing standing there like a dolt? Go in and get undressed. Close the door, of course."

A few minutes later, René came out of the bathroom wearing the deceased man's pajamas. He was frightfully pale and his eye was swollen. Dalia was waiting for him in the dining room with everything she needed to treat him.

"Marvelous, darling! Marvelous! You're a new man. Come here. Sit down. Let me have a look at those rips and tears. Fighting over girls, eh?"

René shook his head so vigorously that he sprinkled Dalia in the face. She let out one of her famous laughs.

"Come on, don't deny it because I won't believe you. Who's the lucky one?" and taking a piece of cotton, she began to staunch the blood gathering on René's right cheek.

René shook his head again and again sprinkled Dalia. Then he stared at the ceiling.

"All right, darling, it's no big deal... I won't demand a full confession. I'm not going to roast you over a slow flame to extract the name of your beloved. But please, don't move your head any more. Let me treat you. I have to leave that face as good as new."

René sat still. Dalia cleaned his black eye. For several minutes the only sounds that could be heard were René's labored breathing and Dalia's hands moving back and forth over his face. She broke the silence by saying:

"It's been ages since I last saw you, darling. Where have you been hiding? You were in the country for quite a while, weren't you?"

Finally she applied disinfectant to the bruises and lacerations.

"Now let's eat. Don't move a muscle because I'm going to spoon the food myself right into your little beak. So, a young lady...eh?"

René lay his head in hands. He began to cry. As he was sobbing convulsively, Dalia, frightened, went to get him a glass of water.

"There, there. Take a sip. What's the sobbing all about? Nothing's going to happen to you. If your rival comes here, we'll send him away with his tail between his legs. Because I imagine you won't have liquidated him, eh?..."

René didn't hear the last thing Dalia said. He was in another world: in the world of Pipo and Samuel. And yet, he wasn't sure whether or not to tell her about the incident. A woman like her, living a life of indulgences and erotic encounters, perfumes, and musical soirées, would certainly find the account of that bloody episode disagreeable.

"Oh, darling, don't cry like that," and she pulled out a tiny handkerchief and dried his tears. "I'm right here, ready to listen to you. Am I not your ever-faithful friend?"

"Mrs. Pérez," and René's voice was faint as a sigh, "this afternoon, I saw an elderly man being murdered..."

His sobbing again prevented him from continuing.

"Oh what a weak child! If you would just finish telling me."

She dried his tears again.

"So, a dead elderly man... And what else?"

"Mrs. Pérez, his own sons were stabbing him over and over again."

Dalia began to laugh; she doubled over with laughter. She took René's hands in hers, plastering them with kisses.

"Ah, I feel so relieved! So, it didn't have anything to do with girls... Oh, my God! An elderly man murdered.

But is that all? Listen, darling, are you pulling my leg? Because if it's nothing but a murdered elderly man, tomorrow night we're going to have a veritable spectacle: a gentleman to whom exactly the same thing will happen as happened to the elderly man, except that it will be done with machine guns rather than knives."

And since she was about to burst out laughing again, René thought she was kidding:

"Trust me, Mrs. Pérez. I swear it was so awful..."

"Hah! We would be paralyzed if we burst into tears over every dead person we saw! I can't fathom all this blubbering over something that has no importance whatsoever. All right, we won't say anything else about the matter. Now, let's eat, and then... to bed, to sleep between heated sheets."

She walked into the kitchen. René went over to the picture window in the living room, drew back the curtains, and took a look at the street. The crime that would be committed under Dalia's balcony the following night had stuck in his mind. But it had to be one of her jokes. How could she know beforehand that someone was going to be shot down with machine guns? Nevertheless, Dalia had laughed out loud when she heard the account of the death of the elderly man. Wouldn't such a sensitive woman be deeply disturbed by a tragedy of such proportions?

"Ah, my little treasure! Why are you standing there?" Dalia asked, returning from the kitchen. "No, it's not tonight. I told you already it's going to be tomorrow... If you're interested, you can come observe the assassination. And now, let's have dinner. There are cold cuts, ham, eggs, and café au lait with toast."

René sat down at the table and Dalia served him a slice of meat.

"No, I can't eat anything, Mrs. Pérez," said René. "I'm very sad. Please explain: is it really true that tomorrow night...?"

"Of course it is!" Dalia exclaimed. "What reason would I have to lie, darling? How do you want me to say it to you? In Chinese, French, German?... Yes, tomorrow at eleven at night they will liquidate Mr. Nieburg. I do believe you know him! Don't you remember him from the guests at that soirée?"

"Nieburg..." René exclaimed. "Sure I know him." He rose to his feet. "Can't we warn him that they want to murder him?"

"Warn him?..." Dalia looked very surprised. "And what for? What does Mr. Nieburg matter to us? No, stop acting so childishly and eat your dinner."

"Please, Mrs. Pérez, call him on the phone. Tell him to hide."

Dalia was overcome by a violent attack of laughter; the laughter prevented her from articulating a single word.

"Oh, what a child," she said at last, "what a child you are! Hide... And what does it matter to us whether Nieburg hides. Besides which, it would be futile, they're going to find him even if he burrows into the ground."

"How did you know about Nieburg, Mrs. Pérez?"

"Powlavski—you remember him, darling: the Jewish jeweler who was also there at my musical soirée. Of course you remember him. Yes? Well, he called me on the phone this afternoon to tell me that tomorrow, old Nieburg..."

"But that guy, Powlavski, or whatever his name is— isn't he a friend of Nieburg's?"

"Bosom buddies, darling! Bosom buddies! He was Nieburg's best man at his wedding."

"That's another reason then to warn Nieburg. They're soul mates."

146

"Their souls, yes, darling, but not their bodies," replied Dalia, running her hand through his hair. "Nieburg's body will provide Mr. Powlavski with quite a tidy sum."

"His body..." and René unconsciously touched his own body.

"Why, of course, darling. Tomorrow Nieburg's flesh, rigid and cold, will provide Mr. Powlavski with quite a pretty little sum. I practically recited an ode. But we've talked enough about Nieburg and Powlavski. Let's worry about ourselves."

She led René to the Recamier, turned off the ceiling light, switched on a red lamp, and sat down beside him.

"Are you feeling ill, love? Open your mouth and tell me what's troubling you."

René didn't answer.

"All right, if you're not feeling well, I'll give you a cordial."

She went to the dining room and returned with a bottle of cognac and a glass. She poured him a drink.

"Have a little. You'll feel better. The cognac, the red light, and my humble person will soon put you at ease."

The taste of cognac reminded him of his first interview with Marblo. He looked at Dalia and it was as if he were watching him: Jovian, massive, implacable... Dalia caught something of René's impression, and to give the lie altogether to what René was imagining, she stretched out along the length of the sofa. At the same time, she flung her arms around his neck and pressed her face against his.

"Listen, my little treasure. You're in great need of tenderness and heat..." and as she spoke, she lay her thighs on René's. "If you cultivate my friendship, you'll find out what an excellent teacher of the flesh I am. Yours, darling, is crying out for heat."

"Teacher?..." mumbled René.

"Superteacher," answered Dalia.

So Dalia too was involved with flesh... She wasn't a run-of-the-mill teacher, but a veritable headmistress. And at what school? So, female flesh was molded as well...

"What's eating you?" said Dalia. "Is there something strange about being a teacher?"

"But of the flesh... Mrs. Pérez, that's what I can't figure out."

Dalia pulled back the right sleeve of her peignoir and showed him her bare left arm:

"You see my arm? Well, that arm is only capable of transmitting as much heat to your flesh as if you had stuffed it into a heater."

Acting as she spoke, she let her arm fall on René's chest, smooth as a slithering snake. Her hand, imitating the snake's head, began to run its fingers over his chest.

"Please, Mrs. Pérez! Get your arm off of me!" René shouted at the height of exasperation.

"Ah hah! Giving in so soon? Is that all you can resist?"

Not wishing to answer her question, René asked her a different one:

"Are you the headmistress of the school?"

"What school are you talking about, my little treasure? No, I'm neither a teacher nor a headmistress at any school. I already told you that I'm just a teacher of the flesh..."

He was about to tell her that there were schools where the flesh was molded, but he restrained himself when he imagined the endless reprisals from Ramón. In any case, Mrs. Pérez, though she didn't belong to any institution of carnal instruction, was almost a practicing professional. How strange! By two paths as antithetical as pain and pleasure one arrived at a single devastating truth: that flesh was the driving force of life—yes, "life," as Pipo himself had called it. Without flesh, the game was over. Play ball! In the end, what was the difference between Swyne's horrible flesh licking the hardened flesh of René and Dalia's perfumed flesh, with her semblance of a gladiator calculating the mortal blow to her adversary?

Dalia watched him with profound anticipation. She said to herself that if she didn't wish to lose the prey, she'd have to bring other charms into play. Without a doubt, the young man was made of hard flesh, and what was worse, flesh that called for truce straight away. She was becoming keenly interested in the whole affair. At first she had considered him a form of amusement, but it isn't every day one comes across flesh as tremulous as this. Yes: tremulous flesh... What a delicious sound, what color, how transparent the phrase "tremulous flesh." Again she let her arm fall on René's chest. Her body shivered in delight. Nevertheless, his chest felt flabby, flaccid; her arm sunk and slid around between his nipples. "Alcohol," Dalia said to herself. "I must give him alcohol to harden up his flesh, and by hardening it, get it to function." She took the bottle, filled his glass.

"Have another drink, darling."

This time René drained the glass. How odd! Mrs. Pérez was giving him cognac to harden him, and it was cognac they had rubbed on him at school to soften him... So, the flesh either relaxed or got harder, according to the situation. Nevertheless, it wasn't altogether unpleasant. The cognac had landed in his gut and was burning there while his brain floated off into a tepid, golden mist. Now Dalia, as if combining her efforts with those of the cognac, gripped his hips between her legs, wrapped her arms around his neck, and pressed her mouth against his. René was about to shout out when he saw Dalia sticking out her tongue, preparing to lick him—or at least that's what he believed as he recalled the scene of the licking tongues at school.

Dalia grasped the situation in an instant. If she let René, with his blushing-maid hysterics, begin to shout, all would be lost. He would get up from the sofa, ask for his clothes with a sullen look on his face, and walk out, leaving her there all worked up. But she wasn't going to let him. She wasn't a superteacher for nothing; that whippersnapper wouldn't have his way. With her arms and legs she squeezed him even harder, and without pausing for even a second, stuck her tongue into René's mouth. His body shuddered, he arched his back slightly, and finally he "hardened up." Dalia perceived that René's flesh was slowly getting harder and that it was no longer a disarticulate mass lying under her body. So she withdrew her hands from around her "victim's" neck, turned off the lamp, and began to take off his pajamas. René pictured a muzzle in his mind, pictured the cold darkness of the classroom. After all, wasn't this just like his first day of classes?

The ringing of a telephone woke him up. He had fallen asleep straight away, and now this awakening seemed remarkably like the first time he had woken up at school: the same bitter taste in his mouth, the same headache. But where was he? At school again? Or at home? At that moment he heard Dalia's voice. She sounded so strident to him that he pulled the blanket over his head. He wished he were a thousand miles from that voice. But he would leave her house that very instant. He'd had it up to here with schools and teachers...

He stuck his head out from under the blanket; he sat up in bed. In bed or the Recamier? He was in Dalia's bedroom. She had gotten him all the way to the bedroom. Dragging him or carrying him? What did it matter. He looked up and saw a small porcelain angel hanging from the lamp. Just then, Dalia appeared.

"Oh, darling! What a funny face! Did you sleep well?" and she leaned over to kiss him.

René turned his mouth away.

"I'm leaving this instant, Mrs. Pérez."

"But no one's stopping you, love. Go and get dressed. When you're presentable, you'll find me seated at the piano singing 'Morning smiles upon you.'"

René walked toward the bathroom. As he walked down the hall, he looked through the windows and saw the snow piled up in the patio, and remembered the death of the old man. His recollection was so vivid that unconsciously he opened one of the blinds, sticking half his body out the window as if he were trying to save someone. A cold blast of air entered the hallway and made its way to the salon. Dalia began to shout and complain that she was going to catch a cold and in two weeks wouldn't be able to sing. René closed the blinds, but continued standing there for a moment with his face pressed against the glass. A dog was leaping in the snow, sinking its snout into it as if searching for a bone. Was it Pipo or Samuel?...

He shut the bathroom door (a basic precaution: Dalia was even capable of following him there.) He turned on the tap and began to wash his face. But his senses were so dulled, his skin so sticky, and his body hurt so much, that he decided to take a shower. Dalia—as hygienic as she was—would consider the decision an excellent one. He took off the pajamas and house slippers. For an instant the immediate reality of the shower made him feel so euphoric that he stretched his arms and legs several times.

Finally, he walked over to the bathtub. The shower curtain was closed. He thought how Dalia, though mad as a loon, was irreproachable as far as the domestic sphere was concerned. This was manifested by the drawn curtain like a warm invitation to submerge oneself in the lukewarm delight of the water. He drew the curtain back with a tug, leaping into the bathtub. His body landed in icy water; his feet collided with a hard object at the bottom of the tub. He let out a shout and jumped from the booby trap, shivering.

To hell with Dalia's domestic virtues! Domestic on the surface, but sheer madness underneath. He grabbed a towel and as he rubbed himself down, took a look into the bathtub. There, lying face down on the bottom, was a human body. Dalia's friend or enemy? But what was the point of that conjecture when she allowed all kinds of eccentricities? He trembled before the idea that he too—like that cadaver—might end up on the bottom of the bathtub and that a young man would right now be looking at him in horror, just as he was now looking in horror at this body. Through the cloudy water, the person looked as young as he.

He turned on the light and contemplated the cadaver at length. At least, he told himself, there's a distinct difference between that cadaver and me: it doesn't have any hair on its head. And if I dared to touch it? Its stiff flesh couldn't be any more repugnant than the flesh of Marblo and company. Deep down, he madly desired to have a look at the poor wretch's face. He didn't dare go that far. Instead, he stuck one arm in the icy water and with his trembling hand, touched it, first its head and then its back. How strange! What peculiar flesh. It felt like anything but flesh. Although, he thought, the flesh of a cadaver is distinctive in its stiffness. He remembered having seen a drowned man. His flesh seemed soft and even spongy, surely due to the swelling. That man had been dead for more than forty-eight hours.

But the one in the bathtub must have been asphyxiated after midnight. He was sure of it. He was so sure that he exclaimed: "Dalia waited for me to fall asleep before she murdered him."

He stuck his hand in again and again touched its back. He ran his hand up to its shoulders, then to the nape of its neck. Behind all this exploration was his desire to turn the cadaver over and look at its face. And each time he touched the body, the cadaverous flesh seemed less fleshy. His hand climbed the nape until it reached one of the cadaver's ears. In a fit of fury, he grabbed both ears in his hands and lifted the body into the air. He had to see its face. Then the cadaver crashed back into the water, leaving René holding an ear.

Revolted, he was about to throw it away when he noticed that the ear had been stuck on with a piece of black adhesive tape. He slowly opened his hand. The ear was like that of a child, or to be more precise, wasn't exactly an ear but rather a type of volute. He squeezed it and the volute broke into fragments of some plastic material. So, neither flesh, nor bones, nor coagulated blood... René didn't know whether to laugh or cry. The sinister cadaver had been transmuted into a grotesque mannequin. That Dalia was an assassin of deposed lovers had a certain logic to it, but to own a dummy and submerge it in a bathtub constituted the height of absurdity. He dropped the shards of the supposed ear, stuck his hand back in, and grabbed an arm, yanking it violently from its socket.

He contemplated it dumfounded. As far as he knew, Dalia didn't work in the line of men's garments. Could she be a clerk in a men's boutique? According to her, a teacher yes, but an attendant no. An attendant of the flesh in any case, but not of mannequins. He rested his arm on the toilet and crouched down to lift up the dummy and see what its face looked like.

He told himself that on second thought, it was preferable to have discovered a mannequin than a cadaver. That thought brought the flush back to his cheeks and even cheered him up. The mannequin would have a face like Don Juan. A Don Juan who seduces women hidden behind parapets of stained glass windows. Well, he'd pull the mannequin out of the tub and give it a good slapping.

He pulled it out of the bathtub. He let out a belly laugh.

"That's just how I pictured the face," he said. And at that moment his laughter froze on his lips. Impossible! But it was his very own face. He let go of the dummy and buried his face in his hands. What was Dalia's reason for owning that mannequin?

He looked at its face again. The similarity with his was astonishing: same mouth, same eyes, same eyebrows, same nose. And its hair? There wasn't a single hair on its head. Why was the dummy bald? His head was exploding. He burst out of the bathroom in search of Dalia.

Her fingers were flying over the keyboard; trills and quavers leapt from her mouth. She was undoubtedly performing "Morning smiles upon you," putting her heart and soul into that ballad. She was so absorbed in her performance that she didn't see René, but a terrible "Mrs. Pérez" made her break off singing.

"Oh! What's the meaning of all this? Why, you're completely naked, love. You're going to catch cold. What's happened? Don't tell me there are ghosts in the bathroom..."

Suddenly she remembered having placed the mannequin in the bathtub in order to wash it. A visit in the morning had prevented her from finishing the job, so the dummy had been left in the bathtub. She imagined René's astonishment and began to laugh like a madwoman. Seeing him with such a pathetic look on his face, she said:

"So, at last you've seen him. But there's no need to make a mountain out of a molehill. He's just a dummy."

"It's my double," René said in a strangled voice. "You have my double also."

"Why of course it's your double," Dalia responded brazenly. "My goodness, what could I do if I couldn't have you in the flesh..."

She wrenched several chords from the piano, as if to say that the whole affair was of no further consequence. Finally she let the piano lid drop with a loud racket and approached René.

"You know something, darling? It all cost me less than fifty dollars. I bought it in a men's clothing store that was being closed for renovation. I painted the face myself, relying on my own memory. I won't say I'm a consummate artist, but the essentials of your face are there on the dummy."

"Then everyone in the world has my double. My own father..."

He left the sentence hanging. There was no reason to tell Dalia the sordid tales of his home and the school. Besides, if Ramón were to find out about such confidences, it would lead to new and awful quarrels. He started to walk toward the bathroom, followed by Dalia, who, as she passedby an armchair, grabbed a blanket and placed it over his shoulders.

"I don't want you to catch cold, love," she said in a soothing voice. "We'll smash the mannequin to bits this very instant since it disgusts you so much. I put it in the water because of how filthy it was."

"Filthy?" René asked her in surprise.

"Filthy. Oh so filthy. Stains all over... (They were now in the bathroom and Dalia pulled the stopper from the bathtub drain. The mannequin began moving around

155

grotesquely.) God only knows how many times I've fallen asleep hugging that dummy."

"Hugging?"

"Hugging it, oh so tightly. Bringing it to tears—insofar as mine were falling on its face. Running my feverish fingers through its silky hair."

René gave a start and set his eyes on the dummy. Now it was moving faster and he could even hear it knocking against the side of the bathtub. He saw its gleaming, bald pate again alternately surfacing and disappearing under the water.

"But he's bald! Can't you see?" René shouted at her.

"What are you saying?" Dalia exclaimed amidst thunderous laughter. "He has a wig. I made it myself with these very fingers which one day will be swallowed up by the earth..." And she showed him her slender fingers, their nails exquisitely polished.

The water swirled around the drain in large spirals making sucking sounds like kisses. The mannequin looked like a foundered boat over which a fly was buzzing. Dalia contemplated it amorously. Suddenly she burst out laughing; she bent down and grabbed the mannequin by its feet, sitting it on the edge of the tub. She grabbed a towel and began to dry it off.

"You've ruined it, darling. It's ruined. You pulled off one of its arms and smashed one of its adorable little ears."

She sat there for a moment, lost in a delightful memory.

"That little ear, which I loved so much. Would you get angry if I tell you that one night I bit it right off?"

René touched his own ears. It seemed to him as if Dalia was opening her mouth and that she was popping in not one but both of his ears, tranquilly swallowing them. He walked toward the door, but Dalia stopped him.

"Young man, how discourteous you are. Help me put your other self back on its feet."

But René was already walking out of the bathroom. Dalia left the mannequin on a chair and reached René in the gallery.

"Now I'll put it away in its boxes. I'll wrap the dummy in cellophane. I'll put the wig in its box and Fifo in his velvet case."

That name sounded unpleasant to René's ears. Who was Fifo? Another double? His own face immortalized in fabric, plaster, cardboard? Immortalized in something infinitely more sinister?

They had reached the elevator. Dalia handed him his overcoat and gloves, wrapped his scarf around his neck. René's face looked like it was about to shatter into a thousand pieces. He entered the elevator. But he couldn't leave that sinister house without knowing who Fifo was. He asked Dalia brusquely:

"Is Fifo another mannequin?"

Dalia experienced a violent attack of laughter. She saw the rubber dildo transformed into a second double of René. At the same time she was laughing, she was also disturbed. He would get mad if she revealed to him Fifo's real "personality." Not knowing how to get herself out of the jam, she embedded herself further with a confused explanation:

"Fifo is the double of your other you."

And she roared with laughter.

"But, Mrs. Pérez, I don't understand..."

"Guess," Dalia said without pausing in her laughter.

And to keep René from asking any more questions, she pressed the elevator button herself.

Goose Flesh

Alone, totally, desolately alone in the elevator. Alone?...
Merely an illusion! That's when the doubling began. It
was as revolting as chewing on a cockroach, as swilling
a gallon of castor oil, as consuming a chunk of putrefied
meat; it was as cloying as stuffing oneself with bonbons
and gallons of syrup; as icy as a piece of bad news, as the
barrel of a revolver at one's temple, as one's ears in
arctic temperatures; or as hot as being humiliated, as a
mad dash to save one's life; as chilling as a piece of chalk
scraping a blackboard against the grain; as suffocating
as a pillow over one's face; in short, as black as the slab
over a grave preventing the livid person inside who has
come back to life from getting out...
The doubling began as the elevator door opened. A
group of four people—probably neighbors from the
building—entered engaged in animated conversation.
They were four human beings, but René saw them as

four mannequins—doubles of himself. Even though there were two women in the group, René saw them each as his own incarnation. And the four "Renés" were looking at him mockingly. They were undoubtedly obeying orders and were undoubtedly involved in something related to him. To protect him? To get rid of him?

In a defiant voice, he told them that doubling a citizen constituted a criminal act of high treason; that nothing in the world justified their doubling him. One of the two men—an elderly man—tried to acquiesce (he undoubtedly believed they had found themselves in the presence of a lunatic), saying that to judge by resemblance and physical constitution, none of them could be the double of a young man like him; to which René shouted at the man, saying he was a shameless liar and that if they wanted to come to some understanding with him, they would have to start by reverting to their true personalities. The elderly man, convinced they were talking to a lunatic, told him that in fact they had been paid by some guy to double the gentleman, and that knowing he was in that building, he had sent them there so that in case of an attempt on his life, the assassins would be confused.

René grew pale. He became weak in the knees. In a faint voice, he mumbled:

"An attempt... An attempt on my life?"

"Why, don't you know?" the elderly man said (and had to work hard not to laugh). "They're going to try it very shortly. That's why the person interested in saving your life is paying a large sum of money to anyone willing to act as your double. We were short of cash and accepted."

"Is the guy my father?" René asked timorously.

"How do I know if he's your father or your uncle..." the elderly man replied in a mocking tone of voice. "Find out yourself. We're going up. Aren't you?"

The four of them entered the elevator. The elderly man, containing his laughter, said to René:

"Now you know. We're going to collect the money now..."

"So what do I do?" asked René.

"Find yourself another double."

And the elevator door closed.

René retained two things from this grotesque incident: first, that in his bewilderment over Dalia's mannequin, he had, for the first time in his life, dared to verbally accost several people who were not even acquaintances of his, and without reason. Obviously he didn't see them as doubles of himself (this would be possible only in a state of madness, and he was in absolute control of his faculties), yet at the same time, he "saw" them as doubles because needing a discharge, any expedient was justified. Furthermore, in a world as dissolute as the one in which he lived—in the world of Pipos and Samuels, of Alfredos and Antonios, of Marblos and Swynes, and of course, of Ramóns— aggressiveness (at all levels) and violence (of all magnitudes) were offensive and defensive shields, norms of behavior for making one's way through "life." The second thing he retained was the word "attempt." On various occasions, Ramón had told him that he would have to confront life from the perspective of attempts on one's life. That a stranger would remind him of this was a confirmation and a healthy warning. The elderly man undoubtedly was participating—in whatever form—in "life." He was familiar with the "experience" of everything that might constitute an attempt on someone's life. He obviously had been playing a practical joke on René, but had chosen as the basis for this joke, an attempt on one's life. This roundly confirmed the general state of affairs. So there was no means of escape.

He would confront Ramón right away. He was going to pay dearly for the previous night. Although more likely than not, Ramón would receive him with a beaming face and even congratulate him on his "feat" of spending an entire night in the apprenticeship of "life." At this pleasant thought, he found himself in front of his house. The door was open. This he found exceedingly strange. The first time such a thing had occurred. Even stranger, the door was not ajar but wide open. Undoubtedly, this was not his house; the door to his house would be shut tight. He looked at the number. There could be no mistake: it was his very own house. So if that was his house, something of grave importance must have happened while he was away. From the way things looked, that something was changing Ramón's "life" so profoundly as to allow a door to suddenly open to the whole wide world, proclaiming that from then on its residents would cease to be people who had anything to hide and fear. Nevertheless, that open door was in a certain way closed to him: he found the opening so unsettling that to enter through it as if nothing were amiss would constitute recklessness.

He tried to reason it out. If the door was open, it was because his parents, troubled over his absence, had gone out in search of him. He immediately dismissed this line of reasoning. It was plausible to think they had gone out looking for him, but not that they had left the door open. Anybody—and to a far greater extent, Ramón—would take the basic precaution of closing the door of his house, even when his abrupt departure is due to a matter of life and death.

He went in and closed the door. He walked through the living room and went to his mother's room. She wasn't there. He walked through his room, leaving his overcoat, gloves, and scarf on the bed. He went to his father's room and found it empty. All that remained for him to explore were the dining room and the kitchen. He walked through both rooms. Deserted. All of a sudden he remembered the "office." He ran there. To his great surprise, the door was ajar. Even when his father was in the "office," he never failed to close the door. René stood there staring at the door. He was about to leave when he thought he heard his father's voice. But, unusual in a man like Ramón, the voice was humming a song. It was unusual, but at least it was his father's voice. So there was no need to put off the confrontation a moment longer. He knocked on the door. Ramón said:

"Come in."

This "come in" sounded odd coming from him. His father never used that phrase. René expected "enter," dry and biting, in that voice his father could assume when he had accounts to settle with René. That "come in" sounded anything but reproachful or threatening; it also sounded like the voice of someone who had just woken up or simply the voice of a drunk.

At last, he went in. There was Ramón, seated in the dentist's chair. But instead of sitting as he usually did, rigid and erect, he was sprawled in the chair and even had his legs draped over the arms. In one hand he held a bottle, which every now and then he brought to his mouth, sucking on it noisily. René couldn't utter a single word.

Ramón looked him over from head to toe. He set the bottle on the floor, removed his legs from the arms of the chair, and sitting up straight, said with great effort:

"I presume you are René."

Of all the affectations his father adopted to admonish him, this sarcasm was the most irritating. He preferred that he come on aggressive and insulting. To make matters

163

worse, the technique of sarcasm required an extremely slow elaboration. Ramón began to ask him stupid questions which, as the game went on, would get increasingly complex in their stupidity until they became simply intolerable. Furthermore, the questions obliged him to give equally stupid answers. Fine; he had to accept the game. He flopped into a chair and answered:

"I presume I am René..."

"What do you mean, you presume!" Ramón shouted. "I'm not here to listen to vague remarks. I need to know whether you are René, son of Ramón."

René responded by saying nothing; he was determined to resist through silence. He would play the part of the mouse in this game (what choice did he have), but would remain absolutely mute. He pressed his lips together and stared at the ceiling. His interrogator stood up, swerved drunkenly two or three times as he approached René, but changing his aggressive tone to a persuasive one, said:

"Do me a favor: don't be so discourteous. Above all, let's not waste any time. If you're not René, if you are a house servant or simply a visitor, say so. I have orders to bring René somewhere. I've been awaiting his arrival for two hours. I've sat in every chair in this house and have finally ended up in this chair. It's very comfortable."

René commented to himself that the game was beginning to take on epic proportions.

"This is the last commission of my career. I'm thinking of retiring to work the land. But before I can do so, and precisely because this commission is of such importance, I must see it through."

His father continued speaking and René scrutinized him. Physically, the man was Ramón, from the top of his head to the tip of his toes. His voice was Ramón's and his movements were in every way, shape, and form those of his father. But "morally," he wasn't René's father, who never got drunk, who never left the door to his house open and much less the door to the "office," So what was the point of such cynical comedy? To disconcert him? But why? If René was an instrument in his father's hands, such comedy was out of place. Could it perhaps be that he had "picked up" on the fact that René was intending to seek his independence? This presumption, more likely than not, was accurate and that's why Ramón had "produced" this comedy of terror.

Now the drunk held his head in his hands and began to look at René's face.

"If we're to judge by family likeness, you don't resemble your father in the least. I would swear you're not Ramón's flesh and blood."

He stamped on the floor as if to indicate his impatience.

"But the situation is such that I can't restrict myself to mere suppositions. And on top of all my other problems, they didn't even give me his picture. There wasn't any time given the precipitousness of the events. They told me: 'Go and bring back René. Don't delay. Every minute is precious. Take the shortest route.' The shortest route! But what the devil is the shortest route when I still don't know if you are René."

He smashed the bottle against the wall, swore several times, and fell back into the dentist's chair. René told himself it was pointless to remain silent. If he remained enveloped in silence the cruel game of cat and mouse would never end. Obviously, he wasn't going to contradict him. With this cat, one had to fight fire with fire.

"Why, yes: I'm René. René, son of Ramón. Of the flesh of Ramón, though you claim otherwise."

"Bravo, boy!" said Ramón. "That's how to talk."

He left the chair and planted a loud kiss on René's forehead.

"I was about to lose my temper. If you hadn't decided to speak up, who knows what I would have been capable of doing. What a jam those guys have gotten me into! To hell with them! I'm really tired of this whole business. Happily, you've now identified yourself. Now, all that remains is for me to bring you to the indicated place."

"Bring me?..." said René, prepared to continue playing the game. "Bring me... Where?"

"They've prohibited me from revealing the place to you. They told me: 'Bring us René without telling him where you're bringing him.'"

"Well, I refuse to follow you unless you first reveal the location," René said, staring at Ramón.

"I can't, I just can't," Ramón shouted, getting worked up again. "I can't reveal it to you, just as I'm unable to reveal what awaits you there. Understand? Orders are orders, young man. You already know the Party doesn't bother with little girls..."

René pointed at the painting of Saint Sebastian.

"That's me captured on canvass. You can take that in my place."

If Ramón wished to play games, he would give him a good run for his money. In truth he felt on the verge of collapse, but as it wasn't under his control to put an end to the game, he could at least make his father know that he was dealing with a powerful adversary. Now, more than ever before, he was determined to set up camp elsewhere. His plan of work and study would not be turned into yet another chimera. No: at this very moment when his father might wish to consider the comedy over, he was going to give him a piece of his mind.

"I'm very sorry," Ramón said, removing his gaze from the ceiling, "but they've given me orders to bring them René in the flesh."

"I'm also sorry," replied René, "but if you won't tell me where you're taking me, you'll have to go back empty-handed."

If his father wished to replay the episode of the train trip, he would not succeed. He would have to bind and gag René, for he wasn't going under his own steam. The long-awaited opportunity was presenting itself at last. He knew Ramón very well; he knew that little by little, his fury would grow increasingly passionate. Then he would see who could shout the loudest. He even thought that his absence the previous night might serve as frosting on the cake of his plans for liberation.

Ramón assumed a supplicating pose. He pressed his hands together, let a few tears fall, pulled out a handkerchief and dried his eyes:

"If you only knew. If for just a moment, you guessed what awaits you, you wouldn't be acting so fresh. For the sake of whatever you most cherish in this world, obey me. I'm telling you this for your own good."

"Well, now I'm definitely not going to accept," René said, heaving a deep sigh that could have been one of discouragement or mockery. "Without knowing what awaits me!... It's enough to make me stay right here in this house. Besides, I've had it up to here with your eternal mysteries..."

"My mysteries?..." Ramón exclaimed. "My mysteries, you say? But this is the first time I've seen you in my life! How can you make such a claim when we've never exchanged a single word before?"

He lowered his head and appeared to be thinking. Could he possibly reveal to this obstinate kid that Ramón had been assassinated that morning and that his corpse was in a house on the outskirts of the city? And if that wasn't bad enough, to have chosen him whose profession consisted in playing Ramón's double—so accomplished a copy of the original that even René believed he was standing in front of his own father. He could wear himself out telling René that he was only Ramón's double, and René still wouldn't believe a single word. On the other hand, did the chiefs intend for René to believe this double was his own father? As far as that goes, though the spoiled little brat might swear the double was Ramón, it was no less true that relations between father and son were hardly cordial. From the first moment of his interview, he noted an open hostility on the part of René. Perhaps this hostility was in some way preventing him from seeing that he was not in the presence of his father. In any case—and apart from his disinterest as to whether they mortally hated each other—the fact was that the time was passing and he was attempting in vain to bring René with him. And if that wasn't bad enough, Alicia, whose presence in the house would have facilitated everything, had been gravely wounded in the attack on Ramón. Very nice: "Open the front door to the house, pass for Ramón, bring us René, don't reveal to him the death of his father..." Not even a photo; they didn't even give him a physical description in their haste. No. Just: "Bring us René..." It's a good thing he thought to ask René whether he was a friend or just the servant. What faces those men would have made, what reproaches and even punishments had he come back empty-handed. Or what would be even more ridiculous: with a friend or with the servant.

René's voice pulled him from these depths. It was a colorless voice, like that of someone who couldn't care less about life:

"Don't imagine I'm going to give in. I'll let up when you let up."

"I'm running out of patience. Put on your overcoat. There's no time to lose."

"We have all the time in the world," responded René with terrifying calm.

He watched his father wringing his hands and commented to himself on what a great actor he was.

"All right," said René, "shall we come to an agreement?"

Ramón saw in René's gaze, in his tone of voice, such terrifying indifference, a spirit so determined not to heed his order to follow him, that he decided to throw it all out the window and declare his true identity.

"Perhaps we can reach an agreement. To show you my honorable intentions, I'm going to reveal to you something of utmost importance."

"Finally you're going to reveal something to me," René said sarcastically. "And what is it you're going to reveal to me?"

"My revelation will chill you to the bones," Ramón said, smiling mysteriously. "You'd better put on your overcoat; you'll see how you start to shiver... I can see you with your teeth chattering, telling me to bring you to the designated location."

Things were getting more complicated. Like a magician who pulls doves, rabbits, ribbons, etc. from a top hat, Ramón was revealing new abilities in dizzying succession. Now it concerned a revelation that would fall like an icy shower over his no less icy spirit. Fine, he would await the icy bath and respond with something far icier.

"Here goes..." Ramón's voice was faltering. "I'm not Ramón..." His voice cracked in his throat. He couldn't go on. It was all so strange: at the end of his career he found himself disobeying orders. The situation was so abnormal that he didn't have the slightest idea how to reveal his true identity to René. To add to the confusion, René said:

"Ah ha!... So now you're the one who doesn't know who he is."

"That's not what I'm saying," Ramón shouted at him, flushed with embarrassment. "I know very well who I am and I'm going to tell you."

"Well, I'm awaiting the metamorphosis," replied René, with such insolence that he was afraid his father would slap him in the face.

"Make as much fun of me as you want. It doesn't bother me in the least. I'm only interested in convincing you. Good god!" and he pounded violently on the table. "Listen closely: for thirty years I've been your father's double, and..." but the weight of his instructions fell over his mouth again like a muzzle. He saw his reputation ruined with each word that left his mouth.

René watched him, and there wasn't the slightest trace of astonishment in his gaze. It seemed totally natural that his father would fall back on the recourse of the double. It was just new evidence of his skill in the game of cat and mouse. Nevertheless, he had to parry the thrust. Sitting as he was in the chair, he closed his eyes and threw his head back.

"Please! Don't go to sleep. I've told you the truth. I was—no, I mean, I am your father's double."

He got scared. A little farther and he would reveal that Ramón no longer existed. He looked at his watch. It was two in the afternoon and the chiefs were still waiting. To have escaped so many dangers and then to fall into the traps of this imbecile. Without a single piece of paper to show him, a single form of identification to confirm what he'd said. All he carried was a copy of Ramón's. Tell him his real name? What for? Obviously he knew his own name, but when a person is called Ramón for thirty years, what the hell is he supposed to do with his real name?

The minutes were passing. He couldn't stand there like a fool without reflecting on something. If the revelation of his true identity had no effect, then it was preferable to continue doubling Ramón.

"All right, enough kidding around. I can see you're not convinced by the sad story of that poor wretch. You're smart to take it as a creation of my fantasy. You know that I'm none other than your father. Let's go; it's getting late. Your mother's waiting for us. Bundle up because it's cold as hell outside."

But René's reply plunged him into a new and terrible state of confusion.

"So now you're passing again as Ramón? However, didn't you consider that I might easily believe you're my father's double?"

"I swear I'm your father!" he said in a supplicating tone of voice. Aware that he was putting too much emphasis on his paternity, he added in a cheerful voice: "Your daddy who loves you very much." He laughed. "Let's go look for mommy... I have the 'buggy' outside that will take us there in a flash."

So his father's pretense could reach the realm of clownishness. But it was admirable in any case. Nevertheless, he would not let himself be underestimated: he would continue to play dumb... He would accept the outing in the "buggy." A simple set change and the game of cat and mouse would continue its downhill progression. He went to look for his overcoat. Ramón followed him. René said:

"Let's go."

The man breathed deeply. At last! He had been that close to total failure. Life contained surprises like that: to have spent thirty years doubling Ramón and at the most critical moment to discover the name of his game. But it wasn't entirely his fault: he had been educated in the elite school where orders are carried out unquestioningly. They had told him to go look for René, but they hadn't specified whether or not to go as Ramón's double. Besides which, there was a contradiction in all this: he was to present himself to René as if he were any man on the street, while at the same time, with Ramón's bearing, face, voice, and all of his tricks, idiosyncrasies, and gestures. Not for nothing does one double someone with impunity for thirty years. So what were those people expecting? That he would suddenly put it all aside and appear to René as the remote Martín from a time when he was twenty? But those men weren't concerned with any of this and like judges, would reproach him bitterly for his delay. He was well aware that his career was over with the assassination of Ramón, but for precisely that reason he would give himself the pleasure of crossing his *t*'s and dotting his *i*'s. For starters, he was going to tell them that in situations like this, their methods were a double-edged sword.

They took off like a shot, just barely avoiding running over two old ladies crossing the street. They took a corner at such speed that the car went up on two wheels. Soon they had left the center of the city and were traveling down an avenue. The double accelerated. René remembered that other trip in Marblo's car. No matter how rushed Ramón was, it was never cause for risking his life. Nevertheless, something very serious was taking place for his father to be driving this fast. The bit about Alicia waiting for them sounded to him like a pretext. Perhaps his mother had been in an accident; maybe she was dead. He looked at Ramón as if interrogating him, but he was unaware of René's gaze. He stared at the highway as he drove. René looked at him again to the same effect. He thought about what his father had said about his double. He was about to ask him, but didn't, for it seemed useless to do so. Ramón would come up with a new scheme and things would become even foggier than they were at the moment. So he stopped looking at him. He restricted himself to contemplating the scenery.

The man kept accelerating. The speedometer was registering one hundred and eighty miles per hour. They had left the city's suspension bridges behind them and were in the open countryside. Houses, trees, animals, people—they all blended together at this frantic speed. Suddenly the man made a sharp movement with his head and his hat fell off, revealing his hair. René grabbed the hat and as he wondered for a very brief instant whether to hand it to his father or to put it back on his head himself, he pictured, so to speak, Dalia's mannequin. And not the mannequin as much as its wig. Was the hair he was looking at his father's real hair, or was it a wig? But a double doesn't necessarily have to be bald, he thought. But he could just as well be. Just in case, he ought to make sure. Pretending to be setting the hat on his father's head, he grabbed his hair and gave it a hard yank. The man cursed. René let go of his hair. That was enough: it was Ramón's own hair. Or it wasn't, for it could just as easily be the real hair of any double whatsoever. Not wishing to give in, and keeping Dalia's mannequin in mind, he came to the conclusion that all doubles aren't necessarily made of flesh and bones, but of cardboard, plaster, or any other material. So, with an irony he fancied masterful, he said to Ramón:

"A son begs his father to accept his most humble apology..."

And confusion, fright, and terror once again possessed him when he heard how the man responded:

"That's fine and dandy when the father can hear the son's apology. I can imagine what you're thinking. I know what you're going to say: 'I have to see it to believe it...' Well, you'll see soon enough! We're about to arrive."

The car entered an uneven dirt road, driving toward the lights of a house located roughly a half-mile from the highway. They were soon in front of a house with a very low roof. The man honked the horn and a man with a flashlight appeared at once. The snow almost completely obstructed the narrow path to the house. The man approached the car with great difficulty. The double stuck his head out the window and shouted, asking whether he should leave the car there or put it in the garage. The man told him to get out, that they were waiting for him, that he would take care of the car. With great effort, they negotiated the few yards remaining between them and the house. The wind whistled furiously and snowflakes whipped at their faces. Rarely had René felt weather this cold. Nevertheless, they didn't have to wait a single second, for hardly had they placed their feet on the doorstep when the door opened, as if someone had been spying on their arrival.

They entered a small, pleasantly heated living room. The person who opened the door for them was no longer standing there. Instead, a girl appeared and attended to their coats. René was disturbed: he was expecting to see his mother. He told the man that he thought it strange Alicia hadn't come out to receive them. The man just smiled, but René didn't have time to reflect on the nature of his smile. As if by magic, a man in his sixties appeared, greeted him ceremoniously, took his hand, and told René to follow him. René turned his head to the double, who was now in a far corner of the room, kissing the girl. René made an effort to free himself from the hand that clasped him but the man didn't let go. Then he said:

"He's in the basement..."

And it was as if by the phrase "he's in the basement," it was understood: "your father is in the basement." He finally was coming to understand that the man had told him the truth. He wasn't Ramón but Ramón's double. So it wasn't Alicia but Ramón who was waiting for him. In the basement meant "another comedy staged by your father." He was already used to them. Nevertheless, the double's words: "That's fine and dandy when the father can..." As he walked with the old man who hadn't let go of his hand, his head was becoming a volcano. They walked through two rooms and entered the kitchen. The old man lifted a trapdoor and René could make out an iron ladder. At the bottom, an intense brilliance could be seen and as they descended the ladder the heat became suffocating. They cleared the last rung, entering a sort of cave. The old man left him there and climbed back up, shutting the trapdoor.

René took a look around him. The red brilliance originated from an oven or boiler located at the back of the cave. The heat was so intense he had to take off his jacket and loosen the collar of his shirt. As a *mise-en-scéne*, this was going to far. He didn't care so much about what Ramón meant by all this as he did about its effects: regardless of how it intrigued him, of how the suspense was wearing on his nerves, his predominant sensation was that of the intolerable heat increasing by the minute as if someone were constantly shoveling coal onto the fire. Sweat was running in rivulets down his body, his temples were pounding, his eyes were red, his throat desiccated, his lips heavy as lead. He took off his shirt and undershirt; his skin was reddened, chapped. Very soon his body would dehydrate and he would perish by asphyxiation. Everything there was burning, even the reflections of the fire flicking over the ceiling and walls like great birds of prey.

His eyes were burning so badly he had to close them. He leaned his head against the wall. In that position, he remembered the plaster statue of Christ in Marblo's school. All that was missing was for him to make his appearance—branding iron in hand—to brand him. Suddenly he heard a slight noise from the other side of the cave, like the creaking of a door swinging on its hinges. René opened his eyes a crack. He heard the sound again. René walked quickly to the place where the sound was coming from; he found a small wooden door about two yards from the mouth of the oven. He got closer and could see a faint light through a crack. His heart began to pound. He waited several seconds, sure that the door would open to let him through to his father. Contrary to his expectations, it remained stubbornly shut. The noise wasn't repeated. A deathly silence now reigned. He was about to shake the door in a fit of fury when it flung open, flooding the cave with light. The vivid brilliance illuminating the cave was reduced to the red spot of the mouth of the oven. René had just enough time to leap to one side.

The same man who had led him by the hand to the cave now entered. When he saw René half naked, he began to laugh. René asked him about Ramón, but the man, without parting his lips, pulled a piece of paper from his breast pocket and handed it to him. He bowed his head deeply and left through the door, leaving it open.

Paper in hand, René stood there staring at the door. That's it, he would run after the man that very instant to demand an explanation. Then he saw that his jacket, shirt, and tie were on the floor. He was about to pick up his clothes—he was bending over—when the piece of paper fell from his hand. Then he realized he had to read it without a moment to lose. He unfolded it feverishly. It contained the following message:

"I hope your flesh meets the same end as mine."
RAMÓN

What did the message mean? Well, he was finding
that out. There was a terrible eloquence in its brevity:
I've been assassinated and hope you perish in the same
fashion. Was this message part of the comedy? He read
it over again. In one minute he read it a hundred times,
for no more time had passed when the man reappeared
pushing a stretcher on wheels. A man lay on the stretcher
completely naked. The man left the stretcher in the
middle of the cave. He signaled for René to approach.

The corpse lying there was the body of his father.
René stood there staring at it. His thorax and abdomen
were savagely riddled with bullet holes. He saw bloody
marks on his arms as if his father had raised them to
protect himself from the bullets. René was covered with
goose flesh; he felt himself disintegrating. Violence
practiced at all levels and in its greatest magnitude. And
his father, a violent man, had been assassinated by
another violent man. But where had he been assassinated? In the street, in his own home, in the living
room of this country house? And when? Yesterday? Just
a few hours ago?... Pointless questions. What is certain
is that he was looking at the body of his father; his father
who, lying there on the stretcher, had achieved his life's
lofty and bloody ideal. Or rather, "Life." But on the
piece of paper he also said that René had the obligation
to meet this same end. So was it his turn now? Were they
going to riddle his thorax and abdomen right now in
this cave? He leaned over Ramón's face as if expecting
to hear an answer from his mouth, silenced once and
for all. But the answer that his father would not give him
had already been satisfied in the office by the double.
Everything was fitting together logically: "I've come for

you. I can't tell you anything. I have to bring you to the place of your destiny." So he was saying that his father must have been assassinated long before the double's visit. And Ramón having been eliminated, René was to take the place of the supreme chief in the battle for the flesh with all of its consequences—included among them of course, his assassination, an obligatory number in the program of "the trigger-happy boys."

Nevertheless, a new objection occurred to him: Might not that corpse be that of the double? One of Ramón's new tricks aimed at a giving him goose flesh? He looked again at the body. He could swear that the dead man was his father in every shape and form... Amidst the bullet holes, he discovered—almost joyfully— Ramón's favorite wound. He was without a doubt in the presence of his father's corpse.

He left the stretcher and swerving like a drunkard, walked over to the man. In a tremulous voice, he asked for an explanation: the funereal character would only point to the piece of paper René still gripped between his fingers. He opened it mechanically and glanced at it. Obviously his father's words could not be any clearer. Ramón had reached his supreme goal; like his father, he could now call himself the Human Pincushion. In turn, he was passing the torch of the Cause of Chocolate on to his son and was recommending that his flesh meet the same end as had his own.

He went back to the stretcher and contemplated that cold flesh for the last time. He thought about how a poet of the flesh like Swyne would apply to the assassination of his father the pompous euphemism of Martyrdom. He was moved as he looked at that completely naked body. He asked the man if he wouldn't be so kind as to cover the body with a sheet. The old man gave him a sly smile. As if he had been waiting for René to make that request, he walked over to the stretcher and with the consummate skill of a butcher, grabbed Ramón by the feet and threw him over his shoulder. He arrived in front of the mouth of the oven and stuffed him in. A shower of sparks filled the cave.

The King of Meat

When the clock struck twelve, René set aside the gloves he was counting and went to collect his pay. It was Saturday and he wouldn't go back to work until Monday. He felt doubly content: first, because it was the weekend; second, because that Saturday he was completing his first full month of work.

His plans had finally become a beautiful reality. An eight-hour work day; at night, instruction in stenography and typing. He took his place in line and patiently waited his turn to get paid. There were more than a hundred employees ahead of him, but he didn't get impatient. He thought of the line in the butchers shop. Whereas there he would wait with death in his soul for a few pounds of meat, here he was bursting with satisfaction. He was about to do nothing less than collect the fruits of his first month of work translated into cold hard cash. Furthermore, he was there entirely of his own volition and not sent by anyone. Everything indicated that the battle for the flesh had come to an end with the tragic death of his father. From now on, he wouldn't find himself forced to stand in line at any meat counter; he now belonged to the world of people who work and build a future for themselves. He had definitively broken with all butchers shops and butchers...

However, this peace had come at a high price. The months following the assassination of his father were, if possible, even more terrible than the years spent under his yoke. To start with, his very life had been hanging by a thread for a month due to a concussion. They had brought him out of that sinister cave unconscious. He never knew who took him to the hospital, who paid his expenses, who left him a note informing him of the hospital where his mother was confined. He was in the hospital for three months and one fine day they discharged him, but not before placing several bills in his hand, which, according to the director of the hospital, was what remained of the money they had left to pay his expenses.

Two days before leaving the hospital, the nurse handed him a letter mailed within the city. In it, they informed him of the demise of his mother and as "consolation" added that "that" was the best solution, for had she survived her injuries, she would have been a wretched woman, both her legs having been amputated. Finally, they included the address of the cemetery where she was buried.

His first trip was to the cemetery. Despite having prepared himself for such a lugubrious encounter, when he stood in front of Alicia's grave, when he saw the gravestone with the name of his mother, he experienced horrible anguish. Standing there on the plot, he confirmed what until then he had known only by reading the letter. It was as if Alicia, laid in her coffin and covered with a few square yards of earth, were ready to start up a conversation with him but at the same time was unable to keep it going. Only now did he know that his mother was dead, only now did he know that she had been murdered, and only now did he find out that he had lost her forever. She, like Ramón, had placed her life under the aegis of "suffering in silence" and had oriented it toward the "cult of meat," but at least in this inhuman lifestyle, her maternal feeling gave her an advantage over Ramón. To a certain extent, she had always protected him against the severity of his father— that is, up to that terrible point where tenderness yields to the necessity of sacrificing the flesh of one's flesh. But at least up to that point she had protected him from Ramón's fury, and now René found himself alone in the ominous life of the Pipos and Samuels of the world.

This was the price of his freedom. A very high price, but considered carefully, it had its advantages. He had never wished for the death of his parents, but having looked for and achieved it, they had at the same time obtained his liberation. And that was the supreme advantage. With them, he lived in their company but in a condition of servitude; they having disappeared, he found himself alone but free.

So then, everything had come to an end and was starting anew. Unless his father sprung resuscitated from the oven, no earthly power would be great enough to force him into the "service of pain" and the "cult of meat." There existed, on the other hand, a beautiful reality: he was standing in a line composed not of servants of the flesh, but of human beings who like himself were waiting there to collect the fruits of their labor. It wouldn't occur to any of them to murder a fellow worker for a few coins or to sacrifice their life for a cause like chocolate or...sardines. People who work don't have to appeal to the flesh of others in order to survive.

These thoughts wandered through his head as he got closer to the pay window. That afternoon he would go to the cemetery and leave a wreath of roses on his mother's grave. Then he would buy books and in the evening would go to the theater.

All of a sudden, the loudspeaker hanging in front of the window pulled him from his pleasant plans. Management was paging him. Someone was waiting for him.

"For me!" René exclaimed, speaking to the loudspeaker as if it were a person.

They paged him again. One of his fellow workers tapped him on the shoulder:

"Your head's in the clouds! Can't you hear someone's waiting for you?"

René left the line and as he approached the waiting room, wondered who could be waiting for him. With the death of his parents, his few friends had also left him. It was sad to admit but true. Ramón's policy, based on concealing him from the eyes of the world, bore such fruit: not a single friend. Of course, he got rid of Marblo and company, as with his father's buddies. All those people had been erased from his life and would never again cross his path. He was about to enter the waiting room when he imagined the person waiting for him could be Mrs. Pérez. He was going to take off, but upon reconsideration, opted to stand up to whoever it might be. If it was she, fine: better to be buried alive than try to avoid her. She would go to the shop on any given day to bother him. Dalia didn't have a crumb of dignity, despite having earned his contempt and disgust on account of the mannequin she used for unspeakable purposes.

He pushed the door open and entered. He looked at all the chairs but none of them were occupied by a

woman. On the contrary, there was only one visitor, and
to top it all, it was a man. René was disconcerted. He was
already retracing his path, certain that Dalia, tired of
waiting, had left, when the man rose to his feet and
headed him off, saying:

"René, don't you recognize me?"

He stood by the door, staring at the man. How could
he recognize someone he had never seen before? Thousands of thoughts flashed through his brain. A friend of
his father's? But if it was one of his father's friends, not
one of his, then the man's "René, don't you recognize
me?" was superfluous. They could subject him to every
kind of torment and still would not get him to confess
that he knew the man. Then he thought another em-
ployee might very well be named René. Seizing upon
this idea as to a lifesaver, he said:

"You've mistaken me for someone else. We don't
know each other."

"Look, friend," the man said calmly, "I haven't got the
wrong person. On the contrary, I'm addressing myself
to you—René, son of the late Ramón." And he added:
"So, do we now understand each other?"

René felt his legs shaking beneath him. All of a
sudden the name of his father was springing from the
mouth of the oven, burning him in the face. Wretched
him, who for a moment had thought the battle for the
flesh was over! Nevertheless, all was not lost. Perhaps this
man (a close friend of Ramón's) wished to see him in
order to offer his sympathy. He fixed his eyes once again
on the man and could not maintain such innocent
thoughts. There was something more to this man than
met the eye. It would not be crazy to think that at that
very moment he was going to pull a slip of paper out of
the depths of one of his jacket pockets and place it in
René's hand. A slip of paper from Ramón, one of those

post-mortem slips of paper... "I hope your flesh meets the same end as mine." Well, at present things were very different and all that was left of his father was that scrap of paper, which he certainly was not about to observe: nor would he in any way obey the first person who might wish to send him back into the battle for the flesh. He looked the man up and down. He said to him:

"I beg you to make it brief. I have to get back to the window to collect my pay."

"I'm not going to stop you," the man said, placing his hand on René's head as if he were going to bless him. "I'll make it quick; very quick. But you really don't recognize me? We've nevertheless met not long ago."

"I'm sorry," René said, trying to contain his irritation, "but you're mistaken. We've never met."

"Certainly," the man said, slowly passing his hand over his face. "Certainly." He remained silent for a moment. Finally he pulled a piece of paper out of his pocket.

"Then you won't have any objection to signing this paper. It's the only requirement I still have to fulfill in order to get my pension and retire to work the land."

At the sight of the sheet of paper, René felt goose flesh rising all over his body. Nevertheless, what the man was saying didn't allude to any message. If he had heard correctly, the man was speaking of a signature... He automatically stuffed his hands all the way into his pockets. No, no, he wouldn't sign anything. He was not about to accede to the sinister machinations of the servants of the flesh with his signature.

"But don't stand there like a dolt. Read what it says," and the man shook him, trying to pull his hands from his pockets. "Take a look."

It was better to get the odious scene over with. He snapped open the piece of paper and read: "I hereby declare that I do not have the honor of knowing citizen Martín Vela."

"Why, I'll sign right away," René said, almost shouting. "If that's all it is, I have no any objections whatsoever. Pen or pencil? Which do you prefer?"

"Pen," the man replied parsimoniously. "But first make sure your memory isn't failing you. Are you absolutely sure you've never met me? You've never seen my face before?"

"What do you want me to say?" René exclaimed, hysterical in the face of the man's uncertainty. "What flavor would you prefer it in? No, we've never met before."

He pulled out his fountain pen, set the sheet of paper on a table and signed his name under the declaration.

"There you go! It's been a pleasure. Now get lost."

"Perfect," the man said, carefully folding up the sheet of paper. "Perrrr-fect... This signature will save me from a second operation. True, I still have the test with the chiefs, but that's just a formality. With this little signature, I'm just about retired."

"I don't understand a single word you're saying," René exclaimed. "You mentioned an operation... What the hell does my signature have to do with all that?"

"Well, well!" the man replied, rubbing his hands together. "So the little gentleman isn't in such a rush anymore. Now his pay can wait. I told you once and I'll tell you again that we've met—briefly, but we have dealt with each other. Nevertheless—heck, when you get your face changed..."

Like someone who repeats the question he's been asked in order to gain time before answering, and like the person who, because of the profound astonishment the question has caused in him, repeats it with the same tone and intention with which it was posed, René repeated:

"...When you get your face changed."

And reacting to his astonishment, as if a million questions were now pressing against his lips, he added:

"You mean to say you used to have another face?"

"Another?... Just one other?" and the man laughed boisterously.

"During the fifty years I've spent in this vale of tears, I've changed my face twice."

"That's not what I mean..." René said, revealing an even greater astonishment tinged with fear.

"See if it isn't," and the man's voice now became almost a whisper. "Until I was twenty, I wore the face God gave me. From twenty to fifty, someone else's face, and for just the last month, the face of the scalpel..."

René felt nauseous, yet these words didn't sound new to him. Where could he have heard them, or in what dream? His anguish was so overpowering as to obfuscate all attempts at thought. He stood there, his mouth agape, as if he had just had a molar extracted.

"I understand your surprise," the man said to him. "That's right: two faces... But you can be sure that this one—" and he touched his face energetically—"will be the last. I dare them to have me double someone else. In the whole wide world there couldn't exist another face like this!"

The man walked over to him until their faces were nearly touching.

"Understand me. A made-over face is unlike anything else. It's nothing but a chunk of meat with eyes. Don't you see they reduced my nose? Don't you realize they sawed off my jawbone? But I'll explain it to you more clearly: tell me, do you remember your father's face? Do you?"

"Yes, I remember it," René said, shutting his eyes.

"All right then. What was your father's nose like?"

"But what does my father have to do with any of this!" René shouted, totally confused.

"Don't get excited young man, and answer my question. What was Ramón's nose like? Big or small?"

"Big," René answered, looking in terror at the man.

"And mine," the man said, trying to seize it between his thumb and index finger. "Doesn't it look to you like a cherry? So we agree that your father had a big nose and mine is like a cherry. Nevertheless, for thirty years this tiny nose was as large as your father's."

"But who was so cruel as to remake it?" René exclaimed. "Is it a crime to have a big nose?"

"It is when that nose resembles another nose and when one's mouth is identical to another mouth and when one's chin..."

He abruptly broke off what he was saying. He pulled the piece of paper out again. He read it with a look of satisfaction and again put it away.

"Good, good... René, I have lots to do as well. Let's not stand here like two little kids deciphering a charade—all the more so since you're not doing anything to help me. So I'll tell you what remains to be clarified (if anything at all) without metaphors. I was your father's double for thirty years. But that's nothing new. I already told you that the day I went to your house. All right, to continue. With your father dead, my work as a double lost its *raison d'être*. So I prepared for retirement, but they wouldn't let me keep your father's face..."

"They wouldn't let you?..." René interrupted. "Who wouldn't let you?"

"Why, who else but the boss! You work and have a boss, don't you? Well, I have one too. And he told me I had to change my face. That was three months ago. When I was presentable, he ordered me to go see you. If you recognized me, back to the operating table."

"But who told you I was working in this glove shop?" René said impetuously. "Who knows so much about my life?"

"You're such a fool!" the man answered. "Who else would it be but the boss himself. He told me: 'Go to such and such a store, on such a such a street. That's where René works.'"

"And he didn't give you any message for me?"

"Nope. Only what I've just told you. And now, with your permission, I'm going, happy and content. You signed."

He placed an icy hand on René's and left.

René let him go. He could have run after him and asked him new questions, but he decided there was no point. This display had been more than enough. He looked at the clock. He only had fifteen minutes left to collect his pay. He ran out of the room and arrived at the line panting. Farewell to his happy plans. The flesh was calling him once again. This very instant they would pay him in flesh instead of money... In his fright, he imagined that everyone would laugh at him when the cashier placed one hundred slices of meat in his hands. Nevertheless, perhaps all was not lost and the visit of his father's ex-double was the epilogue to his old life. Examining things more calmly, the boss hadn't sent him any message—neither verbal nor written. It was simply a matter of confirming that he didn't recognize Ramón's ex-double. That accomplished—if he wasn't mistaken—the episode was coming to a close. And if things didn't stop there? If after a few days, a month, or a year, the same Martín appeared again with another face and another scrap of paper? Although this was highly improbable: with that face, he could double anyone but Ramón, who was dead and burnt to a cinder. No, Martín would go to a different store and would ask to see the René who worked there... For he was certain he wasn't the only René in the city, and this Martín could spend the rest of his life appearing before the

René in turn to ask him in his nasal voice whether he recognized the shining face he saw before him.

In the meantime, he had arrived at the window and the paymaster was handing him his money. He didn't answer the question one of the employees asked him, nor did he accept an invitation to go out drinking. He took off like a shot from the store. He needed air. He was suffocating.

And if this Martín didn't return, but another man showed up in his place? They might call him to the waiting room at any moment. There he would discover the new emissary who would hand him a totally different message. This time it wouldn't be a matter of recognizing a face and signing... This time the message would contain one of those death sentences from the boss: "To whom it may concern..."

He went into a bar. To get drunk, sleep it off, stop thinking. He asked for a cognac, cognac being the drink with which he was most familiar. In critical situations, he had had cognac placed in front of him—at school, in Dalia's house. As the drink warmed him, he began to picture that probable emissary in ever greater detail. He saw him in his room, sitting in his armchair waiting for him. He rushed out of the bar, ready to face that emissary once and for all.

It was two in the afternoon when he arrived at the boarding house. The superintendent received him with an unfriendly look on her face. She told him the dining room was closed, that she had put his lunch in his room, but that he would have to "swallow it cold." René asked her whether anyone was waiting for him in his room. The superintendent laughed in his face, saying that he was putting on some airs to think that someone might wait for him for hours.

He breathed deeply. The room was as empty as his soul. The only thing waiting for him was his lunch, covered with a dubiously white napkin. Feeling the effects of the cognac, he flopped down on the bed. He closed his eyes, but had to open them right away. Martín's unpleasant, inhuman face "materialized" in his mind. Martín was a warning. Now more than ever before, Ramón's fateful words blazed over the depths of his life: "I hope your flesh meets the same end as mine."

He got up and took off his jacket. As time passed those words were developing like a photographic plate. It isn't that at first they lacked meaning or concealed their meaning like ancient hieroglyphics when he read them in the cave, but with the passage of the days and aided by incidents like the ex-double's visit, they were opening their corollas like monstrous flowers and displaying new, revealing colors. At the same time, they resembled the muzzle of a hunting dog that had caught some poor thing, and let it drop only after choking it. It was as if his father, from the black chasm of death, wished to keep him by his side through a sinister appeal to the flesh. Yes, there was more to that post-mortem piece of paper than met the eye... They had crowned René king of the flesh and this symbol would only fall from its carnal royalty with his death.

He nearly cried out in the face of such misfortune. He lifted the napkin and saw a piece of cold meat swimming in grease. He covered the horrible thing up again. Putting his jacket on again, he left the room.

The cemetery was his only alternative. There at least, the flesh had "already" been gnawed by worms and he could now go about opening tombs, for he wouldn't find them full of people roasting themselves over low flames or devouring their own entrails... Kneeling before his mother's grave, he asked her what the great secret of the love of flesh was. Since he was now destined for the cult of meat, the least his mother could do was to instruct him; she alone could tell him from what bloody spring the waters flow that turn one into an hyena hungry for carrion and a tigress who makes a shield of her own body to defend her tiger...

But Alicia remained as silent as her bones. René spent a long time imploring her and not the slightest consolation sprang from the black abyss. His mother could console him in life when, in addition to bones, she was padded with meat. But even while alive, Alicia's flesh had been so bound to her husband's that all her son ever heard from her lips were the rules and precepts of the service of pain.

He was pulled from his self-absorption by the gruff voice of the head gravedigger, an old man who told him that they were about to close the cemetery gate. Since at that moment René was sobbing heavily and as the old man was used to tears, he told René to go cry on the other side of the cemetery wall. René stood up with great effort and began to walk. The gravedigger said to him jokingly:

"Listen, boy. If you like this place so much, why don't you stay here?"

René stopped walking. Mockery and derision pursued him even in the cemetery. He felt like giving the old man a piece of his mind, but all he could say was:

"Stay here?..."

"You've got it," replied the old man. "But not to stay as a deadman, which would mean more work for me. I'm in need of help. I mean stay here alive, as a gravedigger's assistant."

"Gravedigger's..." René repeated.

"Of course," the old man said, "as a gravedigger's assistant. The guy who was helping me 'kicked the bucket' a week ago. I can't wait for the authorities to get me a substitute; that takes time. If you accept, I'll give you room and board and something for cigarettes. Besides, dead people don't bother you; you can walk all over them, no problem."

As the old man talked, René's mouth opened until he had practically dislocated his jaw. He was finally able to express himself, and told the man the job didn't interest him. The old man, who had made him the offer in a joking spirit (although he truly was in need of an assistant) shook his head, indicating to René to beat it. A step away from the gate, he gave René a push, closed the gate, locking it with a padlock, and walked off. But hardly had he taken a few steps when he heard René, pressing his face against the bars, saying:

"Listen, I thought it over and I accept your offer."

The old man walked to the gate and took out the key to open the padlock.

"No, I can't start today," René told him. "I'll start tomorrow."

What was actually happening was that René wasn't sufficiently convinced to grab the lime and start whitening sepulchers... Furthermore, the idea of staying there at night made a strong impression on him and even seemed a bad omen. He begged the old man, who was still grumbling, to let him start the following morning.

He started on his way back to the city. The bus stop was three blocks away. He thought he had made a mistake by not agreeing to stay in the cemetery. Because of his childish fears, he found himself obliged to go back to the city where mortal danger lay in wait for him on every corner. He had had a magnificent opportunity to escape the claws of the emissaries. No matter how mean the old man might be, he would never call him to say that in such and such a tomb an emissary was waiting for him. No, he would just yank on his ears at five in the morning for him to carry out his sepulchral duties... He had to convince himself that the cemetery was his last resort and the work of a graveduster, his only job.

He caught a bus packed to the ceiling with people. He saw all those people as beings without problems who were returning home to sleep the sleep of the just. No emissary would come to disturb such peace and much less would they find their bed occupied by one of those sinister characters. He, on the other hand, was at their mercy and even wished the bus would crash, to get it over with once and for all. His fears grew with each turn of the wheels: the distance grew shorter, the ghost became more corporeal.

If that wasn't bad enough, his brilliant plans had vanished with Martín's visit. Gone was the shopping trip, the wreath, the books, the theater... In its place, a face carved here and there by the scalpel, the gruff voice of the emissary, memories being brought to light which had seemed forever buried, his signature on a piece of paper like the sword of Damocles hanging over his head, the anguish that he would bump into someone in his house waiting to tell him to hurry up, that the knives were ready to maul his flesh. In short, this had been his day off after six days of very hard work and now, exhausted, longing to throw himself on the bed to rest just like other passengers, he found himself obliged to spy, to approach his house fearfully, to sneak in. Wouldn't they ever leave him alone once and for all?

As if the answer were a resounding "no," the bus came to a dead halt. The passengers began to get off. It had stopped right in front of an illuminated sign that said: "Big wrestling match between Blackie, champion of the North, and Santos, champion of the South." René's eyes were riveted on a poster that displayed the wrestlers so

195

intertwined that one couldn't tell where one left off and the other began, their faces distorted by the dreadful pain they were experiencing. He fled as if carried off by the devil himself: he thought the ticket seller was signaling to him, trying to convince him to see the show. He abandoned his mad dash after about five blocks. He saw himself pushed into the ring and caught in the powerful biceps of one of those giants who squeezed him into a purée. His throat was parched; he needed a soda. He entered a bar, asked for a soda, and went to sit at a table, but before sitting down, he bought a newspaper. It wasn't that he had any desire to find out how things were going in the world; he did so purely out of precaution, placing the newspaper between him and the gaze of the public. One of those emissaries might be in the bar and could discover him, sit at his table, and then immediately hand him one of those slips of paper...

He walled himself up behind the newspaper. As he picked up the glass, a corner of the newspaper flopped over, revealing his face. He took a glance around the room and lifted the newspaper again. He held it up with his elbow as he caught the other corner with his hand that was holding the glass. He repeated this kind of juggling act twice, but the third time a corner of the newspaper flopped over again and his eyes again began to explore the room. This time the newspaper didn't return to its original position; René held it down. His eyes were riveted on a table located in front of him.

Sitting there was an acquaintance of René's. Risking being "discovered" by one of the emissaries, René exposed himself to the customers' glances. But did he by any chance have acquaintances? Certainly, now that his eyes were riveted on the man sitting in front of him. He lifted the newspaper again as he murmured: "Powlavski, Powlavski..."

196

Powlavski was absorbed in a complicated arithmetic calculation. He was writing sums on a piece of paper, which he first counted meticulously on his fingers. It appeared as if the result of these calculations was satisfactory, for he was constantly letting out snorts of contentment and gulping down his drink.

René judged that the most prudent thing to do was to beat it. There was more to Powlavski than met the eye. Furthermore, if one was to believe Dalia, he was nothing less than the assassin of Mr. Nieburg, his soul mate. With the aim of determining whether the old man had seen him, René looked at him over the newspaper. He was soon convinced that Powlavski was so engrossed in his calculations that he hadn't taken any notice of him. He took a peso from his pocket and put it on the table. He was getting up when he heard someone asking him for a light.

Halfway to his feet and still walled behind the newspaper, he apologized:

"I don't smoke."

And when he lowered the newspaper, he found Powlavski standing in front of him, who hadn't recognized him earlier, but now that they were facing each other, did remember René:

"Aren't you the same person I had the pleasure of meeting in Mrs. Pérez's house?"

René didn't respond. His surprise at the unexpected appearance of Powlavski at his table made him sit down again and shield himself behind the newspaper. Then Powlavski lowered the newspaper, revealing René's frightened face.

"What's wrong?" he said, aching with laughter. "Does my presence somehow compromise you? Are you engaged in some little 'transaction'? If that's the case, tell me and I'll wait for you at my table. We have the whole night ahead of us."

"I'm not engaged in any transaction and I'm leaving right this minute," stammered René, and added: "Good evening, Mr. Powlavski."

But Powlavski, faster than René, placed his hand on René's shoulder and pushed him back into his seat. Then he sat down, pressed up against him. He told the waiter to serve them two cognacs.

"Look at what you're drinking! Some kind of vile soda. Incredible. No, no, my little friend, we have to celebrate this encounter with something strong."

René tried to get up, but Powlavski prevented him from doing so, holding him by the belt with an iron grip. For a second, René thought of calling for help. There was no reason he should be forced to listen to the summary of crimes which the repugnant old geezer was about to recount. Nevertheless, he restrained himself in order to avoid a scandal. Calling the police would mean having to give himself away. He certainly didn't want anything to do with assassins and emissaries, but neither did he want a run-in with the police. There were always complications.

"You can't imagine, boy, the joy she's going to have when she finds out I've found you at last," Powlavski said, slapping him amicably.

"She?... Who's 'she'?"

"Boy, that's a good one!" exclaimed Powlavski. "She... Why, who else but our mutual friend, Dalia? It's unpardonable that you couldn't figure it out. And even so, she's the only friend you've got."

"That woman is not my friend, Mr. Powlavski," René said laboriously and turning red as a beet as he remembered the night he spent in Dalia's house. "I'm very sorry to say that I wish to have absolutely nothing to do with her, and I would appreciate it if you let her know."

"Tsk, tsk," Powlavski said very cheerfully. "What am I hearing? So you find the enchanting Dalia to be unpleasant? Might one know the reason for such displeasure?"

"Better we just stop talking about her. Besides, I have to go. Tomorrow I have to get up very early."

"Well, if that's the case, I'm sorry," sighed Powlavski. He picked up one of the glasses of cognac and gave it to René. "Let's toast to our burgeoning friendship. I can assure you we're going to be very good friends."

René told himself it would be useless to resist the toast. Mechanically he raised his glass and clinked it against Powlavski's. He barely wet his lips. In contrast, the old man knocked his back in one shot and began to call the waiter, telling him to bring the bottle.

"All right," Powlavski said, lunging at René, "now we can become inspired. As I was saying, we have the whole night ahead of us. But now that I remember... Where the hell have you been hiding all this time that Dalia hasn't seen you? Or rather, where did your father stash you away? No, I'm not pressing you in order to take information to Dalia. If you don't wish to see her, that's all well and good. I'm asking purely out of curiosity. From one day to the next, the birds leave the nest... Ha, ha, that's right—the nest, the nest..."

Once again, his father was being brought up. What did it matter that he was dead and burnt to a cinder when at any moment someone brought him forth and made René sit through an entire speech about Ramón. Was his father going to "spend his death" playing tedious jokes on him? He was sick and tired of his father this and his father that... And what had he won through his death? Nothing. It made no difference at all; he was as alive as ever. Now any Powlavski whatsoever could come up to him to ask questions about his father. He decided to take drastic action. Obviously he wasn't going to mention the business about Ramón's assassination to the Jew, but he was going to respond in such a fashion that from that moment on, he wouldn't dare bother him.

"Listen, Mr. Powlavski, I'm not prepared to make a confession to you. You have no right. I'm not your friend. There is no bond between us, so stop bothering me."

"Tsk, tsk," and Powlavski leaned over ceremoniously. "I understand... To each his mysteries. If you'd rather I not speak of your father, nothing would please me more than to oblige you. As I always say: don't mention rope in the hanged man's house... But you're certainly not going to deny that you vanished from one day to the next... Dalia and I were both very intrigued by your absence during the business with my old friend, Nieburg."

"Nieburg?" René practically shouted, lunging backwards as if he were being machine-gunned.

"Why of course! Nieburg, I said. You promised Dalia you would go to her house to witness the death of Nieburg. I even remember she prepared some meat pastries for you. We ate them on the balcony, while in the street below, old Nieburg was tucking his head under his wing... That's right: under his wing... under his wing..."

And he began to hum that phrase in a ceaseless monotone. René, bent over like a barrel plank, was on the verge of rolling around on the floor. With a sharp blow, Powlavski straightened him up, served him a cognac, and continued his lugubrious tune. René said to himself that without paying a cent to a single news agency, he was receiving the news with capricious irregularity, but no less effectively for that reason. Months after the reprehensible incident, he had the bad luck of bumping into the man who informed on poor Nieburg and hearing the story of the crime from his own lips. He pictured all of Nieburg's possible death scenes as he lay on the sidewalk at the mercy of the hired killers. He realized in fright that it wasn't the imagination of his fevered mind but the details told by Powlavski himself, which he was about to hear. Unable to contain his horror, he covered Powlavski's mouth, saying:

"No, Mr. Powlavski! I beg of you, don't tell me a thing!"

"But what are you imagining? Do you think I'm a reporter? No, I don't belong to that debased race. My friend, I only brought up the business of Nieburg in order to show you that we were expecting you that night. If you didn't wish to, or were unable to go, that's your loss."

"Listen, Mr. Powlavski. I'm very upset about the death of Mr. Nieburg. I hardly knew him, but he was a human being."

"How charming!" Powlavski said, and let out such a loud burst of laughter that everyone turned around to look at him. "Marvelous! A human being... Tell me: what should he have been? A dog?"

"Not a dog. A human being," René stated meekly. "For that very reason..."

"For that very reason... Of course for that very reason. Because he was a human being, he earned me a cash profit of five thousand dollars. Imagine that if poor Nieburg had been a dog instead of a man, they wouldn't have given me more than a few pennies for his hide."

Powlavski's shamelessness was simply intolerable. Not a minute longer with him. René would leave him in mid-sentence. He stood up forcefully and got ready to give the old man a push when Powlavski, getting up as well, said:

"Yes, let's go. I've had enough of this place." He called the waiter, paid for the drinks, and taking René by the arm, left the bar.

"All right," Powlavski said, with his arm around René's shoulders. "We have the whole night ahead of us. I presume you're not going to bed. It's only twelve."

"I'm sorry," René said firmly, "but we're saying goodbye right here and now."

Doing as he said, he yanked himself free of Powlavski's arm. He turned to say goodbye and walked off. Powlavski stood there confused for a moment, and then reacted: seeing his prey slipping from his clutches, he reached René's side in a single bound.

"Please," René said, "don't follow me."

"Wait a moment. Just a moment," the old man whispered. "I believe you're short of money and I know where you can get yourself some."

René stopped in his tracks. Now the wretch was tempting him into a life of crime. He was about to tell him to keep his money, that he didn't need it; and he nearly showed him the pay he had collected that morning, but he thought that if he did, it wouldn't be a second before he was murdered just like Nieburg. Powlavski took his hesitation as indecision which he had to seize without a moment to lose.

"I'm saying you could earn a lot of money. You see... A hop, skip, and a jump from here, right off this street, I have a friend who pays very well."

"I'm sorry, Mr. Powlavski, but I have to get up early tomorrow. Maybe another day."

"No, no," Powlavski insisted. "Don't put off until tomorrow what you can do today... We'll go visit my friend this very instant. In fact, you know what they call him?"

"Martín?" René shouted, certain that Powlavski would answer in the affirmative.

"Martín?..." Powlavski appeared surprised. "I don't know any Martín. No, I'm speaking of Ball of Flesh."

René stuttered.

"Ah ha! So you know him. Magnificent! I'm getting the impression you know a lot of people..."

"No, I swear I don't know him," René said hastily. "It's just such an unusual nickname."

"Heh, heh! Very unusual... But you'll find him even more unusual when you see him. Let's go. We'll be there in no time flat."

"No," René said without conviction, "I have to..."

Powlavski didn't let him complete his excuse. He threw his arm around him and they began to walk.

"Let's not waste the night. I swear you'll be forever grateful to me."

And seeing that René was still hesitant, he said:

"We'll just go visit. I'll leave it up to you to decide whether or not you work for Ball. If you're interested in working, it can be arranged very quickly. You'll see."

"Tell me, Powlavski: why do they call him Ball of Flesh?"

He was being consumed by the most burning curiosity. In a complete turnaround, everything related to meat was of deep interest to him, but at the same time, he didn't wish to reveal this to Powlavski.

"Neither you nor I nor anyone could adequately describe Ball," Powlavski exclaimed, placing great emphasis on his claim. "You'll agree when you see him with your own eyes."

And as he said this, he quickened his pace. René, totally convinced, followed him at the same pace. He had already set aside his concerns. Now, instead of fleeing from the flesh, he was throwing himself into its dark mass. He was now stepping (practically dragging Powlavski behind him) like a soldier marching off cheerfully to offer his flesh to the slaughter. And there surged unthinkingly from his subconscious as from an unstaunchable wound a desperate, dramatic Why? Why?

They walked straight for three blocks, turned left onto an avenue, walked one more block and entered a narrow street. They were in an elegant neighborhood. René said to himself that Powlavski was very well connected judging from the palace they stopped in front of: a mansion made of pink marble in strikingly bad taste, but sumptuous nevertheless. What is called a nouveau riche property: an enclave in an area of houses built in fine architectural style, as if Ball had wished to shout from the rooftops that he was permitted every liberty, including that of bad taste.

A gravel path led them to the main entrance. The (monumental) door sported a large, heavy knocker, but Powlavski walked to the side of the house and knocked on a small door. A servant opened, Powlavski said something into his ear, and the servant let them into the house. The interior displayed the overwrought and ostentatious luxury of the nouveau riche. Powlavski, seeing René's astonishment when faced with such a profusion of chandeliers and mirrors, such lavish frames surrounding portraits (always of the same person: an old tub of lard with the face of a swine), told him that Ball was tremendously rich. He had been lucky enough three days after his birth to meet up with the king of canned meat, who found him at the entrance to the mansion in a tiny basket with a note tied around his neck in which his enemies said that seeing how he was the king of meat and lacked an heir to his empire (syphilis had left him impotent), they were presenting him with Ball of Flesh, who could inherit his empire and millions of dollars.

Powlavski added as René listened in astonishment that the king of meat, on the verge of giving Ball a swift kick, slowly lowered his foot, bent down, and with loving care lifted him from the basket. Then he called all his servants to the great hall to let them know that the chunk of meat he held in his arms was his adopted son, sole heir to his fabulous riches. The servants, seeing such a human monster, were barely able to contain their laughter, but the king cast a withering glance at them. He immediately had a long note sent to the press announcing the birth of a son and adding that at last his empire was assured of an heir.

Powlavski was concluding his abridged biography of Ball when the servant returned to tell them they would be received in a few minutes. Powlavski used the time to finish bringing René up to date. With the death of his adopted father, Ball inherited all his property. At present, he was sixty years old, had never married, and hadn't adopted anyone. His entire life was dedicated to the cult of meat.

The servant reappeared shortly and told them to follow him. They crossed the vast hall, entering an antechamber where the servant handed them over to another servant on duty. The latter opened a small door and announced them.

Leading René by the hand, Powlavski entered the vast octagonal chamber whose walls were covered from floor to ceiling with brilliant red satin. A mattress upholstered in black velvet practically covered the entire floor. There wasn't a single piece of furniture. Located at the back of the room was a column one meter high crowned with a sort of large tray. On it Ball of Flesh was comfortably installed. He had neither arms nor legs. The effect of his obesity was to join his thorax and abdomen, forming a sort of ball, enlarged one might say by his head, which was sunken into his chest to such an extent that it seemed to form part of this ball.

"Good evening, Ball!" Powlavski boomed.

"Welcome, my dear Powlavski!" Ball said, his eyes bathed in tears, while a servant dried his eyes with a silk handkerchief. "Welcome. I am very, very moved..."

His tears prevented him from continuing, and deep sobs gushed from the hollow that served as his mouth. Powlavski took advantage of his crying jag to walk over to Ball, still followed by René. Pulling out his handkerchief and feigning to be crying as well, he said to Ball in a faltering voice:

"What strong emotions tonight, Ball!"

"Very strong, dear Powlavski! You can't imagine anything like him. I have him in the next room, recovering from the session. I swear he's added at least twenty years to my life."

"What are you saying, Ball?" Powlavski exclaimed, overjoyed. "Incredible! But tell me of the wonders you work."

"Oh!" Ball cried, and shook so violently that if the servant hadn't had his eyes peeled, he would have fallen off the mattress. "Oh, Powlavski! First I'll tell you that he possesses the most perfect arms and legs in the world."

He breathed deeply, as if he were out of breath. Once again he had a crying jag, so spectacular this time that the servant gave him a green liquid to drink while another servant dried the river of tears. Calm once again, he continued with great affectation:

"Powlavski, the most beautiful legs! Surpassing even his arms. You know how I adore legs. Oh, Powlavski, I'll never know what it's like to run away! So, as I was saying, his legs more than his arms. You know whether or not I've seen legs in my day; they've been brought to me from all corners of the earth. But never legs like those. And since you're my friend, you'll have the enormous honor of contemplating them. That's right: you alone. I've decided that in order to increase the worth of 'my legs,' I'm not going to allow anyone to see them."

Then he caught sight of René and, as if he had been bitten by a snake, began to shout hysterically:

"And that thing, what is that thing, get that thing out, I don't want that thing in my house. That thing frightens me, I don't want that thing looking at me, get that thing out!..."

And he said "that thing" so many times that with a violent bounce, he began rolling around on the mattress and there, in a flood of tears, he continued telling them to get that thing out of his house. Powlavski quickly dropped to the mattress and bringing his mouth to Ball's ear, said something to him. One of the servants was already taking René away when a high-pitched whine from Ball stopped him as he was leaving the chamber. At the same time, another servant was lifting Ball with loving care and setting him back on the tray, while a third servant hurried to give him a pink liquid which Ball drained languidly.

"You should have told me he was with you," he exclaimed in a faltering voice. "Any friend of yours is a friend of mine. Let's have a look! Let's have a look! Let me see your good taste, you old swine."

René had no choice but to bow before Ball. The latter examined the former with an expert eye. Powlavski closely followed Ball's gaze, trying to discover whether René awoke strong emotions in him, but Ball didn't move a muscle. There was an embarrassing silence which Powlavski finally broke:

"So, what do you think?"

"Hmm! I don't know what to tell you. One would have to see him as he was brought into this world. The measurements look right, but you know... you've got to see the flesh. One must see what his flesh is made of."

Powlavski looked at René as if begging him to strip naked. He could just as well have been looking at a corpse. Seeing how hesitant René was, he brought his mouth up to Ball's ear and whispered something to him. Ball told a servant who was fanning him:

"Bring on the Prince." And turning to Powlavski, he said: "That's what I've named him: the Prince."

In less than a minute he appeared, totally naked, a boy about fifteen years old. His face didn't reflect any great beauty, but his arms and legs were perfection incarnate. He stood insolently by the door casting brazen glances around the room. He was without a doubt a rogue of the worst sort. It was a miracle that his flesh, whole and fragrant, had not yet been marked by the knife.

Ball looked at him enthralled. Powlavski expressed his admiration, applauding furiously. He placed a smacking kiss on each of Ball's cheeks. Then Ball cried:

"Forward, my Prince!"

As if this cry were the initiation of an entire ceremony, a servant placed Ball at the center of the mattress. The Prince immediately began to march regally around to the sound of circus music. Ball's eyes followed him fervently as he marched, but unable to move freely, he fell face down on the mattress. The music came to an abrupt stop, the Prince stopped marching, and a servant was approaching him when Ball's voice sounded like the crack of a whip:

"Come here, Prince! Roll me around!"

Prince took a perfect leap like a greyhound and landed on the mattress at Ball's side. He grabbed him by the head and buttocks and began to slowly push him all around the room. The first bars of the joyful Blue Danube soon began to play. As the music grew more impetuous, Prince quickened Ball's speed, who shouted, cried, laughed, and loudly urged Prince on in his labor. One had to see how Ball rolled from one side to another at such an astonishing speed without falling off the edge of the mattress thanks to the Prince's skill, who in order to encourage himself, was shouting like a banshee and uttering filthy words. At that moment, Ball shouted:

"Spotlights!"

The lights were turned out and four powerful spotlights flooded the mattress with their luminous beams. Now Ball had stopped shouting and laughing and his body rolled silently like a star in the void. The music had also stopped, as had the Prince's shouting. All that could be heard was flesh brushing against the velvet mattress.

A voice shouted "Hup!" As if by magic, Prince froze. Ball lay lifeless at the edge of the mattress. The spotlights went out and the lights were turned back on.

Then a cry, as if from a newborn baby, was heard. Ball was actually wailing: a cry so pure, so forsaken that René was moved. Two servants, wrapping Ball up in a sheet, carried him away. Powlavski signaled to René to follow him to the room where they had just taken Ball. There the second act of the tragicomedy would take place. Appearing to obey, René followed him, but when they reached the bedroom door he let Powlavski go in first. He closed the door, turned on his heels, and looked for the way out. Within a few minutes he was in the street.

He was so impressed by what he had just witnessed that it seemed to him that rather than walking, people were rolling down the street.

The Battle for the Flesh

While René sorted gloves by color, his thoughts focus-
ed on the event that would take place that night. He was
actually about to take the final exam in stenography and
typing. At nine the typing test would be given and an
hour later the stenography test would take place.

He had studied with real diligence. He was certain he
would receive the highest grades. The fact is, he hadn't
allowed himself the slightest distraction. Aside from his
Sunday visits to the cemetery, he used every free minute
to practice. It had been five months since that ill-fated
day when his father's ex-double had made his appearance, five months of tranquillity, of true peace. And
judging from all appearances, it promised to be a lasting
peace. It wasn't the case that he wished to build up his
hopes, but looking dispassionately at the events that
had taken place since the death of Ramón, he had to
admit that they were like the last sparks of a huge fire.

Nothing could be more reasonable than for his father's double, having been at the service of his father for thirty years, to come and request a simple signature from his son. It was pointless to complicate these events and wonder whether the bosses of which the double spoke had sinister designs on him. Countering those thoughts was the fact of these five months of absolute peace. As for his encounter with Powlavski, it could be qualified as pure coincidence. True, he had bestowed it with a terrible gravity, it having occurred on the same day as Martín's visit, and furthermore, having stirred up old memories linked to his past pro-meat life. Finally, the spectacle (as he called it) of Ball of Flesh, despite having been painful, had caused him more than a few attacks of laughter: that mass of flesh with its whining voice and shameful nudity had its laughable aspect—laughter that became increasingly good-humored as René thought how he too had been that close to walking naked before the King of Meat.

He looked at the clock. It was quarter of seven. And what would happen if he feigned a sudden indisposition and left fifteen minutes early? This innocent subterfuge would give him a fifteen-minute breather—actually, half an hour: he never left at seven on the dot.

On the bus, he pulled out paper and pencil and despite the lurching of the vehicle, began to scribble out the stenographic characters. He was sure that as long as his nerves held up, he would pass the exam with flying colors. If he took one of the three top places, he would go to work in the office of the glove shop (so the manager had promised him) with earnings far superior to what he was bringing in working in the warehouse. Then he would leave his room and rent an apartment in the outskirts of the city. All right, he told himself, let's not indulge in such pleasant daydreams. First the exam.

He raced up the stairs. He glanced at the books and notebooks he had left on the table. They lay open, as if someone had amused themselves hastily leafing through them. The superintendent was undoubtedly the one responsible for such a mess. He had already warned her she was not at liberty to poke around in his belongings. He bent over the books and noticed that his typing manual had been leafed through so precipitously that two pages had been torn out. This upset him and he left the room in search of the superintendent.

He found her reclining comfortably in an armchair, petting Monino, her favorite of the band of fifteen cats that was the terror of the boarders.

"Could you explain, Mrs. Juana," René said, trying not to fly off the handle, "why my books are all in disarray and the pages of one of my manuals have been torn out?"

"So I'm the one you ask!" Juana cried. "You come ask me about your damned books."

"All right, Mrs. Juana," René said in a conciliatory tone of voice, "there's no need to make a fuss about it... I'm not blaming you, but since you're the superintendent..."

"Of course I'm the superintendent! And what do you want to make of it? Ah ha! So the superintendent has to know everything that goes on. Well I'm going to refresh your memory. You know who made a mess of your musty old books? You did, young man. You did."

"I made a mess of them?" René said in complete astonishment. "But when, Mrs. Juana? I just got back from work."

"You don't say!" she exploded. "This is one hard nut to crack. He says he just got back from work, this guy who, for more than an hour, was shut up in his room turning things upside down like a madman."

"I truly don't understand..." René said. "I swear I just got back from work."

Judging it useless to hold a discussion with this woman, and to put an end to such a silly argument, he added:

"Fine. It doesn't matter."

"Yes it does. Quite a lot," the superintendent shouted. "I'm not going to let anyone call me a liar."

And then, as if in the back of her mind she had found the devastating proof of her claim, she shouted at the top of her lungs:

"And how do you explain the cup of coffee that I served you? Huh? How do you explain that?"

"Coffee?..." exclaimed René, and he started to feel ill. "I couldn't have asked you for coffee since I wasn't here at the time."

"Well you did ask me for it! And it struck me as pretty odd. You know very well we don't offer coffee to our boarders."

"I swear..." René said, but Juana prevented him from continuing.

"You arrived at six. You rang the doorbell. I opened the door for you. You told me you had forgotten your key. You went into your room. And a short while later, you asked me for the cup of coffee."

"Could it be?" René said, talking to himself. "Could it be?"

And he thought that if she claimed it was so, it had to be true: she lacked the imagination to make up something like that.

"It's the god-honest truth," said the superintendent. "You want to know something else? As you left, you told me you were going to eat in the street."

René was about to tell her that the bit about eating in the street was an out-and-out lie, but he judged it pointless to contradict her. Better to acquiesce: to take what she was claiming as given and try to knock the rest of that nightmare out of her hollow head.

"So I told you I would eat in the street."

"Of course that's what you told me. Just because you regretted your decision afterwards and now want to eat at home is no reason why you have to fabricate all these lies."

René considered the discussion over. He bowed his head and walked back to his room, but the superintendent, far from letting the matter drop, followed him. Entering the room before René, she let out a triumphant cry. She had run to the night table and grabbed a cup. Lifting it up as if it were the consecrated Host, she showed it to him.

"Now what's your explanation?" she shouted, laughing so hard she was about to burst. "Now what's your explanation? This is the cup."

She was silent for several seconds and then, going over to René, whispered to him:

"Could it be that you're losing your memory, or something even worse?..." With her hand, she made a gesture pregnant with meaning.

It was enough to drive a person crazy. That thing called nonsense, foolishness, absurdity, confusion was starting to take possession of his mind. A simple cup abruptly turned into a *corpus delicti*, an offensive weapon, a dangerous animal... The superintendent was no longer her usual dumb self, but a Nemesis, the head of Medusa, Blind Justice. And he, what was he now? Why the victim, the cornered animal, one of the Innocent Saints... He could almost picture the beheading. He wasn't looking for melodrama, the *grand-guignol*, but that cup..., the superintendent... that Mane, Tecel, Phares on the wall of a boarding house room... It was ridiculous, laughable, he had no empire to lose. But yes, he did have one, didn't he? Why of course: he would lose his reign over a place called the tranquillity of the spirit, the soul at rest. No, the superintendent had not been scheming; she spoke the gospel truth, the pure, shining truth, and nothing but: you asked me for a cup of coffee and there it is, right before your eyes. I didn't invent it... So, he was back to the flesh, for that's what it's all about. The superintendent had no reason whatsoever to be plotting against him, but perhaps she too was engaged in the battle for the flesh and was one of its agents provocateurs. So what difference did it make whether it was she or someone else? The fact was that the battle had begun anew. Help! Rescue! But ask help of whom? Whom?

But it was written that he would have neither savior nor salvation. As if to clear his head, he opened a window facing the street and stuck his head out. He let his gaze wander over the spectacle of the street. Suddenly he leaned halfway out the window. The superintendent rushed over to the window. Something strange was undoubtedly happening and she didn't want to miss it. But René didn't give her time. Suddenly leaping backwards, he closed the window with a bang and drew the shades closed. The superintendent left the room in a fury, cursing and swearing that René was crazy as a loon. Outside the door were the two old maids of the boarding house engaged in the "noble" and millenary business of espionage, their ears pressed against the door so that Juana's abrupt exit nearly threw them to the floor. But they quickly overcame their surprise and throwing themselves at her, asked her thousands of questions concerning the grave occurrences which in their judgment were taking place in the room of "the Silent One," as they called René.

But the questions remained unanswered. René burst from his room like a vortex and, like a ship passing within a hair's breadth of another ship, passed within a hair's breadth of the three women, clearing the stairs in a leap and a bound. Now in the street, the vortex deflated. René leaned against a tree, empty and limp, without the energy to take another step. He had just begun yet another station of his pro-meat *via crucis*. No, the superintendent wasn't crazy. When he stuck his head out the window and saw "that thing," he was convinced that the flesh—as he had believed—had not forgotten him; that on the contrary, it was returning with renewed determination to brutalize his own flesh.

He looked toward the corner. *That thing* was still standing in the same spot and was staring at him. *That thing* was really alive, was made of flesh and blood and was not—as in a dream—about to vanish. *That thing* was here to stay. He looked away, but *that thing* changed its position and like two revolvers, aimed its eyes at René's as it began to walk, inviting him to follow. He would be a fool not to obey, for he would once again have it standing guard on the corner or displaying its audacity by entering his room. Then the scandal would blow up like a bomb. He began walking toward *that thing*, which instead of stopping, quickened its pace, constantly sticking its head into bars as if looking for one that would suit its purpose.

They walked ten blocks this way. A red light allowed René to catch up to the object of his desperation. He told him he was on the verge of collapse, but the man, as if he hadn't heard, didn't answer. The green light signaled for the pedestrians to cross. The man quickened his pace, turned into a passageway, and passing several deserted streets, entered a tailor shop.

He told the clerk that he wished to see several styles to decide whether he and his brother would order some suits. René listened to this with great astonishment and was about to protest when the man, pointing to a full-length mirror, signaled for René to follow him. Standing in front of the mirror, he said:

"We're identical. This is my final test. We're as alike as two peas in a pod."

He stared at René and added:

"Now they can't deny me the job."

"What job?"

But the man, leaving René in mid-sentence, went to meet the clerk who was bringing out two catalogues. He leafed through them with great self-assurance and indicated to René a style that was to his liking. The clerk asked them if they were twins. The man said they were and that they were considered identical. Then he shut the catalogue and considering the consultation over, thanked the clerk.

Once in the street, he told René (now mimicking his voice) that they both deserved a drink. René, hearing this voice that reminded him of his own, took a step backwards, but the man, taking him by the arm, made him enter a bar.

They sat down at a table. The man ordered drinks, put a record on the jukebox, and said:

"You know, I like to do everything with music. It's more inspirational."

Then he assumed a serious tone of voice:

"And now I must apologize for all of this..."

"Apologize?..." René muttered with a trace of bitterness.

"Yes, apologize," the man repeated, smacking his lips after taking a swig. "First of all, I owe you an explanation. I like to act properly at all times. Secondly, since you're my superior, I ought to show you respect. Thirdly, because I hope you will be considerate towards me in the work we have ahead of us."

"Work, you say?" René exclaimed. "You presume we have something to do together?"

"Not something: a lot," the man emphasized, lighting his cigarette with affectation. "I don't know what we're going to do, but I presume they wouldn't be paying me a salary to do nothing at all."

"Listen," René said abruptly. "And listen good: I have nothing whatsoever to do with you."

"Uh huh," the man said, sipping his drink noisily, "I have no doubt about it. I don't doubt in the least that you have nothing to do with me, but the fact is that I do have something to do with you."

He sat there staring in fascination at the drink.

"That's enough!" shouted René.

"Please, don't make a scene," the man whispered. "No scenes. Look, I'm as young as you are and I take things philosophically."

"You may," René said with regret. "You may: you don't have anything to lose. But I... Do you know that my very future is hanging in the balance?"

"I don't know about your future," the man replied, "so I can't say whether it is or isn't hanging in the balance. As for your statement that I have nothing to lose, you are totally mistaken. In fact, I could even lose my life. Yes, my life. But I could care less; as long as the money's flowing. Hah!" the man spat. "What good is this flesh to me if I can't feed it, if I can't give it the pleasure it deserves?"

"And you say you're my same age?..." René murmured.

"Twenty-one going on twenty-two."

"All right," René said, resting his elbows on the table. "We've talked about everything except what we have to talk about. Don't you think?"

"You've got something there," the man said. "Except that this preamble had to come first. Now let's get to the heart of the matter."

"Yes, to the heart of the matter. I'm not going to forfeit my exam tonight because you'd like to keep me sitting here like a fool."

"Well said. That's the way to talk. But listen—and I don't mean to meddle in your affairs, but if I were you, I'd abandon your plans to take the exam."

"What! Give up several months' work? Do you know what you're saying?"

"Since it won't be of any use to you in your new life..."

"I don't understand you," René said, horror-stricken.

"Well, I don't know all that much about what awaits you in your new life, but to judge by the exercises I've been put through for six months, I imagine your new life isn't going to have anything to do with exams or schools."

"Could it possibly be?" René exclaimed exasperated.

"Possibly, no. Certainly," the man answered dryly. "But let's not get of the track. Allow me to ask you something: you speak of an exam. Could you tell me what subject it concerns?"

"Typing and stenography," René said excitedly. "If I do well—"

"That's enough!" the man said, cutting him off. "Well, it hasn't exactly been typing and stenography that I've been studying for these past six months."

"What then?..." and René shook him by his jacket sleeves. "Are you going to tell me?"

"Better I tell you the whole story," the man said energetically. "Yes, I think that would be best. All right," he sighed. "I was bored stiff in my neighborhood. That's right, brother: bored... With twenty years under my belt, I was having trouble buying cigarettes, not to mention

women. Sometimes I would spend three months scroung-
ing up one peso to go to bed with a woman. Misery on top
of misery. To make matters worse, I don't like hard
labor. I got a job in a tannery, but the acid was destroy-
ing my hands. I quit after a month and went back to
living on the dole. I was down to my last centavo when
one fine day I met a man—"

"A man..." René interrupted. "What was he like?"

"Nothing special. Up to forty, they're men; after forty,
they're old men. So, the man went into a café where I
was shooting pool. He waited a good half hour. When
he saw me leave, he followed. At the corner he asked me
for the time and we started to talk. He asked me if I
wanted to work as the double of a movie star. I told him
I'd love to if they paid. He said they paid very well. My
eyes lit up. He told me I looked a lot like a well-known
movie star who was in need of a double for dangerous
scenes. He added that with a few touch-ups and some
work on my part, we could complete the resemblance.
I told him it was a deal. He gave me an address and the
next morning I went to his house."

"Does the man by any chance live in the neighborhood to the west of the city?" René exclaimed, recalling
the house where they cremated his father.

"No, he lived right in the center, on the fortieth floor:
a penthouse. Oh!—" and his eyes shone. "The drinks
and the food! Brother, you'd have to have seen it. When
I arrived, he was waiting for me with someone else, an
old man who greeted me in a friendly fashion and told
me that the man had spoken very highly of me."

"That's incredible," said René.

"It might sound incredible, but it's just the way I'm
telling you. The old man pulled out a photograph of
you and showed it to me. I swear I thought it was a photo
of me. I asked him how he'd gotten hold of it. The two

of them began to laugh and agreed that things were off to an excellent start. Then he added that I was hired and that I could live there. The man opened a door and showed me a luxurious room, telling me that he hoped it was to my liking. How could it not be! 'We're eating dinner right away,' the old man told me, 'but before we do, let's complete the first test.' 'Fine with me,' I said. 'At your service.' Then the man, who had disappeared, returned to the hall and told the old man everything was ready. 'Then let's get down to work,' said the old man. 'Let's see how he handles himself.' 'I'll handle myself like a man,' I said. We entered another hall. There was a guy tied up, another old man (though this one really was old) with a goatee. The old man who lived there placed a pistol in my hands and told me that the scene consisted in me—as the movie star's double—having to shoot the Evil One, and he indicated the old man who was tied up. 'All right, I'll do it. But I don't see the danger. The old man's tied up. What harm can he do me?' 'In fact,' the beardless old man said, 'there isn't the slightest danger, but it so happens that the star doesn't like to do this scene; the star prefers romance...' Then the old man with the beard, whose muzzle the old man without a beard had just removed, said to me: 'Listen, young man, this is an assassination. That pistol is loaded and they want you to shoot at my flesh. I know there's no salvation for me, but I'm dying for the Cause.' 'That's what the Evil One says,' said the old man. 'That's his scene. Now he'll repeat it. When he's finished, you press the barrel against his heart and fire.' 'It's a lie! It's a dirty lie!' the old man with the beard said. 'They want to murder me!' As the old man with the beard was speaking, the old man without a beard was bringing my hand up to other man's heart, and when the former finished speaking, he told me: 'Now fire at the Evil

One.' I pulled the trigger and the poor old man writhed in his bonds. Blood trickled from his mouth, his head fell against his chest. Imagine: he was really dead."

"Dead..." mumbled René.

"It's just as I'm telling you. The old man said to me: 'How strange! The pistol was loaded. But no matter. The main thing is that you've learned your part. Now let's go have dinner.' I said to him: 'Well, if the main thing is the scene, there's nothing left to discuss.' He said: 'You'll be an excellent double.' 'I think so,' I said. 'I like it.' And we ate dinner."

René felt so ill he had to hold on to the edge of the table. Meanwhile, the man had abruptly left off telling his story and was swatting flies with the majesty of a lion. At that point the waiter came over and asked if he was going to want anything else; the man told him no, asked for the check, paid, and brusquely shook René who seemed hypnotized. He adjusted the knot of his tie, smoothed back his hair, and said:

"Let's get out of here. There are too many flies."

René followed him like a robot. They walked toward the center of the city. They actually had not strayed very far from the street where René lived, but they had a few blocks to walk. The man hailed a taxi and soon they were in the center. They went into a high-class cafeteria. It was eight in the evening.

"I'll recount the second scene here," the man said, climbing the stairs. "Furthermore, I'm hungry; further-more there aren't any flies; furthermore we're closer..."

"Closer?..." inquired René, dropping into a chair.

"Closer. I have to appear in person at the old man's house at nine. There's time enough for everything, brother. Are you going to eat dinner or not? I'm famish-ed. While we eat, I'll tell you the second scene."

"I'm not going to listen to anymore scenes," René said. "I'm leaving. If you try to stop me, I'll call the authorities to intervene."

"Ha ha," the man responded. "So, the authorities... All right, I'll call them myself."

He told the waiter to find a police officer.

"Let's not waste any time. Would you tell me what your complaint is going to be?"

"If you don't let me leave, I'm going to tell the police everything you've just told me."

"Fine, fine, we'll waste some more time, but if that's what you want to do, go right ahead."

He began to drum his fingers on the table. Seeing him so serene, René became horribly afraid. He was about to tell him he'd listen to his account of the second scene when he saw the waiter approaching, accompanied by a police officer.

"Come right over here, sir. Have a seat," the man exclaimed jovially. "This gentleman—" and he indicated René, "—wishes to make a deposition."

"No, no!" said René, excusing himself. "I have no deposition to make."

"What?" said the policeman. "The waiter called me."

"He's a bit nervous, sir, that's all," the man said. "But I'll tell you. He's a movie star and I'm his double. We make crime movies. We kill people. You follow? The other day, I killed an old man. Not him: he doesn't like to kill. That's why he has me: I do like to kill. Furthermore, they pay me well; furthermore, I don't have to swat flies; furthermore, it comes from down here..." and he made an obscene gesture with his hand.

The policeman began to laugh. Between fits of laughter, he told René that if it was merely a matter of killing, that it was perfectly legal and that he perfectly understood that they were working in the meat business. He bowed, thanked the man for having offered him a cigarette, and left, commenting to the waiter on what a nice bunch of boys they were.

"All right," the man exclaimed. "You see now that resorting to the police is a dead end. We're working in a legal business that pays its taxes to the treasury and that provides the public with moments of diversion. That said, we'll move on to my account of the second scene."

"Nevertheless, I'd like to leave," René said looking the same as when he had stared horror-stricken at Powlavski.

"Now you'll see," the man said, ignoring his appeal. "The next day the old man told me the scene involved me (now playing the role of the guy being cornered) fleeing from one ambush, falling into another, and losing my life. 'Shit,' I said to myself, 'if I lose my life, that's the end.' But, at the same time I was thinking that they wouldn't have hired me just to murder me. I was also thinking that what happened to the old man with the beard could happen to me. 'Yes,' I said to myself, 'but I can't refuse to do the scene.' We went to a larger hall than the previous one. When we got there, the old man told me I would have to sprint across the room with my face contorted as if I were near death; that once I'd made it to the other side of the hall, I should lean panting against the wall. That's what I did. You should have seen the mad dash I made and how I pressed myself against the wall with my tongue hanging out. Then two guys entered the room armed with pistols and fired at me point-blank. I told myself: 'I'm dead.' I looked at myself: no blood was coming out. Then, from the other side of the hall, I heard the old man applauding. Brother, I was alive!"

René looked around and had the strong impression that the people filling the cafeteria (the two of them included) were corpses. The drapery was black, the tables were tombs, and their marble tops were gravestones. Involuntarily, he mumbled:

"There's no escape."

And closed his eyes.

The man jostled him.

"Wake up, brother. I'm not finished yet. The best part's yet to come."

"The worst part..." René said in a faint voice.

"No, the best part. Listen: you must be a big movie star. I'll tell you why. After two days of living in the old man's house, I met his double and the double of the other man. They're the only ones who have them. I guess that if you have me as your double, it's because you're very important. What do you think of that?"

"Nothing," René replied inaudibly. "But if you're not pulling my leg, I ought to set you straight. I'm no movie star. I've never appeared on the big screen, nor..."

He was interrupted by the man's noisy laughter. He was acting so theatrically that he finally knocked over a bowl of salad that the waiter had just placed on the table.

"Of course I know that! I know perfectly well you're no movie star. I've told you what they had me believe at first, but later the old man told me you're the leader of the Cause and that I had to cover you at all times."

"That's what he told you!"

"That's right..." the man said, trying to remember verbatim his conversation with the old man. "He told me that only with my death would I lose my job as a double."

"Or mine," René replied impetuously, remembering Martín's story.

"Hey! How did you know?" the man said in surprise.

"I assumed as much," René said evasively.

"Don't assume. Listen to the real story. The old man told me: 'You would also lose your job if they assassinate him.' And you know what else he told me. Why, he told me that if they liquidate me, they would immediately have another double in place."

"There's no escape," René mumbled again.

"Escape or not, brother, one has to go on living. Now let's eat. I'm starved."

He set about devouring everything on the table. René took advantage of his gluttony to slip from his seat, making it to the lobby. It was eight-thirty at night. If he managed to calm his shattered nerves, he would still have time to get to his house, change, and take the exam. Whether or not he passed the test with flying colors wasn't as important to him now as showing those implacable bosses that he could oppose the plans they had made for him. Anyone had brains enough to sit in front of a typewriter and complete an exercise requiring physical and mental aptitude. He now knew that the die was cast, but those men were not going to have their way. Standing on the sidewalk, he thought about how he could escape from their clutches. Suddenly, he remembered the gravedigger's offer and decided to run to the cemetery and shut himself up there for the rest of his life. He was on the verge of going to look for a bus when the man stepped in front of him, his face all flushed.

"Hey, brother! You have a pretty strange way of saying goodbye. Not even a handshake. And me, carrying this thing around in my pocket..." and he shook a piece of paper in René's face.

"What's that?" René asked, though he knew full well that the man was showing him a folded piece of paper.

"Can't you see?" the man replied. "A slip of paper they gave me to give to you. A slip of paper the old man gave me."

"Tell the old man I do not accept messages from strangers."

"Strangers?... Why, he knows you very well. It doesn't matter. I'll pass on the message. In any case..."

And with a quick movement, he stuffed the piece of paper in one of René's jacket pockets, said goodbye, and running off, disappeared into the crowd.

As if he feared someone was going to pull the piece of paper from his pocket, René pushed it to the bottom. That terrible piece of paper—in addition to reminding him of the two previous ones—made him feel as if he were carrying a hand grenade, his life in imminent danger. His desperation was so great that he was that close to throwing himself under the wheels of a passing car. For the third time they had placed a piece of paper in his hands, and for the third time he had this thought: his father was sending him these lethal messages from the depths of the grave. And if at this very instant, without stopping to think of the consequences, he were to pull the piece of paper from his pocket and rip it into a thousand pieces? In that case, the message it contained would be moot. At the same time, he imagined thousands of other slips of paper like this one waiting their turn to go out in search of him. No matter where he sought refuge, one of those slips of paper would find him and he would be obliged to discover its contents. He decided not to tear it up, but also not to read it until after the exam. He was going to take the exam on a whim. He was accepting adversity but rebelling against it (pardon the paradox), pretending to be unaware of it. The hour remaining before he took the exam, the hour of the exam itself was a period of time not included in that adversity. For that margin of time, he wouldn't be caught in their clutches. Like a person standing on the deck of a boat about to vanish under the waves, he had a few minutes left to "continue living" the enchanting ocean liner life.

He went into his room. The superintendent followed him all the way, reproaching him and telling him to go look for another place to live because she didn't like to have mental patients in her boarding house; that because of his abnormal conduct, one of her friends had suffered a fainting spell. René apologized as best he could and slammed the door in her face. He showered, dressed quickly, and within a few minutes was on the street. He checked his pockets. Yes, there was the slip of paper. But at the same time it "wasn't there" in his pocket. It would only "be there" after the exam.

When he arrived at the school where the exam would be given, he was cheerfully received by his classmates. They even went so far as to give him an ovation. He wasn't the most outstanding student in that class for nothing. Someone suggested that after the exam they go to a bar to celebrate the occasion and more importantly, to pay tribute to René for being a typist and stenographer *par excellence.*

A loud bell announced that the exam was about to begin. That whole noisy world entered the classroom. Despite the display of affection, despite the fact that he couldn't have found himself in a place farther from the battle for the flesh, that was all René could think about. He must have had a very distressed look on his face, for one of the girls asked him if he was feeling sick. René didn't have time to respond: the professor was already dictating the topics of the exam.

The topics presented no difficulty for René. They were all a piece of cake and he could even expound upon them in less than the time allotted. Nevertheless, he felt a tremendous lack of motivation, as if it would be totally useless to complete the exam. That piece of paper sleeping at the bottom of his pocket radically excluded him from the world of normality. Why take the test when other people had already planned his life? While his classmates were furiously writing away, René, pencil in hand, didn't dare begin. Furthermore, he thought that instead of answering the questions, he would, in stenographic code, write down the infamous account related to him by that man. He spent ten minutes on the brink of death until the professor, realizing he was sitting there without writing, came over to find out why. René told him he was thinking. Then right away, he began writing at a rapid pace. Now everything seemed to be running like clockwork, but only for a few minutes. Again he lifted his pencil, pushed the sheet of paper away, got up, and staggered over to the professor's desk. A brief conversation took place in hushed voices. The professor shook his head as if to express deep regret. René shook his hand and left the exam room.

Back on the street, he pulled the slip of paper out of his pocket. They told him "they" were "ready," that they were "awaiting" his call "around the clock," and they gave him a telephone number.

He ran in search of a phone. He wanted to know if this was all a bad joke or whether they actually were waiting for him around the clock. He dialed the number and in a tremulous voice said his name. A nasal voice responded with profuse attentiveness and told him that "they" had been sure he wouldn't fail them. The nasal voice added that if he would be so kind, that he should pass by the Headquarters (here he gave him an address) that very night; that from that moment on they would be waiting for him with great impatience. He was very disconcerted when the nasal voice announced the conversation to be over. René hung up. He repeated the address to himself over and over again. He was so disturbed that he didn't see the building was right in front of his nose. In fact, the imposing bulk of a skyscraper with all of its windows lit up resembled a superhuman lighthouse signaling to him the way of the flesh. René studied it and said to himself that architecture of that size usually goes hand in hand with equally horrible terrors and agonies, like those awaiting him on the other side of those cyclopean walls.

Now almost at the entrance of the building, he looked around. He expected to see the man. No one was there. It was ten at night and he remembered the man had told him his date with the old man was at nine.

So he would have to show up alone, although it made no difference as he was already known at the Headquarters. Realizing this made his blood boil. He was about to turn around and direct his footsteps to the cemetery. But on further reflection, it was worth setting things straight once and for all with those big shots. He firmly resolved to maintain his composure and not contradict his executioners.

He was engaged in such strategies and reflections when the doorman told him that they were waiting for him upstairs, that the gentleman had told him someone was coming up, and since René was in fact waiting for the elevator, that he must be the person in question. René entered the elevator. It was one of the express elevators in the skyscraper. He felt the velocity make the blood pound in his head, producing a suction effect in his body. So, do the people up there require their visitors to arrive without a drop of blood in their veins? The red light at last indicated the fortieth floor.

Hardly had he stepped out of the elevator when someone who had been waiting for him took him by the arm and pointed him to a door located at the end of the hall. A man was standing there, who, as soon as he caught sight of René, hurried over to greet him.

He led René to a vast hall and told him to wait there for a moment. He didn't have to wait for long. Hardly had he set eyes on a magnificent tapestry depicting a bold scene from the world of mythology when an old man appeared, corresponding in every detail to the "old man" described to him by the double. René took a step back and even went so far as to bow, but to his great surprise, the old man responded with an even deeper bow. René was about to answer with another bow, when the old man, humbling himself even further, said in a tone of profound respect:

"Welcome, chief!"

"Chief?..." René exclaimed, with complete astonishment. "What chief are you referring to?"

"You are the chief," the old man explained to him, still in the same respectful tone of voice and maintaining a convenient distance. "Your father passed on to you the torch of the holy Cause of chocolate. For that reason we have been waiting for you around the clock."

He paused and then, as if after deep reflection, added:

"Chief, the moment has arrived to take the field."

"The field..." René repeated, involuntarily taking a step backwards.

"Precisely," the old man concurred, bowing down again. "The Cause awaits our flesh—tender, passionate, and juicy. You herald glorious days. The time has come to send it running through hills and dales."

"Send it running?" René cried out, approaching the old man until their faces were practically touching. "Did you say running?"

"Through hills and dales..." the old man reiterated, bowing so low as to nearly stick his face into René's shoes. He added solemnly:

"At the moment, the Cause is in flight. At the moment, your role is that of retreat. Of course, always inflicting damage on the enemy. From your father's reports, we know that he explained to you in exhaustive detail the vicissitudes of the Cause and its present state. So there is no need for further explanations. But I certainly must make it clear to you that for us the order of the day is flight. We are the great pursued waiting to become the great pursuers. When that takes place, we will hand over to those presently hunting us the complete norms and precepts of the pursued. They in turn will place in our hands the entire archives of the hunter, and the battle for the flesh will continue without cease, forever and ever. The battle for the flesh is eternal. Those simple of spirit believe we are defending chocolate. Leave them to their foolish faith. To you—a chief—I will admit the truth. At the bottom of all this is not chocolate. The flesh itself is on the line. So then, how does one lose it? That's where the precious service of chocolate comes in. Never can such an odorous infusion be praised highly enough. Chocolate looks at the flesh with an imploring gaze, eyes bathed in tears, and says: 'I'm in mortal danger. Save me. My enemies hound me. Don't forget that if you save me, I will offer you what you most desire in this life: your own perdition. I know you long to be a target for bullets and knives.' And with a chocolatey smile, it leaps and shields itself behind the flesh, which is cut down in its prime a moment later by the pursuers."

"That's amazing," mumbled René, looking at the walls as if they were made of chocolate and had begun to implore him.

"Amazing," emphasized the old man, bowing constantly. "Truly astounding. But there is something even more astonishing: every time chocolate goes to shield itself in the flesh of the pursued, the pursuers tremble, waiting to see whether it will reject the chocolate. Then they would have no other choice but to take shelter in the flesh of the pursued. They would *ipso facto* become the pursued, cut down by the thousands."

"And if the flesh...?" René asked, not daring to complete the thought.

"I know what you wish to ask. If the flesh refuses to run, the chocolate is there to put it in check. Don't you see that chocolate and chocolate alone is what keeps it on course? It seems absurd at first glance that something we couldn't care less about forces us to run through hills and dales until one day we fall, shot full of lead or run through with knives, but think how absurd it would be if the flesh, for no reason at all, began to run all by itself through hills and dales. Oh!" he cried out in ecstasy, jumping up and down twice. "Chocolate is a powerful stimulant!"

Immediately, as if he had been caught with his pants down, he blushed deeply and bowed once again.

"I still get ecstatic. At my age! I could spend the rest of my days speaking of the flesh without tiring. A great sorrow gnaws at my heart: perhaps my flesh won't perish on the run. I'm a second-level chief. I could be forgotten."

"By whom?" inquired René.

"By the teeth..." he said melancholically. "Forgotten by the teeth."

He looked at René with noble jealousy and humbling himself again to the floor, mumbled:

"You, on the other hand!... You have a nearly one hundred percent probability of perishing on the run."

"Me?" René cried, burning with curiosity.

"Yes, you," the old man confirmed with unspeakable joy. "Imagine that even now the teeth are approaching your flesh, that the distance is shortening, that you, without violating the norms and precepts of flight, are losing ground, and that in the end you fall to the sharpened fangs, just like your father. Oh, what a beautiful day! How beautiful! How beautiful!"

"You said something about norms and precepts," René noted, thinking he had found a saving loophole.

"That's right," explained the old man. "All flesh, while desiring to be ripped to pieces, must defend its ground tooth and nail."

"To what point, sir?" René yelled, beside himself.

"Ah! There's the hitch. To what point... Why, until there isn't an inch of ground on which to stand. I believe your father told you how, with the passage of years, the ground was slipping out from under him. You yourself participated in those exoduses. Don't you remember the night we left the coast of Europe for the coast of America?"

"We left?..." and René looked at the old man, trying to recognize him.

"Yes, we left... I was the chauffeur who brought you to the airport. But let's put aside these worthless memories. Getting back to what you were asking me: the Cause orders one to run until an insurmountable obstacle obliges the flesh to abandon the race."

"And then?..." René asked longingly.

"Then the flesh sings its swan song. It's the moment of truth."

"I see," and René let out a sigh. "But tell me: Don't you take justice into account?"

"There's no such thing as justice, chief. There is only flesh," the old man concluded. "To go beyond the bounds of the flesh is to fall into a conceptual vacuum and amphibology. Don't build up your hopes. All that exists is the collision of flesh against flesh."

Shaking his head, the old man looked at his watch. With great regret, he begged René's leave. He had to go, as various carnal duties awaited him. He said that if it was all right with René, he would arrange to meet him the following day for the purpose of coming to an agreement, along with his double, concerning an operation of great importance which they had planned. Finally, he said that if René wished, he could install himself in the bedrooms reserved for him in the Headquarters.

"Not right now," said René, thinking about burying himself in the cemetery. "I have a few business matters to take care of, but I'll be here first thing tomorrow."

"It's been a pleasure," the old man responded. "We'll continue waiting for you around the clock."

He took a deep bow and accompanied René to the elevator. He stretched out his limp hand and as he shook hands with René, he stood there contemplating the magnificent flesh tone of the youthful chief of the Cause in fascination. Then, with tremendous bitterness, he stammered:

"Tender, passionate, juicy... Through hills and dales. Tender, passionate, juicy."

Tender and Juicy

One fine day, René received the final confirmation that he was made of flesh. It took a full year and a series of diverse experiences that culminated on a memorable afternoon in the month of June.

After his dramatic meeting with the old man in the Headquarters of the Hounded Flesh, René had taken refuge in the cemetery. The old gravedigger, sticking to his word, took him as a gravedigger's assistant. He stuck a bucket of lime in René's hands and sent him to whiten empty graves, which after having been occupied for several years, would now be occupied by new corpses.

This work as a graveduster was made to order for René's flesh. He didn't have to deal with anything but bones. The diggers would pile them up and he would bring them to the large ossuary. It was far from the flesh, and what a feeling of security to contemplate those bones, knowing that no one on earth was interested in engaging them in the battle for the flesh.

But his cohabitation with his beloved bones lasted only a few days. One morning, he was whitening a grave with lime when he noticed a funeral procession was heading toward the spot where he was working. In fact, they were going to bury the body in a grave near the one he was whitening at that very moment. He barely had time to hide behind a mausoleum. To his astonishment, the five people comprising the procession turned out to be the old man and four strangers bearing the coffin on their shoulders.

At a sign from the old man they set the coffin on the ground. At that moment the gravedigger and two of his assistants arrived. The old man greeted the gravedigger and told him that he would make sure he received the death certificate of the deceased as well as the burial permit; that he didn't have time to attend the interment and so he was entrusting the gravedigger with the sad mission of seeing that the remains were given a good Christian burial. Then, approaching the coffin and staring up at the sky, he said sadly:

"René, may you rest in the peace of the Lord."

He gave the old gravedigger some money and left with his assistants.

As they walked off, the head gravedigger stared dumfounded at the bills the old man had placed in his hands. Not a single one of the hundreds of mourners who came to the cemetery had ever tipped him so lavishly. He looked around as if searching for something. Finally, he shouted:

"Hey, René! Where have you gotten to? Come here. This body brought us good luck."

René left the mausoleum and walked over to the gravedigger.

"Did you hear the dead man's name is the same as yours?"

René didn't respond: he was staring at the coffin as if he wished to look right through it and see the body inside. The old man shook him.

"Your head's in the clouds. Wake up. Look at what that gentleman gave me," and he waved the bills in René's face. "Come on, let's go celebrate this with a drink."

René excused himself, saying that he didn't like to drink in the morning. The old man said:

"Your loss. Let's go, boys."

Once they had left, René walked over to the coffin. He had to see the face of the dead man who bore his name. Could it be that the old man had seen him and to remind him of his estrangement from the Headquarters of the Hounded Flesh, had given the dead man his name? And come to think of it, who could it be? It never occurred to him that the body might be that of his double. He imagined a middle-aged or old man but not a young man like himself. In any case, he was determined to see its face. Though it might constitute desecration, he was going to open up the coffin. He was about to stick a crowbar between two boards in the lid when he saw that it was open, the nails tapped in only for show. He lifted the lid up and inside the coffin lay his double, dressed in the same suit as when they had met. It looked as if he had just been murdered. His suit was stained with blood.

René then ran like crazy to the Headquarters of the Hounded Flesh. The old man didn't seem to think anything of his dramatic reappearance. On the contrary, he responded very calmly to the questions René threw at him and at no time did he acknowledge himself to be in any kind of a bind. "All of this," he had told René, "is the normal reaction of startled flesh, but it's an awfully long way from that to deciding that the end of the world has come."

He added that there was no reason to make a mountain out of a molehill; that he had simply wished to give the mortal remains of his double a decent burial, having died honorably in the line of duty; that he had in no way whatsoever chosen that cemetery with the intention of frightening anyone; that he was completely unaware that René was employed as graveduster in that cemetery; that he had left because he had more important items of business to attend to; that, finally, the lid of the coffin had been left partially open out of pure carelessness.

René made some objections, but the old man finally dissected the facts with such overwhelming logic that he was left with no choice but to accept everything the old man said on face value. Was it that his logic was one of the tactical elements in the strategy of the battle for the flesh? That is, when the old man argued, did one have to accept as articles of faith what he said and how he said it? In a word, in a battle between truth and lies as colossal as this, there was no line of demarcation. Both were instruments that, depending on the situation, could be of service to the Cause.

That was why René decided to take a break from his job as graveduster and accept the new offer to live for several days at the Headquarters. With an eagle eye, the old man had read in his face René's decision to remain noncommittal with respect to the flesh, to determine whether it showed new signs of life or if, on the contrary, it would leave him in peace at last.

In the end, René was not so misguided in his decision. It made no sense to be accepting jobs, taking exams, managing the thousand and one trifling details of social life based on the whims of the flesh. Such actions could never be taken with any seriousness when they were interrupted at every turn by one of those carnal attacks. He was finding that out for the fourth or fifth time at this very moment. The gravedigger as well as the professor would think him mad as a loon.

Voluntarily cloistering himself away allowed him to see his situation clearly. He was made of flesh. Until then, he had never stopped to ponder such a crystal-clear truth. As he passed the days in isolation and in the silence of his room that truth was being revealed to him with unyielding force. So he admitted he was made of flesh and nothing but flesh. It wasn't that he accepted the dirty business of the Cause, but did he possess anything that wasn't flesh which he could use as a convincing argument against the people committed to having him lead the life of flesh? No. No matter how hard he scrutinized his body, he didn't come across anything that wasn't flesh. There wasn't the tiniest scrap of wood, stone, metal, or even straw anywhere in his body. He would stand for hours on end in front of the mirror contemplating his flesh from various angles. If he looked at it from head to toe in the hope of finding something that was not made of flesh, he was forced to look away in horror; if he moved his eyes from right to left: flesh and nothing but flesh, until his maddened gaze flung itself at any object whatsoever that might free it from such great monotony.

The only argument of any weight that he could muster for those who considered him supreme chief of the battle for the flesh would be precisely that there wasn't a trace of flesh in his body. How could he be so bold as to tell them he wasn't going to close ranks in that battle when his whole body, from head to toe, was made of flesh and nothing but flesh? It would be absurd if he were, say, made of straw, for these people to approach him to entrust him with the command of their forces. In that case there would have been more than enough reasons to convince them. But from his position, they were invincible. They didn't come to him with sophisms or figments of their imagination, with fairy tales or casuistic arguments. No: they said to him, plain and simple: "You're made of the same stuff as we are, we who are engaged in a colossal battle. For this reason we demand—yes, demand that you accept the command of our forces."

Nevertheless, he rebelled and appealed to daydreaming. He couldn't admit he had been defeated by such incontrovertible statements. So he imagined appearing before the old man swathed in dozens of suits, and saying to him: "Look, I'm made of cloth." But the old man would smile slyly and begin to strip him of his garments until at last he reached his flesh. With terror, René saw those scrawny hands poking around in the cloth until they reached his flesh. At other times, abandoning the cloth trick, he would appear totally naked, telling the old man in a booming voice that he and his partisans were made of wood, and consequently had no right to bother people made of flesh and blood. The sly old man would not say this is my mouth. He would strip naked, walk over, and press his flaccid flesh against René's own tender, juicy flesh.

So the days passed, with the complication that his provisional cloistering was becoming permanent. One afternoon as he was bemoaning his bad luck once again, someone knocked on the door. He opened the door. He saw a man in pajamas leaning against the doorjamb as if he were on the verge of collapse. He was nothing but skin and bones; his pajamas hung on his frame like a flag in the wind. René said to himself that he was looking at the thinnest man in the world. His bones were barely covered by a thin layer of flesh, his skin was cracked, wrinkled, and sunken into his skeleton. From the back of their sockets, his eyes stared greedily at René's tender flesh. Shortly, two large tears rolled down his cheeks.

"What can I do for you," René said, trying to control his nerves.

But the sad creature didn't utter a word in response, and a thick drool began to drip from his gaping mouth.

"Hey!" shouted René. "Are you feeling sick?"

The creature remained mute.

René led him carefully over to a chair and sat him down. The walking skeleton's forehead was bathed in beads of cold sweat and his teeth were chattering. His eyes were lost in painful dreams: they spun around crazily as if he were unable to bring them to rest on any given point. At last he said in a whisper:

"My God! So very, very much meat!"

"What did you say?" René shouted.

"I said you don't know what a treasure you possess."

"A treasure?" René exclaimed, looking all around.

"Yes, a treasure...a great and enormous treasure. You have meat in abundance, and of prime quality."

René told the man that his presence was disturbing him and would he be so kind as to leave at once; that he wasn't in the mood to have praises sung to his flesh.

"Excuse me," he muttered, "but when one doesn't have what one most longs for in this world..."

As if fearing the man would lunge at him, biting him ferociously, René backed away.

"Explain yourself," he shouted feverishly. "Explain yourself or I swear..."

"I don't have the energy," the man cried out, dragging himself after René. "I beg of you, let me touch your breast."

René was unable to prevent him from doing so. With a superhuman effort, the visitor pressed himself against

René's breast and frantically groped in his clothes in search of flesh. A strangled howl indicated that he had found it. At the same time, he fainted away at the emotion it caused him. René lay him down in his bed and revived him. The carcass felt his breast and even stuck out his tongue. René remembered the scene of the lickers at school. With great effort he freed himself.

"Please!" said the visitor. "Quick, give me something to eat!"

Without waiting for René to bring him food, he grabbed a piece of paper that was lying on the night table and greedily devoured it.

"What are you doing?" René cried out in total surprise. "Wait, I'm going to ask for a sandwich."

"I eat anything. Anything and at any hour. I can't stop eating."

"You want to fatten yourself up..." René observed in horror.

"Why, of course!" he said, as he brought another piece of paper to his mouth. "Sooner or later, these bones will be padded with flesh."

"I don't think that eating paper—"

"You're wrong. Everything is food, everything is transformed into flesh if you put it into the body."

Despite himself, René burst out laughing.

"I firmly believe it. It's just that the day hasn't arrived..."

"What day?"

"The day of my excursion out into the world. It's written that I will make just one excursion and it's written that I will lose my flesh on that excursion. When that glorious day arrives, I will be so fat I won't fit through that doorway," and with a majestic gesture he pointed to the doorway.

"It's written?" mumbled René.

"Written, written!" the man said vehemently. "I've been waiting for the final hour for twenty years now. The Cause can count on my flesh. I will sacrifice it all. I'm certain that four hundred pounds of flesh will land in its jaws."

René couldn't wait for this man to decide to leave. When at last he did, René would go to the old man to demand an explanation. Interpretations notwithstanding, one thing was sure: once again those bones had been able to bring up the problem of the flesh. There they lay like a provocation, like an invitation to strip himself of his own flesh, while at the same time expressing through the mouth of that carcass their burning, eternal desire to be padded with flesh.

"Don't think I only eat paper. I eat meat. They give me everything I ask for. I tell you I only take cat naps. I don't have enough time to eat all the meat they give me. They too wish the day would come..."

"Tell me something," René cried, going over to him, "How did you grow so extremely thin?"

"Ha, ha! Who cares? All that matters is the day..."

He leaped from the bed and headed for the door. René blocked his way. There was such a gleam of anxiety in his eyes that the carcass, possessed with terror, shrieked for dear life.

"Please! Be quiet!" René implored, desperately checking his pockets. He found a few mint lozenges.

"Here. It's a gift. In this way I'm contributing to the triumph of your flesh. But I beg of you, for God's sake: tell me what has turned you into a bag of bones."

"Ha, ha," the carcass repeated. "All that matters is the day..."

He began to hum "the day, the day..." and there was no power on earth capable of keeping him from this refrain. Not knowing what to do, and wishing to get an answer, René gave him several candies that were lying on the bureau. As he sucked on them, he repeated "the day, the day." Finally he stood by the door and signaled for René to approach. With a great air of mystery, he pressed his mouth to René's ear and said that if he really desired to be nothing but skin and bones, he would be perfectly disposed to devour all of René's flesh. Doing as he said, he bit René's ear. René cried out in pain, but judging it useless to fight with such detritus, he jumped to one side and closed the door.

Someone knocked again a few moments later. He was going to call a servant right this instant to come and throw the carcass out of his room. He opened the door, but this time it was the old man coming to ask him for his approval of the new double. Putting that matter aside, René plied him with thousands of questions about the strange visitor. The old man, forsaking his customary solemnity, began to laugh.

"He's a poor lunatic," he said. "We've had him lodged here for several years purely out of pity. All right, he's not a nobody. Not in the least. In his day, he was a strong candidate for the preeminent post in the Party. He's not from this country. He came here years ago to find among our men of science the cure for his mysterious malady that devours his flesh day by day. But it was all for naught. He could never have his baptism by fire. The fellow who held the post I now hold left a curious account concerning The Skeleton (as he called him). This account includes a discussion of The Skeleton's early days with the Cause. I'll get it for you if you're interested. From his father, an obscure chief in a village hidden among the mountain crags, he had received the right to have his flesh perish as befitted the chief he was as well. I believe I've mentioned to you that there are various hierarchies in this business of offering up one's flesh. The slaughtered flesh of a chief is not like that of a simple rank-and-file member. The chief's flesh being defended by one or more doubles (depending in turn on the preeminence of the chief), has limited chances of being slaughtered. Not so for the rank-and-file member, who at every step might sacrifice his or her flesh and in the manner he or she chooses. Imagine the fervor with which The Skeleton would have defended his rights at the moment his father sacrificed his life for the sake of the Cause. He was in line for the position of chief—not the top level, but a chief all the same. True, he didn't have the right to a double (although he was a chief, being a village chief, he could only dissimulate his face with make-up). But still, his flesh would have infinitely more enjoyment than the flesh of a simple member of the rank-and-file, and had a very high probability of coming to a bloody end. And I tell you, he defended his rights, for in the days I'm speaking of, the mysterious malady had already manifested itself. So the Party, without denying him his rights to the post of chief, decided to send him to the men of science to fatten him up as quickly as possible. Disgracefully, nothing could be done. With time, his mental faculties began to fade to the point we find him at today."

"But is it true that he eats meat at all hours of the day and night?"

"Quite true. He's been given *carte blanche* as far as that's concerned. We know it's futile, but we're unable to refuse such an innocent request. Furthermore..."

"What?..." René uttered. "Furthermore what?"

"What I mean to say is that maybe he'll start fattening up and then we could send him to his village."

"And did those men of science eventually discover the cause of his defleshing?"

"Unfortunately not. Had they succeeded, we would have a precedent for future cases. No. But in my humble layman's opinion..."

He abruptly cut himself off, as if implying that his opinion lacked any foundation. He walked toward the door. René barred his way. In an imploring voice, he said:

"Please, your opinion is of tremendous interest to me."

"All right. Though you take me for a fool, I'll tell you what I think. Our patient stripped himself of his flesh in advance. That is: he lived the martyrdom of his flesh in advance and as all can see, his fantasy played a nasty trick on him. I confess that it's in no way a scientific explanation, but on the other hand, it has the advantage of being eminently carnal."

And he began to laugh convulsively as René sank into the darkest cesspools of his mind. If the old man's singular explanation were true, if such a wild thesis could be accurate, then he too would be stripped of his flesh, would become nothing but a bag of bones. They would refer him to the doctors of the flesh. He would devour amazing quantities of meat at all hours of the day or night, and, in the end, would die in his bed far from the bullets and knives, far from the whimpering of the besieged chocolate. Totally useless as a shield.

"Wake up!" the old man cried, shaking him. "My explanation has hypnotized you."

René saw a mocking twinkle in the old man's eyes. He had acted like the father whose young child asks him for the moon and so, in order not to disillusion him, invents the most absurd story as he goes along. No, there was no escape for him, and none whatsoever for that madman stripped of his flesh who actually had the supreme advantage that no human power could restore the flesh he had lost. René's, on the other hand, was thriving more and more every day, and with the passage of every day he was becoming increasingly convinced of his carnality, of his absolute impotence to not be made of flesh.

With his conscience gnawing at him more than usual, he left one morning in search of a little diversion. His choice of locations was not very wise. He headed to none other than his old neighborhood. Something led him irresistibly to the park located a block from the house where he used to live. He wanted to "see himself" in it with Alicia and Ramón, cruel and implacable, but alive. He wanted to "see" Mrs. Pérez knocking on his door. He also wanted to "visit her" as he had on the occasion of that memorable soirée.

He sat on a bench and "saw" all he had intended to see. Time hadn't passed. He had to go this "very" instant. Ramón would be waiting for him...

But "seeing" what he had lived through, he saw what at that moment was alive around him. For example, he saw Mrs. Pérez seated at another bench in the company of Powlavski. This was nothing strange in and of itself. They were close friends. They surely had arranged to meet in the plaza to hatch one of their infernal schemes. Human misery would have to search far and wide to find anything even closely resembling that pair.

He was getting up from the bench when he heard Dalia say: "Well, Powlavski, I like my meat almost raw..." Once again. It would always be like this: that ominous presence in his life, that candescent branding iron. Well then, he would speak with them flesh to flesh. An interview with those masters of the flesh would shed some light on the tangled thicket in which he was caught.

Pretending to bump into them by chance, he greeted Mrs. Pérez ceremoniously and made as if to continue on his way, but she, leaping like a veritable amazon, grabbed him from behind and spinning him around, planted a loud kiss on his cheek.

"Oh, my treasure, what a pleasant surprise! It's been ages since we've seen you. Powlavski, get over here."

Powlavski was a few yards away taking Dalia's little dog to urinate.

"Powlavski, where have you gotten to? Get over here. René has been resurrected."

And now Powlavski was rushing over and now he too wrapped his arm around René's neck, kissing him. Mrs. Pérez was clasping René's hands in her own and was all weepy. The little dog was barking its head off. The picture formed by the three of them was a carnal interpretation of the Pietá, now "enriched" by the presence of Powlavski, who at last said:

"Yes, Dalia, resurrected... That's just the right word. Dead, I said. Dead, said Dalia. Dead, everyone said... And now, suddenly you rise from the dead. But do tell, little friend, do tell..."

"There's nothing to tell," René said disconsolately.

"Of course there's something to tell," Dalia said. "A lot, a great deal. It's been months since we've seen you. But come here, make yourself comfortable (René remembered the Récamier and shuddered). Let's sit on the bench."

One might say she dragged him over to the bench and sat him down between her and Powlavski. The latter poked around in a basket, pulled out a sandwich, and offered it to him.

"Eat this, you poor thing," he said, as if he had just found René on the verge of starving to death. "Eat it with absolute confidence. Dalia made it with those same hands which one day will be swallowed up by the earth."

René took the sandwich and nibbled at it mechanically. Strange: he had told The Skeleton that he could order him a sandwich, and here they were offering him one of pork. Blaah! It was enough to make him vomit. He fell to his knees, bowed his head, and closed his eyes

"No, no, my little treasure!" Dalia exclaimed. "We won't have any reflection. Experiencing some grief? Why, tell it to your friends. Isn't that right, Powlavski?"

"Definitely!" agreed Powlavski. "That's what friends are for. But Dalia, he still doubts we're his friends. With all the evidence we've offered him!"

"Well, those doubts have vanished," Dalia shouted out in jubilation. "Vanished forever. From now on we'll be an inseparable trio. We'll share our sorrows and joys. Come on, my little treasure, out with it."

René was enormously repulsed by such an offer. It would be the height of repulsion to ally himself with people so padded with flesh. He was about to let his muse fly off to the realm of daydreams when he realized that he was sitting on that bench between those two disgusting pieces of meat precisely because he was in search of an explanation for his own. No; how strange that there didn't exist a Dalia or a Powlavski made of marble. These weren't statues of them but them in the flesh. So they weren't really off track in affirming so vehemently that they would constitute an inseparable trio. He looked at them as if longing to see them transformed into marble. Suddenly, he asked them:

"What do you think of my flesh?"

Such a question asked point-blank in the middle of that cheery plaza on such a radiant day, with the sun shining, with a basket of sandwiches, with children and baby sitters, produced an explosion of hilarity in Dalia and Powlavski. They leaned back on the bench and laughed to split their sides while making gestures that undoubtedly alluded to René. At last, Mrs. Pérez, said in a shrill voice:

"Pardon me, my treasure, but you ask questions that... I'd anticipated questions of every shape and size but that one about the flesh." She turned to Powlavski: "You know full well, dear Powlavski, how surprised I'd be for the antiflesh himself to ask me a question about the flesh. Could it be? Am I dreaming?" and she pinched herself and pinched Powlavski. "So young René is asking me what we think of his flesh... Oh! I can't get over my surprise! No, my treasure, don't make that face. Of course we're going to answer your question. This very instant. A disturbing question. Isn't that right, Powlavski?"

"Very disturbing," Powlavski said, staring off into space. "The surprises of life, dear. But I yield the floor to you. Tell him what you think. Then I'll respond."

"All right," Dalia said, taking René's hand in hers and examining it the way palm readers do. "All right, my little treasure. Your flesh is of the highest quality. Prime among prime."

"Excuse me," René said in a strangled voice. "I'm not asking you about the quality of my flesh. Rather, I'd like to know how you find it since the last time we met."

"You astonish me anew, my little treasure. You are simply stupendous. Why, I'll tell you that your flesh is better now than ever before. One can now say that it's at its peak."

And without another word, she bit him on the lips.

"Watch out, Dalia!" Powlavski shouted at her as their mouths parted.

This warning seemed to herald some hidden danger. Mrs. Pérez looked at him for an explanation.

"Yes, watch out, Dalia. How could you dare...with such seductive flesh. René, you asked us how we found your flesh since the last time we saw you. Well, I will confess to you: frankly irresistible. You've made astonishing progress."

"But where do you see that?" cried René in utter anxiety.

"Tsk, tsk. Why, I see it in the flesh itself. Those things are only seen in the flesh. Now you are truly made of flesh. A few months ago, you were made of a collection of inanities that need not be enumerated."

"I thought—" René noted timidly.

"Give up your false convictions," and Powlavski shook his head energetically. "Give up your false convictions, which even you don't believe. Don't act like a fool as far as your flesh is concerned."

"That's what I say," emphasized Dalia. "Listen, Powlavski: I always thought that my little treasure was made of the finest flesh, but..."

"But what?..." Powlavski said, surprised there could be any objection.

"Please, my dear Powlavski. How could I contradict you? How could I go against our Gospel? I wholeheartedly share your opinion. Just that my little treasure must take great care of his flesh."

"Uh huh, Dalia! Uh huh," emphasized Powlavski. "Great care."

René sat there staring at them. Powlavski's "uh huh" floated in the early morning air. Did they know? Did they belong to the Headquarters of the Hounded Flesh?

"I don't understand. Am I in danger?"

"Why no!" cried Dalia. "You see, Powlavski? You've frightened my little treasure. He has sensitive flesh," and she hugged him to her bosom. "Don't be afraid, there's no danger. They're not waiting for you right around the corner to finish you off like old Nieburg. No, nothing of the sort. What I mean to say, my little treasure—don't get me wrong—is that this adorable flesh of yours is pure dynamite..."

"Where do you see that?" René inquired.

"It shows, that's all. Neither Powlavski nor I could be more specific. We could spend a month poking around in your flesh, probing it, and wouldn't come up with the precise factor."

"Oh, Dalia!" said Powlavski. "There is no such precise factor. His flesh is like a—let us say, a mystical rose. It embraces all the carnal points."

"So am I condemned?" asked René.

"You damn or save yourself; it all depends on how dedicated you are to your flesh," Powlavski told him. "If you live in a carnal world, be carnal and you will be saved. But if you think you live in a world of fairy tales, then you'll be damned."

"Exactly. It's no coincidence that you, Powlavski, are our Gospel," Dalia exclaimed. "If the flesh demands its due, we must satisfy it."

"But if it means putting one's life on the line," objected René.

"The call of the flesh cannot be ignored, young man," Powlavski said. "Even when putting one's life on the line, one must follow its orders."

"Don't think about it any more, my little treasure. Throw yourself headfirst into the thick of the battle for the flesh."

"But is there in fact such a battle?" asked René, feigning ignorance.

"A colossal battle," said Powlavski. "We are all engaged in it. And listen: there are neither victors nor losers."

"Then what are there?"

"Pursuers and pursued. In accordance with the rules of the game, the pursuers can become the pursued and vice versa."

"If I were you, my little treasure," and Dalia looked lasciviously at René, "I would give my flesh over to pleasure. One loss for another..."

René turned red. He thought that even by accepting Dalia's carnal invitation to wallow in the mud by throwing himself in her arms, that they would come looking for him. The chiefs would not be convinced by the argument that he was living the life of the flesh as pleasure. They would undertake to compile reasons to demonstrate to him that there is flesh and there is flesh: that some flesh is good for some things and other flesh for other things.

He stood up. He mumbled something in the way of excusing himself. Dalia clung to his neck and began to wail plaintively. She told him that he was awfully wretched, that she would be forced to return to the disagreeable use of the mannequin. Tearing at her hair, she shouted that she was sick of the dummy, that her flesh imperiously demanded flesh, that it was inexplicable for flesh not to seek flesh. In her frenzy, she could only utter the word "flesh" mixed with a copious flow of saliva. Powlavski signaled for René to leave. Then he attempted to contain Dalia's carnal effusion by covering her mouth with a handkerchief.

For a moment, René contemplated Dalia. He appealed to the heavens for some saving grace but the heavens remained sparkling bright. Its bulge didn't burst to let the miracle through. Then René appealed to himself. He contemplated his body in the vain hope of being able to offer it to Dalia, but his imploring gaze found nothing but flesh for torture.

He arrived at the Headquarters of the Hounded Flesh with his tongue hanging out. The old man was waiting for him. With a trace of irritation in his voice, he told René that they had been waiting for him for a good two hours to duly certify his weight. It was all that was needed to complete the monthly report.

"Weigh me, you said?" And then René saw the gleaming scale.

"Right away," the old man said. "We can't release the report to the press until we know your exact weight."

As he spoke, he walked over to René and began to strip him. René offered no resistance. Everything had now been consummated. The needle of the scale indicated his exact weight. The old man looked, noted it down, nodded his head in satisfaction.

"Coming along."

"What?" René asked.

"Your flesh is coming along. And at a quick pace. You've gained five pounds."

The Eridanos Library

Eridanos Press, Inc.
Horticultural Hall   300 Massachusetts Ave.   Boston MA 02115

*This book was printed in April of 1990 by
R.R. Donnelley and Sons Co. in Harrisonburg, Virginia.
The type is New Baskerville 12/14.
The paper is Warren Sebago 55 lb. for the insides
and coated Warren Flo 80 lb. for the jacket.*